# WHEN HER TIME COMES

# DAVID VELLA

**TP**
TAILWINDS PRESS

Text copyright © 2023 by David Vella
All rights reserved. Except as permitted under the U.S. Copyright Act of 1976, no part of this publication may be reproduced, distributed, or transmitted in any form or by any means, or stored in a database or retrieval system, without the written permission of the publisher.

Tailwinds Press
P.O. Box 2283, Radio City Station
New York, NY 10101-2283
www.tailwindspress.com

Published in the United States of America
ISBN: 979-8-9853124-8-5
1st ed. 2023

# When Her Time Comes

# 0

I'm hunched over on a toilet in one of the stalls of The Glaze Indian Restaurant.

*Marmara Spicy Kebab*, I say to myself, as I rock to and fro. My fingers are pressed against my temples. I take long breaths in and out.

*I have to go to Marmara Spicy Kebab.*

There's a piece of squashed red meat on the floor in the corner of the stall. It resonates with a vivid menace as I sway and breathe.

I don't know how long I've been here. Half an hour? More?

Dina might have left the restaurant already. She could have taken my long absence the wrong way. Perhaps the juicy lamb madras has kept her still . . .

Nausea is rising in my throat. Around me, the stall walls seem to quiver. My vision blurs. Everything collapses into a watery mush.

*I have to go to Marmara Spicy Kebab.*

I hope she doesn't leave just yet. I have to try and get her to my place. A few drinks can take care of that. Then again, it wasn't easy to ask her out for dinner.

If she's left, I'll have no choice but to get back to that pickup line. Do my act all over again.

My hand slides down my face and scratches my right cheek. Fiercer and fiercer.

*I have to go . . . I have to . . .*

*David Vella*

One thing is certain about tonight. It will be very difficult to find another Dina. She's one of a kind.

I met her three days ago at a party at the Noli Noli Club. *Groovy Wonderland: So Funkin' Fresh* was purring in intense pink over the entrance to the most iconic venue of the club. *I remembered* the moment I stepped inside. Tonight, this entire space was an iceberg lounge. The glass walls were arrayed with space alien masks, their vacant almond-eyed faces lit in a cool blue. Eighties electronic-dance was playing and projector lights cast the shapes of rings, diamonds, and squares across the floor, converging, diverging, overlapping, swirling around to the hyper rhythms. Everyone and everything was replicated upside down, from below in the ice mirror floor and from above in the ice mirror ceiling, as if they all existed at once in foggy parallel dimensions.

I headed toward the bar with its row of champagne glass chairs and ordered a bourbon neat. She was sitting only two chairs away, cross-legged in a latex dress, alone. She tugged her violet hair behind her ear as she sipped from her cocktail. I remembered *again*. So I sat beside her, two chairs away.

"Forgetting or celebrating?" I said without looking.
"Drinking," she said without looking back.
"Bummer."
I took a sip of my whisky. Then, as an afterthought:
"Was hoping it was forgetting."
"And why's that?" Now she turned to fix her eyes on me.
"That way I can make my move."
I made a toast.
"What's your move? Try me."
"I'd play it off as the intriguing stranger, your shining knight who steals you from the clutches of the foul dragon you're currently seeing... who's probably... most probably some Frank who's very handsome and very fit but very boring. The type who hashtags 'gymning it' with every second photo and pretends to love missionary when what he's really into is some good old

puppy-eyed oral wrapped up with a face shot. Five minutes? Just in time for a benchpress session and the game. The rest of the times, he confuses his Alfa Romeo with his lunchbox, but secretly . . . *secretly* . . . " I emphasized, wagging my finger, "he claps whenever his plane is landing. How did I do?"

"You sure think highly of yourself," she replied.

"Well, here's to bruised egos."

"Hear hear."

I moved to the chair right beside her and we clinked our glasses.

Some minutes later and I was touching her shoulder lightly as we chatted. From her shoulder, my hand slid down to her elbow, and I leaned forward to speak to her in her ear. I could smell the strawberry lotion in her hair. She was doing most of the talking now, so I gently brushed my lower lip against her earlobe. She didn't shrink back. So I did it again. My hand found her thigh while my lips kissed her lightly in the snug place behind her ear. Soon I would venture the comment that there were way too many people in this place, to be followed by the natural conclusion—that we should get out of here and brave the night.

I remember every single detail of the night I met her. I remember it all because it made me forget. She gave me a diamond moment of reprieve—a memory in which I *was*.

*Not this evening. Not on this date.*

It's passing. I can breathe more easily now.

I get off the toilet and open the door of the stall. The world around me has regained its reality. It has resumed its old familiar sights, smells and noises. Plain and clear in the white fluorescence are the walls of glossy beige tiles and the rectangles, cuboids and hollowed hemispheres that extend beyond them.

A toilet is a place where you leave behind what's happening, *anything* that's happening, and postpone it for later. It's in fact a tiny pocket of suspension: a floating moment that's outside of it all. Nothing feels as if it's going to happen here. Time is at a standstill. A toilet is always neither here nor there: a cosy corner where the quiet absence of any event, any world is comforting, sometimes even exciting. I used to feel this way in toilets . . . But not now. That was before.

Before Marmara Spicy Kebab. The place where I was diagnosed.

I pass by the row of urinals, sinks, and mirrors. At the corner of my eye, I can see that a reflection is desperate to get my attention.

I see my diagnosis, as plain as day, in the mirror. My diagnosis is attached to my face. It's stuck there like something alien that's also mine.

I call it the fly. The fly determines me and my every action. It's my own parody protruding out of my face. I make an expression and the fly distorts it. I say something and the fly opens it to other interpretations. I make a movement and the fly lends it significance. The fly can twist whatever I do into something funny or ominous and I would never know about it.

I stroke the fly at first and then I rub my fingers against it.

# 1

Exactly a year ago in September, on the same evening, I was sitting down, smoking a cigarette in the toilet at the Marseille airport. I had just arrived to France and before I ventured out to this new world, I decided to pay the restroom a little visit. Take a pause, collect my thoughts.

This is it, I thought as I lit up and took a few long drags.

*This. Is. It,* as I focused on the message scrawled in blue on the door.

Let us take care of you. Call 0146 21 46 76.

Here I was with a one-way ticket and no plans. A month back I was surfing the web when I discovered the town of Saint Laurent, 30km north of Marseille in the south of France. I took a liking to it instantly. Actually, it was more than that. As I did my research, I had this hunch. This place, I thought, might well give me the experience I need to create great works of art. This place, I thought, could well be the Beatrice to my Dante, the Laura to my Petrarch. It could define my work to come, make it shine.

Trust your gut, it seemed to say. So I did.

I felt for my Cardiff home keys in my pocket, took them out, and started etching letters on the stall door.

A town of Parisian chic deep in Provence, *WanderingOmies* said, Saint Laurent is all class. Seventeenth- and eighteenth-century manors line its boulevards and public squares, interspersed with fountains that date back to Roman times. The sculptures of

Impressionist painters guard its majestic avenue, café-laced Euphoria Square, where stylish locals pose on pavement terraces sipping overpriced wine.

Saint Laurent, *Forks in the Road* claimed, has seduced the hearts of many a great painter along the generations. So many of Paul Cézanne's masterpieces were conceived under the spell of this town! Today it is still a home to several accomplished artists. Take a look at the museums that can be found across this fairytale city and behold works that have defined our very culture.

My hand fumbled inside the toilet paper holder nearby. It was empty.

I pulled up my jeans, flicked the cigarette into the water, flushed, and left the gents. A new proud message was now engraved on the stall door.

*Gabriel is here.*

# 2

Once I arrived in Saint Laurent, I managed to find a cheap one-room apartment on a third floor. The place was located in a very narrow side-street full of old Provençal buildings, lined with obese garbage bags heaped against their mouldy walls. The street went by the name of Our Lord.

I decided there and then to make myself known in this town of culture. I would start off by displaying some of my finished oils and hope to turn some heads.

After googling a couple of people in the Saint Laurent art world and making some calls, I got myself an appointment with the chief and assistant curators for the Hermès Museum. When I met them, they gave a cursory glance at my samples and *instantly* accepted my work for an exhibition in a fortnight. If I was supposed to be wowed by this, I wasn't. The title for the exhibition was *The Hopes and Sorrows of Love: Absolute Selflessness.*

"*Three* principles," the chief curator said with a shifty glint in his eyes. "This event is based upon *three* principles."

My mum had always warned me against people with deadpan faces and sly eyes. So I was prepared for this.

"Such an event, you see," he pointed out, "is designed to promote any budding artist with a contemporary style. The more contemporary the style, the better, you see."

But I was certain he required some translation. I'd wager that what he really meant was: "We don't give two tits if your art looks like multi-coloured poop. Give us a used rubber and your last empty tuna can and they'll make it into the exhibition."

"Secondly," he added. "*Secondly.* This event is also for a most excellent cause, you see. Your participation will help contribute to the refurbishing of the Saint Guerlain Chapel. That's the chapel right next to the museum."

What he meant was, "The *only* reason we're actually doing this stupid exhibition is to refurbish the chapel nearby so that we'll have space to hang our paintings. The *real* paintings."

"And the third and most crucial principle," he said, taking a suspenseful breath. "There's a prerequisite to pay a little something for displaying your works in this world-renowned heritage site. A little fee for each painting is only fair, given the cultural significance of this museum for Saint Laurent, France and the rest of the world, you see."

In translation: "Did you really think this exhibition was for real? This is a fundraiser, you tool. We need your money to restore that damn chapel. And we're going to need a lot of it because we take a huge cut for ourselves. We're in a recession. A man's gotta eat, you see."

Oh, I saw.

The chief curator was a dick. But I agreed to pay anyway. I was in, at least. If he was right about anything, he was right about the venue.

The Hermès, *Away We Whoa* claimed, is housed within the monastery of the Knights Hospitaller and is one of the most outstanding museums of archaeology and fine art in France. Most of France's finest painters from the sixteenth and twentieth centuries can be found within its permanent collection. Over the past twenty years, it has acquired eight Cézannes.

Any event that took place within the halls of this museum was always going to attract attention.

I saw that much.

It didn't make the curator any less of a dick.

# 3

So the day arrived—September 11, the day of my debut in the Saint Laurent world of art. For the occasion, I decided to sport a Che Guevara teeshirt and green ripped jeans. I added a royal blue slim-fitted blazer with tails that went down to my knees. Last but not least—in case folks didn't get it—a black beret.

At half past six in the evening, half an hour late, I walked into Hall 7 of the Hermès Museum, where my collection was being exhibited. Expensive champagne and tasty nibbles were being served, probably thanks to one of the contributors. I was dead certain that this had nothing to do with the chief curator.

There were six other collections by different artists in this same hall. Mine was at the far end, next to a grand marble stairway that led up to another gallery. A few visitors had arrived already but none of them were looking at my paintings. Instead, they were all crowded around the collection of the famous Saint Laurent artist, Michel Moreau, who, as it turned out, was this exhibition's guest star. I can't say I was overjoyed by this realization. His participation meant one thing and one thing only: that all the other works would be overshadowed by his. "The Hopes and Sorrows of Love" would be Michel's "Hopes and Sorrows of Love." "The Absolute Selflessness" would be Michel's "Absolute Selflessness." What happened to the whole giving-voice-to-budding-artists point of this exhibition?

The logic, of course, couldn't have been clearer. I could imagine what that chief curator must have been thinking.

"If it's all dilettante," he must have reasoned out, "this exhibition would look just about as attractive as my half-dead granny in full-fledged makeup. The only visitors who'd bother coming would be those relatives who had given these participants their false hopes to start with. No, we need a highlight: something real that would get a lot of people's attention."

I had to admit nonetheless that in the asshole-land of business this was a sound marketing strategy.

I spared a glance at the figurative-expressionist paintings of the one and only Michel Moreau. One showed a naked ageing woman with large love handles and cellulite chicken thighs gazing hopefully, with a clueless look on her face, at a skyscraper from her window. It was the kind of painting that left you wondering *why* she was so hopeful. Three other paintings were homage portraits of classical artists who were unrecognisable. There was another one that showed a crowd of people all screwing up their faces as if they had constipation issues. And another depicting several sumo wrestlers bending down and sticking their asses up in the air. How in hell these paintings were related in any way to the hopes and sorrows of love and selflessness, I had no idea.

I had the uncontrollable urge to steal the felt-tipped pen next to the guest book and put in some of my own tweaks to these works. I was about to consider actually doing this when new visitors arrived. I positioned myself near my own works and pretended to observe them very intently. A tall middle-aged couple in designer shirts and scarves walked in my direction.

"Fascinating, aren't they?" I told them. "Simply fascinating!"

They looked, nodded and climbed up the stairs.

# 4

Three quarters of an hour into the exhibition and I was getting pretty bored. A couple of steps away, I spotted a girl who must have been in her early thirties, dressed in a skirt suit and a ruffle-collar shirt. She was concentrating on one of my minimalist paintings, with curvy outlines and a strong focus on the Burnt Sienna 3 in the Daler-Rowney tint range. I had called it, "To Sleep in Fire." The girl's athletic figure screamed fitness—today's one and true religion, followed by veganism.

"Don't look at it," I begged her. "It's terrible. Abominable even."

"Aren't you the artist?" she asked.

She pointed at the poster photo of my face hanging right next to the painting, above the bio and blurb.

"Oh . . . That . . . " I said. "That's my evil twin brother. That guy . . . that guy's evil."

"So what does that make you?"

She stared at me with grave eyes.

"The good twin brother," I replied. "The shining example, the golden boy. See, we were raised by different parents. His parents used him in experiments."

"But enough about me . . . him, I mean," I ranted on. "What about you? You don't seem to paint. And you probably don't study art. And yet curiously . . . very curiously, voilà, here you are."

"How do you know that?" she asked, her eyes crinkled in

accusation.

Suddenly she bared her pearly clenched teeth, giving me a skull grin.

"That was a wild guess, wasn't it?" she then said.

"Well," I replied, "you look fit. And you're beautiful. You're so beautiful, you're almost ugly. And you know what they say, 'Fitness is to artists . . . as . . . as reason is to ISIS . . . as the concept of boners is to *The Lord of the Rings.*'"

"Where'd you hear that? There are always exceptions."

"Because all artists do is paint, think, and drink. And not necessarily in that order. In fact, usually not in that order."

Her mouth burst open and flashed its gritted teeth at me.

A waiter stopped by with a tray of drinks. I took two glasses of champagne and offered her one. She refused.

I shrugged and drank a glass.

"I don't know about artists," she said, "but it's important for everyone to take care of their body." The fitness lecture began. "After all, you are what you eat. And drinking, that's certainly not good for you. You should cut that out. There are lots of calories in alcohol as well."

"So they keep on telling me," I said. "And I hear you. I really do."

I downed the second champagne.

"But," I continued, "with all these filtered fitness selfies and fake wellness gurus around, I guess I need a little bit more to go on. Proof beyond doubt that *your* brand of fit works. I'd have to see you disrobed."

"You'd have to see my drawings first," she said. "And yes, I draw."

"Yikes," I muttered. "So much for artist clichés. Now I'm piqued."

Her lips flew open again, revealing her clenched teeth. It was as if her mouth was doing this on its own and she wasn't even aware of it. Perhaps it was the involuntary result of something she was trying to hold back, something she didn't want to let out, something she didn't want to control her. And her mouth betrayed these tortuous efforts.

"Do you have a paper and pencil?" she asked.

"No. But that's what guest books are for, right?"

We went to the table near the hall entrance. She took the pen attached to the book and drew a stick girl: a circle for the head, five lines for a body and limbs and a little triangle for the skirt. When she finished, she didn't wait for me to say anything. She turned her back and left. Just like that. I stood there staring at her as she walked away.

I took a closer look at the stick girl. She hadn't even put eyes and a mouth on the girl's face, it had no face at all.

A few moments later, I walked across the hall toward the central stairway. Behind it on the far wall was an oak door with an aluminium bar in the middle. I gave the bar a slight push and the door opened to a corridor with a grey pixel pattern on its walls and three doors. I went for the second door. The ladies' sign was right above it.

The sign displayed a stick girl with a triangle for a skirt and no eyes or mouth on the face.

I pushed open the door.

She was there, right in the middle of the toilet, posing as if she was expecting someone at any instant to snap a picture of her.

"You have potential," I told her.

She simply stared at me with no expression.

I approached her slowly. She followed my every step with alert eyes. When I was close, she didn't pull back. Not one single step. I leaned in and kissed her lips. They gave in to my tongue. Her snogging was long and hard. Without notice she seized my shoulders and jumped onto me. As I held her up from her haunches, she wrapped her toned legs around my waist. With our mouths still glued together, we staggered for a while around the bathroom in no direction until we hit a sink. I hauled her up onto it as she started fumbling with my belt and zipper. I pulled her skirt up, peeled off her panties and flung them away. She instantly set the rhythm with a bounce that varied from fast to hysterically fast. On occasion, one of her legs passed under a hand-dryer nearby, releasing an intermittent drone. I imagined the sound to be a round of applause by some unseen audience that was watching us. At one point, in the mirror above the sink, I saw another person standing behind us. He was right by the entrance, plump and beaming. Clearly he had no intention of leaving.

"This isn't an exhibit mate!" I pointed out. "The art's that way!"

He nodded but stayed where he was, watching us with a grin. I gave up and concentrated on the more urgent matters. The next time I glanced at the mirror, he was gone.

When we were finished, I took a leak in another sink.

"Got to get going," the girl said as she was readjusting her skirt hurriedly. "I've gym in half an hour."

"Consider me converted," I replied as I gave it a couple of shakes.

She didn't bother about looking for her panties. She flashed her gritted teeth and nervously rushed out of the toilet.

I zipped and studied my reflection for a short period of time.

# 5

Leaving the toilet, I returned to the corridor leading to the exhibition hall. And that plump man was suddenly right before me. Psychos did that in slasher movies. The person in question, however, had a permanent childish yet sleazy smirk on his face and his belly was squeezing out of an undersized grease-stained teeshirt which said, I WOKE UP LIKE THIS.

"Do you always creep up on people like that?" I said post-recovery.

"Very good! Very good!" His eyes were directed to the wall rather than me. His grin seemed to hint at some secret conspiracy that only he and I shared.

"Back there," he said again. "Very good!"

"Kudos."

"So you're the great Gabriel, the man of the hour. I saw your artworks at the hall—awesome, man, awesome."

"You American?" I asked.

"That's right. From Wisconsin, the land of cheese and farts."

He chuckled to himself.

"I came here with some buddies from the States," he said. "We decided to have a wild random adventure in another country, but we never left. Now they're picking grapes in Arles and I'm a chef. Your French rocks, by the way."

"I had a lot of practice way back."

Way back was a year before when I was seeing this Parisian girl who refused to learn any other language because it wasn't French. I was left with no choice but to practice French with her on those rare occasions when we had to communicate. I learned quickly and she had a thing for my accent. In fact she used to enjoy making me conjugate a litany of verbs while banging. For some reason she often climaxed while I was reciting the verb "to be."

"You're getting a lot of practice here as well," he said. "If you know what I'm saying."

He sniggered and grunted.

I didn't bother saying anything.

"But that's good, man," he continued. "What you did over there, man, was awesome. That was *badass!*"

His watery eyes now roved around as he talked. It was as if he was too shy to make any eye contact.

"You seem to have enjoyed it more than I did," I said.

"I really mean it. Respect, dude. Respect."

He gave me a wider shit-eating smile.

"Right," I said. "And I got to go now. The fans are waiting."

"Sure thing, man. You're awesome. I'm your fan, too."

He moved aside. I walked past him. I was just about to breathe out a long sigh of relief when he crept up on me again and tapped my shoulder.

"By the way," he said. "I work at Chez Corsi and that's a restaurant that provides catering services for all kinds of events. So if you ever plan to have one of them exhibitions anywhere and need some drinks and munchies for the occasion, I'm your dude. I'll make sure you'll get them at a very fair price."

He winked at the wall and then his hands started fidgeting around and scratching his face.

"The name's Gregory. Here's my number."

"Cheers."

"Anything for you man. Anything!"

Back at the exhibition hall, there was quite a crowd. I eagerly glanced over at my section. A toddler was gawping up at my paintings with a terribly confused look on his face.

# 6

On a Friday evening a month later, I was having a smoke in front of a six-foot poster of my face hanging above the arched entrance to a building known as The Refuge. My magnified features gazed down at me from above with a disenchanted expression. My vacant eyes and dishevelled hair added to the overall weariness. That person seemed to have seen and been through a lot . . . or perhaps he was just hungover or stoned. Right under the stubbly chin, in a funky horror font, was the name of this evening's special event:

MOONLIGHT STRIPTEASE: AN ART EXHIBITION BY GABRIEL CORE

I had landed it—my first solo exhibit. And all thanks to the new proprietor of this building.

His name was Angelo Casablanca. Around seven months prior, he had quit his job as a senior sales manager for Casewise Company and for some inconceivable reason decided to open a space for budding artists. He accepted bookings for any artistic event *as long as* the art in question was transgressive. The Refuge's hallmark was *transgressive*. Transgressive theatre, transgressive salons, transgressive gigs, transgressive readings . . . you name it, it all happened there. Transgressive parties were welcomed as well as long as they had some relation to art. Angelo Casablanca hosted it all.

The Refuge was advertised everywhere as having one principal objective in mind: to be *the* haven for all those artists who could not find a voice in the money-grubbing insensitive world out there. Come all ye who have been misunderstood. Fear not. Come to the Promised Land where your art (as long as it is transgressive) will be celebrated rather than condemned. Angelo Casablanca will take care of you.

There was of course a catch to all this. Casablanca couldn't tell the difference between a three-year-old crayon drawing and a Chagall. *Transgressive*, for him, had one meaning and one meaning only.

Sexual.

The Refuge was basically a wank heaven.

All the same, my rise to fame had to start somewhere.

I had already planned what I was going to wear two hours before the exhibition: a blue-striped autumn suit jacket over a black shirt along with shocking red leather trousers, bright green sneakers and a fedora hat.

Once that decision was over with, I thought that it would be highly appropriate to watch an entire episode or two of *Face and the City*. This highly promiscuity-driven comedy-drama TV series, with a title that was obviously a lazy ripoff of the HBO series *Sex and the City*, had been an instant winner since its first season. It had it all: a lot of sex, boobs, swearing and general debauchery. What else can you ask for? *Seriously*—and I repeat—what else can you ask for? The sixth season had over nine million viewers from all over the world, which was three million more than it had in its first and second seasons. There had been as yet no news as to whether the series would return next year, though there were fan rumours that a seventh season was in the works. Either way, I had to content myself with rewatching some of the best episodes.

*Face and the City* follows the racy lifestyle and adventures of Vincent Face, a forty-something writer who regularly escapes from his writer's block—which seems to happen to him most of the time—with the use of three age-old creative lubricants: drugs, drinking and shagging. Though there is no indication that these *actually* help him write afterward.

This evening I opted for the season one pilot, "Welcome to the Jungle." Vincent Face wakes up looking like he was run over by a truck that reversed and ran over him again.

# 7

There was a glitch in my event this evening. Lailah, a performance artist, was going to be doing her own show on the second floor *during* my exhibition. Wearing only a man's shirt, she would be pouring water, then ketchup and then honey on herself while reading extracts from Heidegger's *Being and Time*. This was worrying, particularly because her body was a walking sex billboard. It was perfectly rational that any sane person would choose to go see her get all wet and dirty rather than come see some oils on canvas.

When you entered The Refuge, you found yourself in a long wide passageway with walls of peach subway tiles as far as the eye could see. Above you, the constellation of cove lights in the pale pink vaults flooded the large tube-like space with an intense metal-halide light. As you strode along, you felt as if you were walking across the blank emptiness of an endless hospital waiting room. The ever-present smell of chemical disinfectant in the air didn't do much to dispel this impression. On the way, a few abstract cubist sculptures could be seen at regular intervals, each and every one made up of a particular combination of the five Platonic Solids. Their geometrical abstraction seemed to have just materialized out of the lucidity of a mathematical equation.

My gallery was the first on the left. You climbed up some glass stairs and you were in a hall with ceramic subway tiles. Minimalist chandeliers illuminated it with the flat glare of LED. My twelve paintings hung in this white space like windows opened to a night.

*Moonlight Striptease* was a series I had started long before I arrived in France. I had just finished the last two works some two weeks before. The style merged contemporary realism with an underlying surrealistic ambience.

All of the paintings were untitled and each one showed an enticing woman in a short, high neck dress slipping off in different parts. She had black hair that fell around a pale, diamond-shaped face with high cheekbones and she stared at you as she grinned with purple lips. She had metallic green eyes, lit up with intense determination. In each image a railway track serpentined behind her across a junkyard that was heaped with engines and other bits and pieces of trains. From the horizon rose the skyscraper silhouettes of some unknown metropolis. A half-crescent moon feebly lit the landscape.

There were only a few differences between the paintings. The woman's state of undress and her pose changed. So did the position of the moon and the light and shadows it cast upon the woman. They concealed parts of her body in some paintings and uncovered them in others. Here, her hands were hidden, and there, they were revealed, very long with knife-sharp red fingernails. In all of the paintings there was one part of the woman that was always hidden: the right side of her face.

Number 12 was a painting that stood out from the others. In the distance, a man in a yellow horned mask and cape could be seen running frantically toward the woman, almost like a comic book superhero.

A waiter came up to me, breaking my reverie.

"Sir, the food delivery hasn't arrived yet."

And the exhibition was due to commence in *twelve minutes*!

The food had been ordered from the Chez Corsi restaurant, or more precisely, over the phone from Gregory himself, the very Yankee who had proclaimed himself my undying fan, the one and the same who confessed having had such a great time seeing me hump in the toilet.

On the phone, he had made me an offer I could not refuse, insisting I pay him once the food was delivered on the day of the event. I accepted without hesitation.

I picked up my cell and called him. There was a series of hopeful rings but they were soon interrupted by the fatal voicemail. I tried again and again no one answered.

I asked a waiter if he knew where Casablanca was. The waiter said that the last time he had seen Casablanca he had been staring at my paintings with a funny face and then he had instantly sprinted to the toilet. Chances were that he was still there.

In fact he still was. When I called him from outside the toilet stall, he answered back, out of breath, that he was certainly not going to send anyone to pick up the food. The food delivery, he gasped and panted, was my responsibility and not his.

"Let me be!" he added.

It was too late to drive over to the restaurant anyway. Chez Corsi was in Marseille, more than an hour away by car. I'd have to call his potbellied highness again later on.

A few people arrived just before the starting time. At 19.30 sharp, the wine was flowing. There were glasses of Pinot Noir, Langlois-Chateau and Jaboulet. I took whatever wine came my way as I waited for a delivery that would quite possibly never arrive. Soon, there were fifteen guests in the hall studying my paintings.

I called Gregory for a third time.

"You have dialled 0147 07 87 38. Please leave a message after the tone."

Beep.

"Hey Gregg, if your food isn't here in one hour, I'll hunt you down, I'll find you, and I'll deliver you as food to your restaurant."

*Click.*

I picked up my fourth glass and downed it.

# 8

"What you've painted here bears an indisputable resemblance to the phenomenon of the postmodern posthuman virgin whore," someone said right behind me as I went for my fifth glass and grew more and more depressed by the second.

The speaker was a stringy man with eyes, nose and mouth that seemed too small and close together for the size of his oblong shaved head. Almost instantly, I spotted the very large lump of his Adam's apple protruding from his throat.

"Your woman indeed reminds me of the protagonists of Georges Bataille's texts of transgression or those messiah characters in J. G. Ballard's New Wave sci-fi. In fact, in her gaze and her demeanour she seems to wield a defiance of all human beliefs, values, and conventions. Her being is resplendent with sovereignty and abjection."

His deep voice had the gravity of some end-of-days preacher, but his face was completely inexpressive and still. The mouth was the only thing that was moving. His eyes looked so blank and dead, they could have been plastic. I wondered whether he was really talking to me or to someone else I wasn't seeing. Maybe he was just talking to himself.

"I also see that you've been influenced by Julia Kristeva's seminal works, *Powers of Horror* and *Black Sun*. Are you by any chance a poststructuralist existentialist? Or perhaps a nihilist phenomenologist?"

"No idea," I answered, "but I'll ask my therapist in our next session."

"There's more. I see more here."

"Oh boy, you do?"

"This here is a woman who lives for abandon. She uses fornication to push away and forget a terrible memory that keeps on visiting her like a spectre. Fornication for her is an amnesiac. She lets go to its movements and sensations with a savage excess in order to escape from what is tormenting her. For her, it's the only route that will set her free. She has bestowed upon it the fascination, the import, the power that one bestows on God and his salvation. For this woman, fornication *is* God."

His Adam's apple suddenly spasmed up and down.

"You know what?" I said. You should use those lines with the performance artist upstairs. She'd do you. Right here, right now. Guaranteed."

"Maybe I err in my judgement of these artworks," he continued in his funereal voice. "It's often admittedly quite difficult to express the experience of art in mere language. For doesn't art free itself from its maker's intentions and acquire a mysterious life of its own?"

"Not upstairs, it doesn't. Art's very naked upstairs."

"Maurice Blanchot calls this mysterious life of art, art's 'essential solitude' among other things. Mind you, analogies can be found in Umberto Eco's notion of the 'open work,' and the 'trace' as well as 'différance' with an 'a' in Jacques Derrida's oeuvre."

The ball in his throat jolted to life again. It lurched upward, a hidden bulbous being with a blind force of its own.

"The origin of the work of art, claims Martin Heidegger, comes from the Fourfold," he pointed out.

"Is that the name of a new planet?" I inquired.

"Well . . ."

"Let's put a pin in that. I've to make a phone call and it's a life-or-death situation."

"That shouldn't be a problem," he said, extending his spidery hand. "Samuel Dubois. Dr Dubois, soon-to-be, actually."

The little bulbous being made a few fierce jerks as if it was struggling to burst out.

I shook his hand.

"Professor Core. But you can call me Gabriel. Or maybe not . . . I changed my mind."

"Very pleased to meet you, professor."

"I'm sure the pleasure is all yours. Or mine. Or ours?"

"Until our next discussion then. On the Fourfold—I'll remember that."

"Can't wait. Drink some more."

I noticed that the number of visitors in the hall had dwindled to ten.

*I knew it!* Lailah was stealing everyone from me. Maybe if the food delivery arrived, it might attract some more visitors. I whipped my phone out and made one last call to his spherical twatness.

"You have dialled 0147 07 87 38. Please leave a message after the tone."

Beep.

"Last chance, asshole. Or I'll be sending you in different packets to Ethiopia to feed all the hungry little boys and girls."

Out of sheer desperation, I decided to look for Casablanca again. Maybe I would finally be able to convince him to send someone to fetch the delivery. At this point I didn't care if the food arrived late, as long as it got more guests. A waiter told me Casablanca had gone upstairs to *experience* Lailah's performance.

I went up, but he wasn't watching Lailah anymore (she was in the ketchup phase now) and he was not in any other hall or office on this floor. So I checked the toilets as a last resort and there he was. His voice quickly answered back from behind a locked stall.

He asked me what I wanted now. When I told him, he repeated that the food was my responsibility and not his.

"Let me be!" he shouted out again and then started gasping. I gave up and left The Refuge.

# 9

I know now that had I not walked out on my exhibition on that Friday night, at *that* point in time, things could have been different. The fly wouldn't have revealed itself on my face. Had I stayed inside, safe in The Refuge, sheltered among my paintings, my face could still be mine. It's a real torture knowing you could have prevented it all in retrospect.

So I went out at around 21.30 and one thing led to the other. And it finally came to this.

Outside, I lit another cigarette. I wasn't about to go home just yet. The night was young.

There was a group of five girls standing in front of a nearby club called Electrique. They were talking to each other in conspiratorial voices while passing around a joint and a bottle of tequila. I went up to them.

"Are any of you rich and interested in marrying me in the not-so-distant future?" I asked them.

I was met with suspicious stares.

"Shit that spliff smells good," I added. "Can I take a drag or three?"

"Why?" one of them asked.

"Hell I've just been rejected by all of you," I answered. "A little something for the pain, maybe?"

One of the girls, probably Chinese-French, snatched the spliff from her friend and offered it to me with a laughing face.

"I'd marry you in a blink," she said.

I instantly struck up a conversation with her. And she chatted away, her arms gesticulating as if they were swatting invisible flies while her feet were constantly on the move, taking one step back, then one forward, now to the left, now to the right. She spoke urgently and devoured whatever puerility that came out of my mouth with a starry-eyed enthusiasm that bordered on frenzy. That was Osanne: relentlessly ecstatic, relentlessly full of joy and sunshine.

Osanne introduced me to the rest of the gang. There was Nina, extraordinarily pale and tired-looking in her summery floral print dress. She nodded and said a quiet hi. To her right, Sybille in her tight sequined minidress designed to set her DD cups into prominence. She struck a pose, squinched her eyes and pouted her mouth. I couldn't tell if she was inviting me or rejecting me. Maybe it was both. Then there was Arienne in her austere denim skirt and blouse. Sporting a crushed expression, she was all silence with an occasional stuttering reply if asked a question directly. There was also a fifth girl whose name I didn't catch. She had a pixie haircut and a chic beige trench coat on. As Osanne introduced her, she raised a pencil-thin eyebrow and observed me with a haughty cynicism that was somehow enticing.

"We've to go now!" Osanne then shouted out in a busy voice. "Le Divin has opened!"

Then she turned to me and said, "We're going to a club outside of town. Want to join?"

I agreed without even thinking about it.

Le Divin Club was quite far away and we were going there in Osanne's car. She had left it at a nearby parking lot. On our way, Arienne suddenly confessed that she wasn't feeling very well and she had better go home. There was a lot of cheek-kissing and hugging and goodbyes before we finally reached our destination. All the others decided to sit in the back, so I took the passenger seat.

*When Her Time Comes*

The moment we started driving, an odd whistling sound filled the car. It went on and on, its pitch fluctuating. Sometimes it went up so high it was close to unbearable.

"I crashed into a road sign a few weeks back," Osanne shouted out above the din. "It's been making this noise ever since."

"These are good times!" she yelled, changing the subject. "Life's beautiful!"

She turned on her hip-hop playlist and put the music on at full blast. At first it seemed to drown out the whistling. But then it came back, continuous, persistent like the low buzzing of a fly.

The girls in the back erupted into hysterical laughter every now and then. They produced another tequila bottle and passed it quickly between them while smoking one cigarette after another.

I asked Osanne why they had become so party crazy all of a sudden.

"Don't mind them," she said. "They get like this every weekend since I crashed my car. It's the whistling sound. They're trying not to hear it. They're trying to forget it's there."

We left Saint Laurent and took the A51 motorway toward Bouc-Bel-Air. Nina's head suddenly popped out between Osanne and myself.

"We're hungry!" she shouted into Osanne's ear. "We want to go back to Saint Laurent to eat! To eat!"

Osanne told her that we were already halfway to Le Divin.

"*Fuck Le Divin!*" Nina shrieked. "*I don't want to go there anymore! I'm hungry! Do you hear that? I'm hungry! I want to eat! Eat!*"

"*We want a kebab!*" Sybille screamed behind us, pounding her high heels against the floor over and over again. "*Turn this stupid car round. Now!*"

"*Right now!*"

"*We want a kebab!*"

"*A kebab!*"

In a frenzy, Sybille burst out punching and punching the back of Osanne's seat.

"*A kebab!*"

With a cheerful face, Osanne suddenly made a sharp U-turn, the tyres screeching violently against the concrete. Once we were on the other side of the street, we roared back the way we had come from at a maniacal speed. We were going to drop Nina and Sybille at their favourite kebab restaurant in the world.

"Marmara!" Nina sang out with no tune at the top of her voice. "Marmara! Marmara here we come!"

"Yum yum!" Sybille sang back. "Yum yum!"

"Marmara! There when you need it!"

"Yum yum! Yum yum!"

"Marmara! Best kebab in the Provence!"

"And the tastiest place in the world!"

The girl with the pixie cut was quiet during all of the ride back to town. She stared out of the window, smoking and drinking from the tequila bottle. When we arrived again in Saint Laurent, Osanne drove into Euphoria Square. Marmara Spicy Kebab was only a street away from here. Nina and Sybille clambered out of the car before it even stopped. They took each other's hands and walked away singing and skipping. We drove out of town, heading once more to *Le Divin*.

"They aren't just going to Marmara Spicy Kebab, you know," Osanne laughed on the way. "We all know where they *really* want to go. They just don't want to say it."

"They're going to see the Duke.

"Marmara Spicy Kebab is close to where he lives."

The girl with the pixie cut checked her face in her handbag mirror. She made some careful touches to her eyelashes with her mascara wand.

I asked who the Duke was.

"The Duke," Osanne explained, "is a certain figure who's very notorious all over Saint Laurent. Many are obsessed about him. He has these charms. People go to his place to play in the Game, which can last days, even weeks.

"Sometimes when you visit him, you keep going back. You

see, it can get very addictive. Many of those who see him want to see him again and again. They just can't help themselves.

"No one wants to reveal this, however. To admit that you see the Duke is to admit that there's something very wrong about you. The Game isn't something you'd want to talk about . . . with anyone. So there's this unspoken agreement all over town that the Duke shouldn't be mentioned. But the truth is that a lot of people go to him regularly. Any person you meet, your best friend, your own mother or father even, could be secretly visiting the Duke. You never know."

In the backseat, the girl with the pixie cut stared out at the rushing streets with a sullen face.

# 10

Somewhere along the A51, the car broke down. It just stopped moving as a cloud of smoke rose out of the hood.

We were stranded in the middle of a highway in the dead quiet of the night. There was no traffic at this hour and the lack of street lamps made it blindingly dark. A distant dog barked out a couple of times and then fell silent again.

The pixie girl got out of the car to take some air and call a towing service. Osanne didn't seem worried at all. She laughed and rambled on and on about her cooking style and how fun and funny her job and colleagues were. She worked as a government clerk. After a while, she informed me that she was slightly tired and was going to catch a few winks before the tow truck arrived. She nodded and passed out a few seconds later with her mouth open. She started snoring like an old motorcycle.

I went out for a smoke and spotted the pixie girl. She was standing in the quartz-halogen spotlight of the only streetlamp on the road. I approached her. When I stepped into the spotlight, it was as if everything ceased to exist except her and me. It felt as if we were the protagonists of a play that was about to begin on the little circular stage cast by the light above.

She was smoking and swiping away at a series of photos on her phone. All the photos showed a baby girl.

"Yours?" I asked.

"My sister's," she muttered at the screen.

"Cute."

She kept sliding the pictures in silence.

"You're not much one for talking, are you?"

"Depends if there's anything to talk about," she snapped.

"Given the circumstances, you bet."

"It also depends whom I'm talking to."

"Nothing like the comfort of strangers."

At this, she glanced up at me with a deadpan face.

"I don't trust strangers," she stated with a cold finality.

"Not all strangers are psychos with chainsaws. I just do some killing on the side when I'm having a bad day. And I use a samurai sword."

To that she didn't reply and she went back to the pictures on her phone. She had cut me out once again.

"So who's this Duke exactly?" I persisted.

She took her sweet time and then glanced up from the screen and said:

"He's known for the luxurious parties he hosts. And the special chocolate he offers his guests. After many of his parties, most guests are invited to play in the Game."

"What kind of game *is* the Game?"

"The kind where you become someone you're not."

She checked her lips in her handbag mirror and then calmly lit up a fresh cigarette. I waited for her patiently.

"You go to him," she said, "and he creates for you a world where you don't have to be you. He frees you of yourself for as long as you stay with him."

"How does that work for your friends?"

"It's all they want."

"All they want?"

"Yes," and she lifted up her face to the streetlamp and idly exhaled a fine line of smoke. "My friends are scared. Sometimes it's not just fear. It's dread."

I kept my eyes on her, waiting for a further explanation.

"They feel that something's going to happen to them soon.

Before long, something will come . . . and then everything will change."

"What will?"

"They don't know what or who. What they do know is that this moment is drawing closer every day. It'll come when they least expect it, a surprise in the most surprising possible way. They won't be able to escape it. It's already too late."

"And the Duke?"

"They're horrified," she said, "and the Duke takes the horror away. His Game takes them to another world where that horror doesn't exist. In that world they're free because time there is different."

She got back to her phone as if she had lost interest in what she was saying.

"There's no time in the Duke's world," she then murmured.

"You've been?"

But at that moment, the tow truck arrived.

Not that she would have answered that kind of question.

We didn't make it to Le Divin on that night. I never did. I did, however, manage to do something far more impossible than try to reach that place.

I got her number.

I asked and she gave it to me, just like that, without a moment's hesitation.

Her name I had forgotten and I didn't bother asking.

Sometime in the early morning hours as I was going back home, I took a picture of an attractive restaurant I passed that went by the name of Happy Days. I sent her the photo along with a message on WhatsApp.

> Sent to: 0509 75 83 51
> Pixie Hotness
>
> Saturday, October 10, 2015
> 03.40

## When Her Time Comes

> How about round 2 with some vino at this place?
> Next week in the afternoon.
>
> Best Regards,
> The stranger who's not a psycho

# 11

The night I met pixie girl, I had the most vivid dream. It was one of those dreams that convinced you that it was real while it was happening; the type you would often have had when you were a kid. I'm not sure what had triggered it. It might have been the weed those girls had been smoking. Maybe it was just a random incident. Or perhaps it was something else—something I knew about but hadn't been aware of for a long time.

In the dream, I was in a dim attic stored with canned food and boxes full of old unused furniture. I had climbed into the attic from the window.

There was a narrow staircase leading down. As I was about to touch the last steps, something heavy fell into the attic above.

The stairs ended in a washing room that opened into a peach bathroom.

From the bathroom, a door opened into my bedroom. Pendant lamps lit the room with amber light. Dust covered the colourful quilts on the two beds, the wooden cabinets over them, and the wardrobes on either side. Two Playmobil medieval castles and a pirate ship were on the topmost cupboards.

I was given that pirate ship on my birthday. Ma had prepared a treasure hunt for me just a few hours before the party. The hunt had finally led me to the little bathroom downstairs and it was there right in the shower tray: a giant pirate ship.

My old drawings were hanging here in my room as well. All of them depicted the landscapes of a faraway land that had long since gone.

Footsteps were clacking down the attic stairs.

I crossed the bedroom and left from the door on the opposite side. I stepped onto the landing. Little bits of plaster from the ceiling fell softly all around me and they looked like snowflakes. A classical pendulum clock hung between two mahogany doors. It showed 02.05. I picked the door closest to my bedroom door. It opened into my parents' bedroom.

Pa used to have a siesta here on his days off. He had probably picked up the habit from the Greek cousins he had once visited in the village of Dimitsana.

The footsteps got closer and closer.

A Victorian crystal chandelier laced with cobwebs cast ma and pa's bedroom in an old golden glow. Several cracks spread out from the ceiling where the chandelier was suspended. In the centre there was a blue double bed covered in dust, surrounded by the mirrors on the wardrobe doors and on the dressing tables. On the bed were some of my brother's teddy bears with faded messages on their sweaters.

Forever Loved
Forever Free
Forever Wild
Forever Happy

A plain cross hung right above the cabinet mirrors and above the headboard was a painting of Christ the Redeemer. It was so faded that I could barely make out the robed bent figure with the massive cross on his shoulder.

I caught a glimpse of myself in the mirrors. A younger version of myself looked back at me. His hair was parted and combed from the left side and he wore a dark blue tracksuit with "Sahara" written on the top. I used to wear this tracksuit a lot. It was my favourite one.

The footsteps could now be heard coming from across the

peach bathroom.

    Cream silk curtains were drawn over the bay windows on the east wall. I parted the curtains. The panes were white with fog. I rubbed the glass with my palm. Outside, I could see a tarmac road with Georgian houses on either side, interspersed every couple of blocks by the ruddy halos of streetlamps. Over all, the sky was an absent grey. There was not a soul in sight.

    I grabbed the window lever and tried to turn it. It didn't budge. I tried again with both my hands but it still didn't move. I tried the levers of the other windows, but they were all stuck. The windows couldn't be opened.

## 12

I opened my eyes. Everyday reality slowly dawned on me. I grew aware again of where I was, what this was.

It was probably morning and I was in bed in my shabby studio flat in the street of Our Lord in the town of Saint Laurent. The bathroom door was in front of me, slightly ajar, inviting. On the shelf above the sink were heaped a few packets of noodles and a cereal box. On the table between the plate rack and the fridge were several unwashed wine glasses. Up there in a corner, right above the desk, the wall was stained with a little patch of mould. Three filled garbage bags were piled near the flaking door. The fridge drummed on in the stillness.

Yesterday had seen the launch of my art exhibition. The food delivery had never arrived. Few people had shown up. I had left early and met those girls. Today I had to buy coffee and more cereal and I had to look around town for acrylic gesso, a new filbert brush and a tube of 526 Phthalo Turquoise for a new series of paintings.

It was 10.14 and I had one unread message on WhatsApp.

I turned to my right side and saw the laptop open on my desk. An episode of *Face and the City* had been paused. Vincent Face was staring right at me with a disastrously stoned face, bedraggled hair and a half-smoked cigarette dangling from the corner of his mouth. I stared at him for some moments and then forced myself to get up.

At that instant, Jerome Casablanca, the masturbating manager of The Refuge, decided to call. He said he wanted to congratulate me on my most excellent *transgressive* artwork, "which is quite frankly an *explosive* feast for the eyes." He also wanted to congratulate me on the most excellent attendance. It appeared that quite a large number of people showed up after around 21.00 and the hall was crowded an hour later. He counted more than a hundred visitors.

When Casablanca hung up, I made some extra strong coffee and opened the unread WhatsApp message.

> Sent by: 0509 75 83 51
> Pixie Hotness
>
> Saturday, October 9, 2015
> 08.37
>
> Okay, how about Tuesday at 15.00? Happy Days.

# 13

I had nailed it.

Pixie Hotness was hot . . . very hot. I couldn't wait to meet her.

On the days leading to our date, I did a lot of painting to distract myself from all the excitement. On the day in question, I went for a jog in Park Ailes de Joie to calm myself down. This was followed by a light lunch at Sensi Restaurant, an immaculately cool space with coned lamps and grey furnishings. A fly buzzed around me while I ate. It wouldn't go away. My body tensed with every swoop the bug made. The fly stayed with me till the very end of my lunch.

My general peace had been shattered. That's the reason I now call this thing on my face a fly. It's always there, *no matter what*. You can brush it away and you can try to ignore it and it can leave for some time, disappear even. But no matter what, it will come back. It will make you remember it. It will let you build your inner peace, and as soon as you do, it will shatter it all over again.

A fly is your constant ridicule.

You can kill it of course and be done with it. You can devote some of your time and energy to wipe it out of existence.

*This* fly, however, cannot be killed.

It was because of the incident at the Sensi restaurant that I *had* to watch an episode of *Face and the City* just before meeting Pixie Hotness. For the occasion I selected season one, episode six. The episode went by the name of:

## Fun at Church

In this episode, Vincent goes into a church to shelter from the rain. At first there seems to be no one there. But then, close to the stairs leading to the apse, he sees someone kneeling in prayer. The first thing he notices is her wavy brown hair that tumbles down her paisley shirt to her thighs in tight jeans. He walks closer to her from the side. And she is stunning. The candles beside her seem to make her skin glow. It's as if a soft aura is coming out of her, illumining her with the presence of another world, some place far, perhaps mystical.

She sees him. He puts on an astonished face and points at himself. He approaches her.

"You know you remind me of Arwen the half-elf in *Lord of the Rings* when she saves Frodo and she's all glowing and shit," he tells her in a hushed voice. "You literally look like you're emitting light from here."

She smiles sweetly at him.

He extends his arm and offers her his hand.

"'I've come to help you. Hear my voice. Come back to the light.'"

"It's ironic you're telling me that in a church," she answers.

"I'm sure the big guy up there would approve. If he were around, he'd probably be high-fiving me. 'Good one,' he'd say. 'That's a damn good one.'"

"You know you've a very original way of praying."

"I only pray to what's beautiful."

"I know that's heavy," he then adds. "It'll make sense."

"And I'm beautiful?" she asks sarcastically.

"That depends on which angle I see you from."

# 14

There were ten minutes remaining until my date with Pixie Hotness. I was about to leave my apartment when I received a message.

> Sent by: 0509 75 83 51
> Pixie Hotness
>
> Tuesday, October 13, 2015
> 14.56
>
> I'm at Happy Days outside on the terrace.
> I see that you're going to be late.
> I've a very low tolerance for people who don't respect times.

On my way to Happy Days, at 15.06, I received yet another message.

> You're late!
> I'll be leaving in a few more minutes.

The Happy Days Café was situated in Place de Martyrs en Extase, a little square surrounded by manicured bistros and restaurants. The air here was full of the aroma of fried chicken and bolognese sauce. Cooing pigeons pecked at breadcrumbs on the street. A couple of Asian tourists were taking photos and videos of this ornate place.

I spotted Happy Days right away. She was sitting there in the sun, upright and tense. Her elbow was on the table, her arm up with a slim cigarette posed beside her cheek. The black halter-neck dress she wore was like a second skin. Its tight miniskirt reached to her upper thighs, leaving the winding landscape of her crossed legs bare. Her gelled hair glistened in the sunlight and its boyish cut emphasized the nape of her neck and the large silvery hoop earrings she wore.

She had noticed me before I noticed her. She had that sharp fight-or-flight alertness of a cat. As I sat down, she slid her Versace butterfly sunglasses down her nose to have a better look at me.

We ordered a red Bordeaux and she scrutinized the waiter pouring wine in our glasses. She swirled the wine, smelled it and took a careful sip.

"I returned here from Paris two years ago," she said in a bitter voice. "It was a very bad decision. Saint Laurent bores me. It bores me to death."

Her features were so even and her skin so smooth and clear that she reminded me of the androgynous faces of top models. She looked so perfect that there was somehow nothing distinct about her appearance. Her face seemed to blend and disappear into all the plastic faces in magazines. After this date, it would probably be quite difficult to remember exactly what she looked like.

"I felt free, very free in Paris," she said. "So many places to discover and things to do. I got to know my limits there. And I broke many of them."

She smiled but her smile was strained. She uncrossed her legs, pulled her retreating miniskirt down her thighs, and crossed her legs again.

"Nothing seems to happen here, though. This town's like an airport. People come and go and everything stays the same. Changes here don't matter. They're just repetitions, all the same."

A flicker of dismay passed across her face and she frowned. She took a long and hard drag off her cigarette.

"Saint Laurent is a place you go to for your studies, a temporary job, a holiday, an experience. It's an interval, a short-term getaway, a refuge before real life, with its demands and responsibilities, hits in. We're living in a bubble."

Her eyelids blinked repeatedly.

"Time here can be too slow. It doesn't pass easily. It's always stretching. The kind of time that makes you angry, that makes you want to smash things and leave forever."

Again, she uncrossed her legs, pulled at her miniskirt, and crossed her legs again.

"What keeps me in Saint Laurent is my work. I babysit a couple of kids from time to time. I'm too attached to them to leave now. I adore children. I always wanted to work with them. In Paris, I used to work in a children's library in Montrouge and when I came back, I worked as a summer camp counsellor for some primary schools. I can't live without children around me."

Her mannequin face winced briefly. She downed her glass and crushed her cigarette into the ashtray.

I was about to pour some more wine for both of us when she refused, explaining that she had an appointment with the beautician in a quarter of an hour.

She stood up, put on a leather jacket and checked her phone.

I raised my glass to her.

"Here's to hoping the next chat will be with candlelight, violin, dinner, some awkwardness, the walk home, a leg-lifting kiss . . . Did I mention rain? Yeah, there should be rain. The kiss should be in the rain."

She didn't reply; she was carefully reading something on her phone.

"Or maybe you're more of a cut-to-the-chase type," I carried on. "Skip the frills and get down to biz. Romance is for high school right?"

She tapped away at her phone for a few more seconds, then she calmly looked up at me.

"The restaurants here bore me," she said. "I've been to most of them. Come by to mine Friday evening. We can have another chat there. Bring some good wine."

She put the phone to her ear, and turned to go. A couple of steps away, she stopped, turned and glanced back at me.

"Good wine."

## 15

Pixie Hotness had left without telling me the address of her apartment. I decided not to ask her and let her send it of her own free will. If she didn't send anything, well, it simply meant that she had no interest in my company.

I received no other messages on Tuesday, and there was only silence on the days following. By Friday, I was quite certain that she hadn't really wanted to invite me over.

Late in the morning, however, I found a new message in my inbox.

> Sent by: 0509 75 83 51
> Pixie Hotness
>
> Friday, October 16, 2015
> 11.06
>
> My address for 20.00 tonight:
> Apartment 15
> 16, Sommeil de Diamant Street,
> 13090
>
> Don't be late.

For that evening, I put on torn laurel green skinny jeans, old neon purple sneakers and a loose anarchy teeshirt. Over this outfit, a carmine, slim-fitted suit jacket with green patches.

I went into the bathroom and switched on the bright halogen

light clipped to the top of the mirror frame. Before me, my face and half my body lit up in the gloom.

I styled my hair with a texturizing wax to give it a dishevelled look. I observed my face and started going through the ritual thoughts that provoked *the* attitude. If women used makeup, I used a mindset. Gradually, I went through the ceremony of recovering it.

*I am that person who has been through so much—too much. I have been through so many things that now there is nothing new left to feel. It has all already happened. All the great and terrible stories have passed, gone. My life now is a leftover.*

*I am a leftover and my time is meaningless.*

*Today will always be different from the way things were in those early years of world-shattering emotions. Anything that can take place today has already taken place a zillion times before. It has all been exhausted. All the hope and excitement in this world, its soul, has been nipped out. Nothing is real. No place or moment can bring me back to the vividness of the past.*

*The fire has been snuffed out. Poof! All landscapes are a faceless plain of ash and rock.*

*I can now play and not get burnt. This wasteland can be my playground.*

In the mirror, I saw the tension in my face melt down, my features relaxed. My face grew tired and dazed as if I had been stupefied by some drug.

Here I am, it said. Let's have some fun.

# 16

Sommeil de Diamant Street was outside the town centre on the D64 motorway. On either side of the main rood was a row of five-storey concrete buildings that seemingly stretched on forever. The buildings were identical, all their faces exhibiting the same rectangular windows and steel rail balconies. It was like wandering into a life-sized Tetris game.

Pixie Hotness was supposed to live in the fifteenth apartment in Block 16. The streetlamps near that building weren't working, so the area was shrouded in darkness. I had to use my phone's flashlight to pass through the courtyard and find the main entrance. On one side of the gate was a column of glowing green buzzer strips.

Number 15 read *Angelique Duval.*

Her flat was thick with a musky vanilla fragrance. Ambient trance music hummed in the background. On a wall hung the pictures of vast obscure landscapes belonging to a world seen only in dreams. They showed plains and forests with ruins of old castles and sometimes a lonely figure looking ahead at the horizon with a wild wind battering at his cloak. Others showed a peaceful world of tilled fields with cottages and wagons and a few ducks flying overhead in warm amber light.

Facing the bed, other paintings were hung that displayed naked bodies entwined in passion. Others showed the close-up faces of men and women, young and old, eyes closed, mouths slightly open, all surrendered to ecstasy.

It was a tiny studio flat. Angelique approached me from the open-plan kitchen with a cheese platter, rapping the floor with her high heels, the batwing sleeves of her blouse fluttering with her every step.

We went outside on the balcony. A bulb above us blasted the parapet with white light.

The balcony was a stage and we were in the spotlight performing. Out there was the darkness of the auditorium, silent, expectant. The occasional rumble of cars was the appreciative applause of the unseen audience.

We sat half facing each other, half facing the void.

"This kind of feels like we're the only two people left on the planet after some worldwide disaster," I pointed out.

"Is that so?" she replied.

"Everything's gone. Only thing left is this balcony with the two of us. And this balcony will soon crumble down as well."

Angelique tapped her glass with one of her varnished nails and stared at me briefly. She drank and then she looked at the darkness beyond without a word.

"When all the past is gone and there's no future, you can pretty much do anything you want," I suggested.

"That's just depressing," she observed.

"Sure it is."

I moved my chair closer to her.

"But it can be liberating as well," I said. "Us two being the sole survivors in the middle of an apocalypse."

I placed my hand lightly on her lap.

"What would you do if that happened?"

Her eyes blinked furiously and she shook her head as if she was trying to wake herself up from something.

"Why are you even talking about this?" she spat. "It's ridiculous."

She took my hand and put it back on my lap. But I leant closer to her until my face was only a few centimetres away from her ear. I could smell the mousse in her hair and the perfume on her neck. But I could also sense her icy tension.

"I can think of a million things I'd do," I said with a low voice.

"A million things like what?" she asked.

"Like desires you're usually too afraid to follow," I whispered in her ear. "Dreams you could make real because nothing else matters."

With that, my lips nudged her earlobe ever so slightly.

She flinched as if my kiss was acidic. She sat further back, stiffer than before.

I made eye contact and kept speaking in a low voice.

"Everyone's got wild fantasies. Few are brave enough to go along with them."

I put on an over-the-top seductive face and said—

"You *must* be brave."

I leaned forward and tried to kiss her neck, but she shrank back again.

She drank the rest of her wine. When she put the glass back on the table, she winced for a second.

"I've a much better wine," she stated. She stood up and went inside to fetch the bottle.

Upon her return, she found me standing near the balcony door, waiting for her. I went up to her and held her gently around her waist. She looked up at me with a sceptical face and raised an eyebrow, just like that night when Osanne had introduced us. I could feel the timid ghost of her silent breathing on my neck and it was quickening, deepening. Without saying anything, I closed in on her glossy lips.

She backed off once more. The third time.

"What's wrong?" I asked.

She flicked my cheek with her long fingernail.

"I'm just not buying it."

# 17

It was getting quite late so I asked her if I could sleep over. There were obviously taxis working at this hour but I didn't want to leave just yet. The night was still full of possibilities. Surprisingly, Angelique said yes.

We decided to go to sleep right after the second bottle. She went to the bathroom, and in the meantime, I stripped to my boxers and slipped under the quilt. While I waited for her, I tried and failed to devise a plan. Finally, the bathroom door opened and she emerged in a pink kimono.

She wanted to leave the music and the lights on while we slept. It made sleep feel less crucial, less decisive . . . less of a something that she had to do. The prospect of sleep didn't seem so urgent anymore. This made her sleep.

She turned around, back to me, and went still. I couldn't sleep for a long while. For a long time I stared wide-eyed at her nape.

Then, I too gave in.

Until I woke up suddenly, very vividly awake, my heart pounding in my ears.

I looked around. Everything was as I had left it. Her back was still facing me, her sides heaving slowly, the room cluttered with paintings—all still, the same. The music had stopped. There was a perfect silence inside as well as outside. Everything seemed to be waiting for something.

Angelique suddenly jumped and spasmed. Then she jolted again with another spasm. This time her shoulders shook, her head vibrated and her back jerked backward. The bed squealed. It was as if something was beating inside of her to get out.

Just as abruptly, she went still and quiet again. It was as if nothing had happened and I had just imagined it.

I couldn't go back to sleep. I climbed out of bed and started poking around the room.

First, I looked into the wardrobe through the forest of clothes. Then, I opened its drawers and found an array of glittering designer shoes and handbags. The bedside drawer and cupboard were stacked with lifestyle and beauty magazines and cluttered with face creams, moisturizers, lipsticks and every other kind of cosmetic. In the desk drawers there were travelling documents, bank statements, receipts, flyers and a couple of Blu-ray romantic movies. On the desk I found a small pile of loose crumbled papers covered in a spidery handwriting. There were various words and sentences that were crossed out and corrected in shorthand. It took me quite some time to figure out what I was looking at. It was a series of short stories.

Under the papers was a hardbound book with lined pages. Some of them had dates and were filled with the same handwriting. It was her diary.

I glanced behind my shoulder. She was sleeping peacefully, her arms hugging her pillow, her knees bent up. I folded the papers with the short stories and stuffed them into my jacket pocket. Before I put the diary into the jacket as well, I had a glimpse at one of the early entries.

*Monday, 16 October, 2013*
Today, an eye has opened in my head.
It was bound to happen sooner or later.
I had always known it was there, closed, asleep. Even when it was asleep, I had sometimes felt it stirring.
The stirring had been increasing lately. I had felt the signs coming all along.
And it finally happened today.
It awoke in me unsuspectingly. It was a bit of a surprise.

# 18

I left Angelique's flat the moment I found her writings. I suppose there was no other reason to stay any longer.

When I got home, I couldn't sleep, so I took her diary out and read her next entry. It also spoke about the eye. Not one of her two eyes but another one. A third.

> *Tuesday, 24 October, 2013*
> The eye can close for some time. For minutes, an hour, or even several hours occasionally.
> Then it opens, and when it opens, it doesn't blink. It glares.
> It casts a very strong light.
> This light burns everything I have, everything I know. I am naked, too naked in this light.
> I am in a spotlight, naked, for very close exhibition.
> The light of the eye bathes me from head to toe. I am this light.
> But this light is not me.

I didn't understand what she had meant then.

But today, right now, as I stare at my face in the toilet mirror of The Glaze Indian Restaurant, I think that I do. Now, I see how she saw. Now, I share her world.

Or maybe, it's all in my head. You can never be certain about people. There's always this infinite distance that separates all of us.

And yet, if there's anything certain, it's that at some point in her life something had awoken in Angelique and it gave her a fresh vision of the world. It was probably like an epiphany of unenlightenment.

And perhaps, just perhaps, this something . . . this eye was a *thought*: a certain thought, singular and irremovable. She felt it not just in her mind, but also in her body.

What is too intimate is what can't be felt, can't be thought. In order to get along in your day-to-day life you have to push it away to the margins of your consciousness and forget about it. You go about your life as if it's not there, as if it doesn't make up a part of who you really are.

But then one day a thought dawns upon you and you wake up to your secret. At long last you are reminded of it.

"*This! This!*" the thought announces. "You'll always live with *this!*"

And the obscured and ignored is suddenly displayed under a surgical light.

"*This! This* has always been with you and you've always looked the other way!"

I wonder how she felt in that moment when it was all revealed to her.

"There's something in me that isn't me," she could have said. "It's coming out of me but it doesn't belong to me. It's taken away all that is my own: my world and my body. Everything that was me it now owns. Nothing exists for me anymore. In myself, I'm no longer myself. This is still my skin but it's now also *its skin*.

"A whole new life has just begun."

# 19

In the days that followed our second date, she didn't text. It was as if she had disappeared. Or more likely it was because she didn't like the fact that I had left her flat while she was sleeping, even though I did text her when I got home, letting her know that I had a good time and had to leave early to catch up with my painting.

I gave it two weeks and then decided to break the silence. She messaged back two days later and I messaged back and it went on like that for a while. She often took quite a long time to reply, sometimes even up to three or four days. Whenever I asked her to meet, she would always give me some "plausible" excuse about why she couldn't make it: "On that day I've cardio." "This week's going to be super-busy." "I need some me time this evening." "I'm afraid that week's all full."

I kept on texting her anyway.

One rainy evening, I searched for the Duke on Facebook. I typed "The Duke of Saint Laurent," and then "The Duke's Game," "The Duke Parties," and every other permutation I could think of.

Nothing came up.

# 20

On a Thursday morning in late November, I took a break from my painting and looked out of the window. The sky was a flat grey with nothing to show and nothing to hide. It hovered over the huddled houses with their cracked walls and sagging clotheslines.

My mobile rang at that moment. I tapped on the unread message.

> Sent by: 0509 75 83 51
> Pixie Hotness
>
> Wednesday, November 26, 2015
> 10.13
>
> It's first snow!
> I've taken the day off
> and I've been dancing and playing in the snow
> for the whole morning.
> It's liberating!
> I feel like a child.
> There's always hope with snow.

I sent a reply and went back to my canvas. The work-in-progress was entitled *Soapy Dreams.*

The painting depicted a bathroom with walls covered in a maze of water pipes, water pumps and siphons linked to valves, cylinders and a main generator. The bath in the centre was also embedded with brake cylinders, connecting rods, pistons, valves, camshafts, tubes, axles and other engine components. Reclining amidst the bath was the same woman shown in the *Moonlight Striptease* series.

I had originally planned to draw another female figure for this one, but from the first rough sketch, the face and body already resembled hers. It was as if there was no one else I would rather draw—or perhaps, *could* draw.

Her arm rested on the safety rail enclosing the bath. The foam climbed up the left side of her body to her neck and covered the right side of her face. Out of the froth, her full leg stretched while her half-exposed face, with the sharp green eye and purple lips, grinned as if she knew something unbearably intimate about you.

Right above the bath was a little round window, misted with vapour. On the other side of it, a man's face peered in, his nose flattened against the glass. He gaped at the woman not in lust, but in despair.

> 11.05
> I'm coming to town for some shopping.
> I'm going to shop till I drop.
> It's the season to be jolly.

> 16.20
> Just finished shopping and I've bought so many clothes!
> I'm at L'Essence now, drinking tea and reading a book.
> Life can't get more perfect.
> Care to join me for some aromatic tea?

## 21

L'Essence was only a ten-minute walk from where I lived. The streets were covered with white and brown slush. In the teahouse, the air was hot and heavy with several different aromas. Mural paintings full of glittering colours hung on all the walls. I instantly felt safe in this snug place. It was as if I had entered a tiny corner of the world that was always the same, where time never passed. L'Essence was not unlike a bathroom.

I found her sitting erect and cross-legged, surrounded by heaps of embroidered cushions, designer shopping bags and three kettles of oolong, black and pu-erh tea. Proust's novel, *In Search of Lost Time*, rested in her lap.

"I went shopping. Now I'm drinking tea," she said. "I feel good things are about to come. This morning was full of promises. It reminds me of the time I was in Corfu. My sister and I had gone there for a holiday. Today was like that."

She looked down at the carpet underneath her.

"I like to remember Corfu as that feeling you have when you hear an old melody from far away."

Then she gazed at me but her gaze was distant.

"There was a bay there. In Palaiokastrista. A tiny place it was, secluded by cliffs, and on these cliffs there were a lot of olive groves and citrus orchards. On some mornings, my sister and I would go there to lie down for hours, just lie down and observe the sunlight playing on those heights and the way it changed as the day wore on. When the afternoon grew late, wild birds would answer one another in shrill cries from different places hidden in the cliffs high above.

"On other early mornings, we'd head to the countryside in Kanoni to play hide-and-seek. This area would be so pale with all the mists in the morning that you wouldn't be able to see past a metre. I remember staring at the wet leaves while I hid and waited for my sister to find me. Some leaves had a drop of dew poised on the tip, never letting go. There were a few trees that had the shape of a fish or an eye etched on their trunk. When the sun was up, the air would suddenly be filled with the scents of so many strange flowers and herbs, and everything would emerge out of the mists, crisp and colourful.

"Once we grew tired of our games, we'd buy some olive oil, potatoes and drinks and go down an incline nearby to a pebbly beach where we'd buy some fresh fish from the fishermen and start a barbecue. We always set our barbecue near a grotto that served as a boathouse. I don't think I've ever had more delicious fish since.

"Then came the evening, when we'd sit on wicker chairs on the balcony of our tiny hostel room, sip frappe and lemonade and read verses from *The Odyssey* to each other. On a shelf on the balcony wall there was an old kerosene lamp that was always lit and there were always a few moths flickering around its glass chimney. Behind it there hung a small faded painting of the Virgin. As we'd read, the quiet of the evening would deepen and then the crickets would start chirping.

"There isn't anything like it in the world."

We moved on to chat about other things and at some point during our conversation, I slid close to her to kiss her. But she instantly pulled away from me.

"Is it the chainsaw again?" I said.

"Why can't we just talk?" she replied, and she moved further away.

"Here, have some tea," she offered.

She poured some black tea and raised her arm to hand it over.

Then she froze, her eyes glared. Her raised hand trembled. The cup rattled frenziedly in its saucer. Carmine spilled out of the cup, dripping from the saucer onto the carpet underneath. Her head quivered.

# 22

The following Monday I found a new friend request on Facebook. It was from Samuel Dubois, the stringy doctorate preacher fellow I had encountered in my exhibition at The Refuge. He looked very serious and pensive in his profile picture. Most likely he was meditating on the meaning of life. There was also a new Facebook message by Angelique.

> Monday, November 30, 2015
> 17.12
>
> Two streets away from mine by the Opium Path, there's a children's playground.
> During the day, the place is usually empty.
> But in the evenings, it is full of children who go there after school.
> They play on the swings and merry-go-rounds and slides and seesaws till the late hours.
> On Monday and Wednesday evenings,
> you can find me there, sitting on a bench, watching the children play.

> Wednesday, December 2, 2015
> 17.03
>
> Yesterday, I read a most beautiful poem.
> It's called "A Fan."
> I found out who wrote it: his name is Stéphane Mallarmé.

## When Her Time Comes

> I'm going to go buy a book of his poems from my favourite bookshop.
> I can't wait.
> Want to come?
>
> You can find me at the playground.

It was bright and cheerful when I got there. Tiny children jumped and ran and climbed up and went down the brightly coloured park toys. She was on a bench by herself, motionless, attentive. She was observing all the playing children with a silent intensity.

"You're late again," she said without as much as a glance in my direction. "I was just about to leave and go without you."

She stood up, snatched her handbag and slung it over her shoulder. Without a moment's notice, she walked away, hammering her high heels on the paving stones.

"I hate waiting," she snapped, waving her hand around. "I really hate it."

She took me to Morpheus Bookstore on Verrerie Road to buy her book of poems. It was a cosy little place with a tea bar. She instantly cheered up at the sight of all those books around us.

She walked to the French Literature section and started browsing through the shelves carefully.

"Sometimes I write," she said as she searched around. "I write and I become so many people and see so many places I've never seen before. I go through so many feelings. When I finish, there's nothing like it: it's perfect. The peace that comes after creation."

She stopped and batted her long eyelashes quickly a couple of times.

"I'm not sure if I'll live without writing."

From then on, whenever I passed by Verrerie Road I would spare a glance at Morpheus Bookshop and sometimes I would see her there behind a window, reading. She would be lost in one of Paulo Coelho's novels and on some occasions I saw her holding the third volume of Proust's *In Search of Lost Time*. There were always a lot of books on her table. I bet she barely even looked at any other book save the one in her hands. All those others were always simply there, like a fortress around her, waiting, just in case she needed them.

There were a couple of her short stories in the diary I had stolen from her flat. Most of them were similar. The island was always present, mystical, enchanting. At first you witnessed it in a dream, but then it found you. You would wake up on one of its ivory white beaches. From then on, you would explore its wild lands and behold the sacred magic that haunted its skies, forests, plains and mountains. And then, one day, you would meet a beautiful girl or handsome boy with whom you would travel from then on, the girl or boy who would eventually become your lover—the person you had been waiting for all this time.

There was also one entry in her diary that struck me in particular. It gave a new insight into why she wrote, why she did what she did.

*Sunday, 16 February, 2014*
This is wrong. It is beyond wrong. It is the kind of wrong that makes me want to write to make it right once more. At least for the time I'll be writing.

My aunt has done it again.

I saw her in bed face up, with her eyes glaring and her mouth gaping. She was still, very still. We called her name. We called her name again. She did not reply. She did not move at all.

She was sleeping with her eyes wide open.

We were told that's a sign. But the signs are everywhere.

The seizures have increased by at least twice a day and there are times when you wave at her and she does not see your hand, when you talk to her and she does not know it is you. She is stupefied by something that we are not seeing.

Her words got simpler as the weeks went by. And yet they now carried an echo they never carried before. The echo was so hollow that it kept me awake on some nights.

"God help me," she used to say. "God deliver me."

She used to be religious.

Then her phrases became questions.

"Where is God?" she said on many mornings, afternoons and nights. "Where is God?"

"*What* is God?" she started saying one day.

"What is this?" she asked later. "Where am I? What am I?"

"Where? How? Why? I? Who?"

Now she is silent. She has given up on words.
The tumour in her head does all the talking for her.
My writing outtalks its nonstop talking.

There was another reason why Angelique wrote.

It was not just her aunt's tumour that forced her pen to paper. There was the other tumour and it was not in her aunt. It was *in her*. Not in her brain . . . but in her *mind*.

One day, it was just there, before her, without invitation.

Once it showed up, it would not go. This shapeless lump stayed on. She was the host in which it thrived. It held on to her with the stubbornness of a parasite. Its persistence had that same blind indifference you would have found in any terminal disease.

Yet even this could have been tolerable for her. She would have learned to ignore it like so many of us learn to ignore our weaknesses, our defects, our ageing, our failures. She would have looked the other way. But this blind lump refused to be forgotten. It stuck out, with an obstinate resolve, right through her thoughts, right through her being. In its mute and dumb way, it would flaunt itself right in front of everything she did.

# 23

On the night I read Angelique's entry about the tumour, I played a video game about a guy who wants to quit his dead-end office job. He needs to tell his boss that he's quitting, but he never shows up to work. So one grey evening, he goes to his boss's house, which turns out to be a villa surrounded by a vast garden. The garden is awfully quiet, shrouded in a ghostly mist. From the distance, the house looks old and boarded up. In the description it said that this game was a survival adventure, although I encountered no one on the way to the front door. The enemy could be inside.

Perhaps it was this game that brought about the dream I had that night. It started in exactly the same way as the one I had several weeks ago.

I climbed into the attic of my Cardiff home from the window. I went down the narrow stairway and into the washing room and from there I went into the peach bathroom. The bathroom led into my bedroom and its other door led onto the landing. On the landing, I chose the door to my parents' bedroom. I couldn't open the bay windows in that room.

The footsteps were clattering across the bathroom. Soon they would be in my bedroom.

I returned to the landing and passed through the other mahogany door. It led to my little brother's bedroom, but he never liked it so much. Sometimes, late at night, a group of people from the neighbourhood would meet up right under his window and get drunk and shout. On these nights, Adonai would go to sleep in ma and pa's bed, but more often we would find him sleeping in the little bathroom downstairs, wrapped in blankets. For Adonai, that tiny room was the safest place in the world.

I could hear the footsteps now in my bedroom. They were uneven. One footstep sounded like a sharp clack, while the other was a quick light tap on the floor. Whoever it was seemed to be limping.

I could look inside my room. I could *see*. I took the stairs to the ground floor instead.

Bits of plaster from the ceiling were falling on the stairs. Old brown photos of my family tree lined the wall, which was veined with fissures. Some of the photos were too pale for me to identify the people in them.

When I reached the final stair, I found myself in the middle of a small corridor. To my right, it ended in an arched entrance to pa's study. To my left, it split around two sharp corners that faced each other.

Upstairs, someone was limping terribly onto the landing right above my head.

I went to the left side of the corridor and took the right corner. The entrance hall greeted me, enclosed by four white columns in every corner coiled with golden tinsel. An unlit Christmas tree knitted with cobwebs stood by a column. As I crossed the hall, I passed by a colossal baroque mirror suspended on the wall.

I reached the main entrance door. I turned the handle and pulled. The door didn't open. The keyhole had no key. I was locked inside.

I woke up just then. It was very late in the morning and the fridge was drumming.

# 24

The dream left me heavy—like I carried an unbearable weight.

So I started the morning with some *Face and the City*. Today I went for episode ten of season one—

### Freedom Bound

Vincent has fallen in love with Laura, the girl he met in church in episode six.

"Let's get away from here," he tells her. "A new world, a new life. Start anew."

She says she would like that. So together they hit the road, cutting themselves loose of everything and everyone, driving wherever the journey might lead, with no plans, no memories, no destination—just enjoying the here and now. They stop only for swims and to eat and sleep at nearby motels where they never stay longer than one night. On the next day they always move on toward the next moment, the next experience.

"We're going somewhere where we can be really free," he says.

# 25

On a warm Monday evening, I met Angelique at the playground again. She was sitting on her bench, staring at all the children playing with a vacant expression on her face. Two dry leaves had fallen on her shoulder and she hadn't noticed them. She only realized I was there when I was standing right in front of her. I had asked her to come with me to Museum Hypnôse to see the Michael Sisyphe Collection, which had opened for the public just a few days ago. I thought she'd say no, that she had other things to do. She said yes.

The exhibition consisted of around a hundred and twenty works of impressionist masters and prominent contemporary artists. There were Pablo Picasso, Jean Dubuffet, Pierre-Auguste Renoir, Claude Monet, Vincent Van Gogh, and Paul Gauguin, along with Georges Braque, Paul Klee and Nicolas de Staël, among others. We split up to look at different works. She wanted to look at the contemporaries and I preferred to start from the classics. From time to time I glanced at her from across the hall.

I noticed that she had been observing the same painting for quite a while. Something about it must have captured her complete attention. Whenever I glanced at her, she was still stationed in the same place, staring at it. I couldn't tell how it was making her feel. Her face rarely made any expression I could really understand.

The painting in question had the realism of a photograph. It showed a girl with tousled hair and a gossamer dress with one strap loose, resting her head on the naked lap of someone who was cut off from the picture. The girl's eyes were closed and kohl-stained tears streamed across her face, down her nose to her open mouth. She looked completely lost in ecstasy—an image not unlike those images that hung in Angelique's flat. The signature was of Balthioul Lovelace. The painting was entitled "The Edge."

I put my arm around her waist and touched her hip lightly. She jumped and stared back at me with a blank face. She shrugged me off and moved toward the next painting.

We observed the next couple of artworks together. The sixth or seventh we passed was signed "Rose Dumas" and it had that blur that made it look like a scene from a vague dream or a scene brought about by some hallucinogenic drug. It featured a man with a smooth chest in a fur-lined cloak, reclining on a velvet throne, holding a jade cigarette holder. His protruding belly hung over his groin in tight trousers. His face was a smudge, which made his features unrecognisable. Next to the painting was the title in elegant calligraphy: "The Duke."

We observed the smudged face in silence.

"You went to his place, didn't you?" I asked.

She said nothing but kept on observing him.

"Maybe once? Twice?"

"His world doesn't attract me," she replied after a long moment of silence. "I don't want fantasy. I'm looking for love."

I was behind her again and I stepped closer toward her.

"Who says fantasy and love are incompatible?" I asked. "As far as I'm concerned, they're one and the same."

"You know exactly what I mean," she said.

"But people *do* make a big deal out of some neurons firing up in the brain," I said. "For all intents and purposes, being in love's a chemical reaction in our brain that makes us see unicorns farting rainbows."

I stepped close enough that I could smell her delicate perfume radiating from her neck.

"But I guess the fuss—the fuss is all about the fact that there's no stopping those crazy neurons. Once they kick off, oh boy, there's no knowing what we can do."

I touched her hand. I started tracing my fingertips along the lines of her palm.

"At that point, there's no going back," I continued. "You finally get to realize that what's really making the big decisions in life is not you."

My thigh brushed against her bum.

"It's your body," I whispered in her ear. "It's always been your body."

I placed my other hand on the small of her back. She instantly went tense. But she didn't flinch. She didn't move away. Not this time.

"We are the sum total of the chemical reactions inside of us," I told her.

My lips went down to the slope of her neck and shoulder. They brushed her skin for the briefest of seconds. Her skin was hot.

"So give in to it. Give in to your body."

And then I went for it. I kissed her neck.

She tore away from me and, calm as ever, marched on to the next painting.

# 26

I can say with complete certainty that the Sisyphe Collection was one of the richest collections I had ever witnessed to date. I could have easily spent two or more days there. All the paintings, sculptures and video clips seemed to be screaming out for my attention *all at the same time*, leaving no time to think about anything else other than their competing images and colours and sounds and movements. I experienced an artwork even as I was already anticipating others after it. The enjoyment of one experience was already being blitzed by the thrills of oncoming others.

Some minutes after our little chat on love, Angelique got bored of the museum and I had to leave with her. And yet the Sisyphe Collection stayed with me long after that day and in time helped me perhaps understand her more. It reminded me of when I used to see her in the window of the Morpheus Bookstore, reading one book in the midst of so many other books all around her. It reminded me of when I saw her in the thick smoke of L'Essence, surrounded by shopping bags filled with clothes, mounds of cushions and different teas. It reminded me of her place, cluttered with so many paintings and the music that went on day and night. I could see a connection between these memories of her and the hypnotic experience of being in the vertiginous middle of all those artworks.

It was my guess that Angelique crowded herself with all these little pleasures to *crowd out* the dismay and emptiness that came when a pleasure ended or was going to end. She choked out the awareness of time passing with all these possible pleasures at hand. Their presence reassured her that close by were so many other opportunities for pleasure. That way her feelgood was secured for an indefinite time.

For this same reason Angelique sometimes squeezed some of her days with an almost impossible amount of activities and events. She would babysit in the mornings and afternoons, head to the gym right after, then shop for food and clothes, then plan a complicated meal for dinner, then meet friends for drinks and finally head to a musical concert or the cinema. Being busy gave Angelique a sense of direction; her tight schedules overwhelmed the day with purpose.

They made sure there would be no gap in between what she was doing then and what she would be doing after that. The gap made her anxious even *while* she was still absorbed in her current activities. It gave the sense of an impending end, the approach of that moment that was stripped of any distractions. Without a distraction, the hole would reveal itself.

It was often in times like these that *it* happened.

The eye would open.

## 27

There were times when I was out with her and she would stop in front of a children's boutique for a few moments to observe all the little clothes on display. She would stare at them in complete silence with an intense gleam in her eyes and her lower lip would often tremble.

"I've always loved children," she muttered once. "I'd love to have my own. It's my dream. I'd give them my all."

On the Friday before Christmas, we went shopping for presents and she bought a lot of clothes for her little cousins and her one niece. When we had bought enough for everyone, she said she wanted to tour the other kids' stores to buy toys as well.

"Or alternatively, what say you to a drink with a view?" I suggested. "All this thinking of others makes one thirsty."

I showed her all the full shopping bags I was carrying.

"Maybe I'd rather go home now," she said with a tone of defeat.

"Oh, your home would do."

"My balcony has no view."

"I'd have to settle for you."

She blinked. Dismay quickly darkened her face.

"Besides," I continued, "your ladyship requires a loyal servant to help her carry all this shopping for her. And loyalty is in short supply these days. So you see, it'd be like hitting two stones with one bird . . . or however that goes."

"You can come," she murmured, as the tension seemed to leave her body. "Yes, you can come."

But it didn't matter to her if I came, if she shopped, if she cared for someone or enjoyed herself. All this I understood much later on. A static had turned everything that was around her—places, experiences and people—into something unreal. All the vivid reality of the world had disappeared, and what remained was a silence that turned everything that was present into everything that belonged elsewhere. The now she was living in was not really here: it had withdrawn to an infinite distance, immediate yet remote, indefinite, like smoke.

The vanilla musk at her flat was so strong it made me nauseous. We went out on her balcony as the sky grew dark. She switched on the spotlight and it blazed us with its clinical light. Again, I had the impression that we were actors and out there in the deep darkness lay the attentive auditorium.

She had an Isabel Marant miniskirt wrapped around her thighs and she crossed and uncrossed her long legs. I placed my hand just above her knee as I talked to her. My hand slid up very slowly and then slid down again. Her skin was as smooth as a peeled plum.

"You like to touch, don't you?" she said.

"It's a condition," I answered. "My dad gave it to my mum. And they both gave it to me. I suppose my future child will face the same . . . predicament."

I gave her a stoned smile. I didn't take my hand off her and she made no effort to push me off either. She was actually letting me touch her.

"Be that as it may," I blurted on, "here's to Christmas," and I made a toast. "May it be full of red wine and bad decisions."

We tipped our glasses.

"There's still seven days left," she pointed out.

"Well, I'll be leaving in three days to Cardiff. I booked the flight just this morning." I raised my glass again. "And here's to getting through all the family pleasantries with duty-free Welsh whisky."

We tipped our glasses again. My hand crawled a bit higher up her thigh.

"You're going to miss my birthday then," she stated.
"When's that?"
"Two days just before Christmas. It's going to be fun."
"How fun is fun?"
"I guess you'll never know."

I decided to leave soon after. A blank canvas awaited me tomorrow morning and I had no idea what to do with it. As a matter of fact, I hadn't had a single idea in weeks.

We went to the elevator and I got in. I was instantly surrounded by the starkest three reflections on the mirrored walls. All four of us pressed the button to the ground floor. The doors didn't respond at first. We pressed the button a couple more times. She waited politely outside for the lift to close and go down.

The steel doors finally rumbled to life, slowly starting to move toward each other to shut me in. She said bye.

I raised my arm in between the doors, grabbed her elbow and pulled her inside. She staggered forward into the lift, surrounded by her three other astonished replicas.

"You want to," I told her.

I put my arm around her and drew her gently against my chest. Our chests were heaving together.

"You *know* you want to."
"I don't," she said with dead certainty.

She stared at me for a while, deadpan.

"But since you insist . . . " she then said.

Still holding her, I shoved her back against the mirrored wall with the buttons. Her bum clicked some of them. The doors started closing again. I stroked her right cheek. My lips played with her left ear and then went down the side of her face, down her neck and then up against her chin, toward her lips.

The doors slammed shut. The elevator around us rattled and

then started humming.

I brushed my lips against hers. My other hand slid down the curve of her thigh.

I then slipped my tongue into her small mouth, and it opened up for me, letting me enter its warm and wet world. In that darkness my tongue met her tongue: liquid-quick, restless, challenging. She answered my kissing with an equal ferocity and this made hot blood rush into my head.

I opened my eyes at that moment and caught a reflection of myself snogging her in a mirror. I winked at it and it winked back.

The elevator bumped to a rough halt and rattled all over again. The doors shuddered and then slowly began juddering open. She broke away from me and took a few steps back. I went out into the entrance corridor.

"If only I'd known it was this easy if I used the lift," I told her, "I would've stopped using the stairs a long time ago."

"Don't try again," she replied. "I don't like you in that way."

She pressed the button and the doors were closing again. There was only a small gap between them—when her head started quivering on its own.

Then the doors slammed shut. The elevator groaned and went up.

# 28

When I got home, I couldn't sleep a wink and I kept on tossing and turning in my bed. I had finally done it.

How different I was on that night, in those days when I could forget myself in a moment or in a memory. Back then, I could lose myself and *be* the experience or *be* the memory. Now all that is gone: the spell shattered. That time is a distant fantasy.

Now, a year forward, as I gaze in the mirror of the Glaze Restaurant toilet, I know that every so often, in whatever I see, in whatever I do, in whatever I feel—I am *reminded*. I see and do through this reminder.

I am reminded that I have *this* face.

Seasons change but this face remains. It is the only constant in the endless movements, the repeated cycles. This face is the still point of my turning world.

The skin on one side is stretched too tight. It is so taut that it feels as if it might rip open at any moment. This skin neither feels nor looks as if it is mine. It has sensations of its own.

I'm jealous of how pure and strong my emotions were back then, jealous of my innocence on that night when I could not sleep because I had kissed Angelique.

# 29

On Saturday morning, I found out on Facebook that Samuel had just invited me to a party he was hosting on that very same evening. The event description read:

*Before the World Ends*
Today at 18.00

These are the last days, the very last hours, lived in the grey light. Very soon there will be nothing and we will be no more. The empty darkness will swallow all.
You are therefore all cordially invited to the place where we shall dream the short future away one instant at a time. Let us all play and pretend and dance in our dreams as the darkness slowly descends upon us.
Come hence to the last haven near the edge of the world.
Come to the Dream House.

Any poison of your own choice is welcome. Do not bring your wits with you.

For the occasion, I slipped into a loose white shirt with a Chinese collar and crimson jeans torn at the knees. Finally, a Matrix-styled leather trench coat.

I went into the bathroom. The bulb fastened to the mirror cast its halogen illumination over me.

My face stared back at me, tense and severe.

I told myself:

*I am old with so many tragic stories. My exhaustion has knocked the life out of anything that can happen to me.*

*What remains is a wasteland. This is the leftover world where nothing has value anymore. It is the world swept perpetually by the blight of exhaustion, a blight which has drained up all feelings, taking everything I have, everything I care about away. And because it has robbed me of it all, this same blight empowers me. It becomes my secret weapon.*

*In killing off all my fear and shame, exhaustion has set me free. It has allowed me to do just about anything.*

*Here, in the leftover world, a decision, any decision does not have consequence. I can do this or I can do that and it makes no difference. No decision can ever intimidate any longer. If nothing is important, it does not matter what I do.*

*So any possible experience that I can have is an opportunity that I can taste without guilt, without regrets, without fear. Whatever I want, I can do just like that without the least iota of hesitation. The sky is the limit because nothing has gravity. Anything can be tasted for the sheer fun of it. The world has become my party. All experiences have been turned into holidays.*

*And I cannot stop this dance from one holiday to the next. Boredom is the foundation of my life and it creeps into anything I do. I must not rest for even one moment from my dance. The fun show must continue distracting me from the hollowness it is a symptom of.*

*I have grown so old that I have become so young.*

To my face in the mirror, I recite:

"Nothing is real. Everything is permitted."

And then my face loosens: it surrenders. My eyes lose their intense focus, my tight scowl slackens . . .

A new face now smiles back at me.

# 30

Samuel's place was close to Saint Laurent's bus terminus. After a couple of rings, the door buzzed open and I went upstairs to number 3. "Dream House" was sprayed lazily in red above the door left ajar. Electronic music was beeping and meowing and womping from inside.

I walked into an empty corridor in the dental light of a row of LED tubes in the ceiling. The walls and floor were white ceramic tiles and identical grey aluminium doors were on either side. I made my way toward the electronic music and the corridor opened into a large white space that was also filled with the glare of ceiling LED tubes. The place was bare save for a few zinc tables and some cheap plastic-covered camelback sofas and steel chairs. Samuel was in a corner playing the funky music from his laptop and some people were chatting and drinking. No one had noticed me yet.

I helped myself to some vodka from one of the tables. There were also some lines of coke on the stainless steel breadboard in the kitchen. I snorted two lines.

I was rubbing my gums when I suddenly spotted someone I recognized sitting on one of the plastic couches. He was digging his hands into different bowls of crisps and then stuffing the crisps into his mouth one fist after another, spilling bits and pieces all over the belly bulging out from under his teeshirt.

Gregory, the chef who never delivered, had deigned to grace me with his bulbous presence once more. He was gawping at a wall with a slimy childlike smile, and in the intense light, his skin had an oily sheen.

I went up to him.

"Hey jackass, that wasn't cool. That wasn't cool at all."

Gregory turned to me with his watery puppy eyes, munching frenziedly and beaming.

"I bet you had one hell of a laugh about it with your other Neanderthal buddies. 'Hey guess what? There was this artist dude shagging in the toilet and he fell for my prank. That's so funny, right?'"

"But you know what the truth is?"

"No," he replied.

"That you've probably been sacked and you're probably broke right now. That's right, I called your manager. That's right, I insisted that she fire your sorry ass."

He reached out for the crackers next. With the first cracker he scooped up most of the salmon dip in a bowl.

"Do I ring any bell?" I then decided to ask.

"Yeah," and he gave me a bashful look.

"Then why are you looking at me like I'm your girlfriend?"

He popped the cracker into his mouth.

"*Dude*, you *never* showed up."

"Why?" he pleaded as he munched away.

"Because you're an asshole!"

"I don't know, man."

He cleaned what little dip there was left in the bowl with his two sausage fingers, which he then stuck in his mouth and sucked.

"It's good man. This is good," he said after a while. "I'm Gregory," and he took his fingers from out of his mouth and extended his hand to me.

I just turned my back to him, returned to the kitchen and snorted another line. I was about to do yet another when a girl with blue eyes and a cat ears headband came over to pour some orange juice. She had curly voluminous hair full of ribbons that fell over her shoulders.

"Bump?"

I offered my straw to her.

"Oh thank you. I . . . I have to work tomorrow." She smiled fiercely as her hand slipped into her hair and scratched inside at her neck.

"Not if the world's going to end tomorrow," I pointed out.

"Why's it going to end tomorrow?"

"Party theme. We're supposed to go along with it, right?"

"Oh yeah, right."

She flashed me a smile that was too wide to be believed. She scratched her neck again.

"Are you an actor?" she asked.

"I guess I can act out the last-day-on-earth scenario pretty well if that's what you mean," I answered.

"How would you do it?"

"I'm doing it right now."

"But what are you doing right now?"

"Sweet-talking a beautiful girl to join the act that nothing will matter by tomorrow. So might as well do *anything* today."

"That's a pretty feeling—that everything will end tomorrow."

With her eyes glaring, she showed me all her teeth in a fanatical smile. Her hand slid into her hair and scratched and scratched.

"And it's romantic," she pointed out. "You seem to be a romantic person . . . and a convincing one as well."

She grabbed a bottle of green absinthe from the table and quickly filled up half a highball glass. Clearing her throat, she swallowed it up in one go.

"I don't know about romantic," I said, "but I usually mean what I say and say what I mean."

I brushed away a long curl that had fallen on her face.

"Then you're also very honest!" she exclaimed. "And that makes you even more romantic than I thought!"

Her hand went back into her hair and hacked away.

"You could be right," I replied. "Show me a sunset or a picture of Mother Teresa and I'll start crying."

"You're also very intelligent," she continued. "And most importantly of all—*funny!*"

"Oh."

Her face suddenly made a twisted grimace but then quickly recovered its excited expression.

"Now I've to go to the bathroom," she stated. "And sometimes I forget to lock the door."

"And they say romance is dead."

# 31

I went up on my knees and peeled off the Durex Pleasuremax condom. Beneath me, the girl with the cat ears was sprawled on her back in the bath. She had lost her cheerful expression and was staring upward with dejection. Her hair was spread all about her head, exposing her neck. On her neck there was a red patch of swollen skin the size of an apple, as if she had been branded by a hot iron.

She caught me noticing it.

"My hand does it," she said. "Sometimes I don't even know it's doing it."

I asked her why it did it and she said, "It does it when something is ending and something else is going to begin."

I told her I didn't understand.

So she said: "I think there's another life going on inside me and it's not mine. I can see quick glimpses of it but I don't really know what they're showing me, what's taking place there. They're so vague. And it's all happening on the edges of my day-to-day life. It's like a movie going on nearby and I'm always focusing on other things, never stopping for a moment to watch any part of it. But I'm dead certain it's there. *I know it.*"

Her hand raised itself and the bracelets clanked and the nails hacked and hacked at the patch on her neck as if they wanted to rip it all off.

"But why the scratching," I asked her.

"I think my hand scratches me because it wants me to feel something definite. It wants to reassure me. It's its own way of telling me that this at least is familiar, this is real."

I climbed out of the bath and went to the sink to take a leak.

"I don't think I want to see that," she said, "that other life. So my hand takes care of that in those moments when I'm about to see it—when something's going to end and something else is going to begin. When my hand's scratching, it's forcing me to focus on itself. Its scratching is a scratching out."

My mobile rang. Someone had just sent me a message on WhatsApp.

> Sent by: Angelique Duval
>
> Saturday, December 19, 2015
> 22.04
>
> I'm having prebirthday drinks with some friends at the Hieroglyph in Saint Paradis Street.
> Great vibe, great times.
> Are you coming?

"I have to go," I said.

"Me too," she replied, still lying in the bath.

Two bright streams of blood snaked down her neck.

I opened the door and left the Dream House.

# 32

It was my first time at The Hieroglyph—a techno electronic club, lit with ice blue neon.

I ordered a whisky neat and walked around looking for Angelique and her friends. It took me quite some time since many of the Baroque disco couches were crowded with groups drinking shooters and making out. Finally, on one of the sofas, I glimpsed the back of her head with the familiar short gelled hair. Approaching, I realized that she was alone. She was sitting up in a rigid manner, swirling a glass of red. She was glancing at the empty sofa in front of her with an imperious frown.

"My friends got hungry," she said as she noticed me. "They've all gone to eat."

I sat next to her.

"They've all gone to eat at Marmara Spicy Kebab." Her lower lip was quivering.

"I want to have fun tonight," she added.

She downed her glass. She refilled it with the bottle close by.

"I *need* to have fun tonight."

I took her to the clubbing area beyond the lounge. We plunged into the people swinging to the hammering techno. In the spastic lights, she looked like a spectre flashing on and off continuously. Groin to groin we swayed together, my hands on her waist, her arms on my shoulders. She leaned her head back and closed her eyes to the whirl of lights and bodies.

Suddenly she jumped as her body spasmed. Her eyes glared and her face twisted. I took my hands off her and drew back. The spasm ran through her like a high-voltage current rapidly jerking her legs, waist, torso, arms, shoulders, neck, and head in different directions. She shook her head savagely to shrug it off. There was a hateful and determined anger on her face now.

Without warning, she grabbed my wrist and wrenched me away from the dance floor. She dragged me across the lounge to the large glass tube that led to the exit. She spotted a large mirror panel behind her on the wall. Pushing her back against it, it swung open to the inside as a door. It led to the toilets. She pulled me inside. Before us were three plain doors to three stalls. On one of them was a message sprayed in violet.

*Come hide in the lights.*

She shoved me against that door. It flew open and I stumbled in. A circle overhead instantly turned on, casting a beam upon me. The stall was a bare white little room that reminded me of the glossy cubicle of an airship. Another message was sprayed on the wall.

*The faeces are outside.*

There was a long fine crack across the ceiling right above the toilet. From this crack, a saffron yellow liquid was dripping. Every drop made a hollow plop and a tiny spatter as it struck the floor.

I see now that this everlasting dripping was the rhythm of her life. Plop. And then the stretch of quiet. For how long, she wouldn't know: half an hour, a few hours, a day? Sometimes she hoped that it would last long.

And then, again. Plop. And she was knifed. Plop. And she lost herself. It was the only moment that felt alive every day.

The time in between was an interval: a space for some respite. It wasn't real because its quiet was false. It was only a matter of time before the next one came . . .

Will it come soon now or will it take its time? It *cannot* not come.

And after that, there will be another and another. Plop . . . Plop . . . plop.

If the thought was anything, it was an alarm clock. It reminded her of the next time it would arrive. It reminded her of time, *her* time, as a series of arrivals.

Her world would then shrink into a little cell. The air would go stale and scarce.

In the graphic light, she slammed me against a wall and unbuckled my belt.

"This is what you want!" she said. "This is what you came for tonight!"

She pulled down my jeans.

"This is why you meet me!"

She ripped down my boxers.

She grabbed my member and kneaded it with her spotted nail-polished fingers. She jerked it back and forth ruthlessly, kneeled, swallowed it all with her mouth, and jerked it back and forth with her lips as her restless tongue licked its glans. As she sucked, she goggled up at me with greedy bright eyes, gurgling with every swallow into her mouth.

Upon releasing me, she grabbed her Hervé Léger miniskirt from behind and tore it apart. Turning around, she bent down, held onto the toilet and thrust up her ass at me.

"This is what you want!" she shouted hoarsely.

Parting away the flaps of her torn skirt, I gripped her shoulder with one hand and with the other her thigh. My first thrust went in deep and shook her forward with a moan. Withdrawing, I did another with the same force, and then a quicker halfway pace was picked up.

"Faster!" she roared. "Go *cunting* faster!"

I dug in and out as fast as I could until my thumping synchronized with the techno beat outside. With every entry, she shuddered and moaned, and her moans crawled out from deep inside her throat. A particularly ferocious push knocked her so far forward that she clutched at the wall, clawing it down, snapping off two of her fingernails. Without a moment's notice, she was squirming and squealing. Her orgasm finally ripped out of her.

## 33

The eve of my departure to Cardiff for Christmas finally arrived. On that afternoon, I was walking down Lotus Street when I passed by a restaurant with a sign that said "Marmara Spicy Kebab." I could see from the glass windows that it was a fairly large place. I went inside.

A few customers were eating kebabs at the Formica tables. A boy, probably nine or ten years old, was serving them and taking orders. There was a shelf under the counter displaying a very generous variety of toppings and shish kebabs. Behind it was a stainless steel kitchen cluttered with plates, saucepans, cutlery and an electric oven. A middle-aged man with dark skin and a jolly-roger bandana was busy frying chips. He was speaking in Arabic to one of the customers waiting to pay. A rather tall woman with a silvery Cleopatra bob was cutting some meat from three greasy, slowing rotating kebab grills. Her thickly lined eyes with spidery eyelashes and intense red lips contrasted with the whiteness of the foundation on her face. A screen on a high shelf was displaying a fashion show on MTV.

I was hungry, so I walked over to the counter to ask for a menu. The woman noticed me and came over. Under her oily apron she had a long vintage silk dress on.

"How can I help you?" she asked, placing the stained kitchen knife on the table.

Her voice was three octaves lower than mine.

## 34

I managed to make it just in time to the airport, thanks to one wine bottle too many the previous night. I had just taken my seat on the plane when I realized that I had left the presents I bought my family back at my apartment. I would have to make do with the Heathrow Airport duty-free and pretend that all the stuff had been bought in France. Some perfumes with French names would do. They always do.

It was really hard to think straight on that morning. My hangover was the saint of all killers. I could think of only two things that could remedy this. The first was the classic hair-of-the-dog, so I ordered a double whisky. Once I had a good sip, things started to look bright again. After that, I looked for my second. I checked the seat-back screen to see what was available to watch. And there it was! *Face and the City*! On impulse, I went for season two, episode six—

It's All Physical

Vincent Face is being interviewed on TV by Dr Kristeva, one of his archenemy critics, who also happens to be a feminazi academic.

"Why is the concept of love nonexistent in all your novels?" she asks.

"Why does everything have to be about love these days?" he slurs. "We're all putting that word on a pedestal it might not deserve. As far as I'm concerned, love's just a stimulation that triggers a bunch of neurons in the brain."

Dr Kristeva's mouth twitches a couple of times with extreme irritation.

"Don't you think that your exposition, Mr Face, is rather degrading? The love I'm referring to can be defined as the subject's freely willing openness to another person's absolutely unknown identity. It would also entail a particularly intense sensitivity to that person's needs. Ergo, love as an unqualified sacrifice, an unconditional givingness to the other."

"It still doesn't make that hard-bone fact less true. Love comes about because a certain stimulus from outside affects our brain, hormones, genes, and ancestral evolutionary traits—in a word, our biology. Like everything else."

"Mr Face," and she visibly quivers as her eyes glare at him, "are you saying that you cannot love someone out of your own free will? Ergo, are you conclusively denying the existence of free will?"

"What, me?" Vincent points at himself and makes an astonished face. "Well . . . as far as I'm concerned, free will's just an impulse caused by a certain code in all our genes and brain traits. You do what you do, and it's all a reflex, a knee-jerk kicked off by some neuronal activity through some laws of chemistry and physics. *ERGO,* we're all just the sum total of our chemical reactions."

Vincent raises his eyebrows and purses his lips. Then he takes out a hipflask from his jacket, opens it, and raises a toast.

Finally, the doctor asks, "So if we shouldn't talk about the universal significance of love, Mr Face, what should we talk about in this misogynistic day and age?"

"Bodies," he replies. "In the end it's our bodies that tell us what to think, what to feel, what to do. It's all physical. We're moral when we're in a good mood and in good health. We want pleasure or power when we're not.

"And right now, I'd wager, you're all in for power. And I'm all in for pleasure."

"Can we just agree on pleasure?"

Suddenly Dr Kristeva stands up and slaps Vincent hard across his face. She grabs his collar and wrenches him up to his feet. She pulls his head down toward her. Her lips crush into his. She starts kissing him furiously. They take their clothes off and start banging on the chairs of the conference hall. At some point, both of them raise their heads together toward the entrance. Laura is standing there, still, silent, staring back at them. There is an expression of defeat and resignation on her face. Just as quietly as she has entered, she leaves.

# 35

I stayed in Cardiff for sixteen utterly drab days, returning to France on 6 January of the new year. On arriving at the Marseille airport, I went straight to the gents' room. I sat on a toilet, lit one up, and contemplated the largest message etched on the stall door in front of me.

*Gabriel is here.*

I was just about to take a sip of the duty-free whisky in my hipflask when the phone rang.

> Sent by: Angelique Duval
> 17.43
>
> My birthday was a blast.
> You've missed so much and you need to make up for it.
> I know you're back.
> So meet me this evening at Rêves de Soie on Boulevard Résurrection at 21.00.

I instantly replied that I would be there. It was 17.43. The bus ride to Saint Laurent was only around half an hour. There would be plenty of time left to unpack and shower.

I wheeled my luggage through Arrivals and walked over to the bus stop. There was only one other person waiting for the bus, a tall, toned dark-skinned girl, with braided hair in a scoop midi dress, who seemed to have just stepped out of a plastic surgeon's wet dream. She was standing with one hand posed on her hip and as I checked her out she did that wild hair flick they do in the L'Oréal commercials.

Exactly fifteen minutes before my date with Angelique, I was climbing up the stairs to my place two, three steps at a time. When I arrived at my door, I managed to stick in all the wrong keys first before I got to the right one. Once it clicked, I kicked open the door and darted in, tripping over the garbage bags that permanently guarded the entrance. Cigarette ash and stubs poured out of the bags, along with pizza delivery boxes and empty wine bottles that started rolling out across the floor. No time for that now. No time to unpack. I had around ten minutes—just enough time to do the more crucial one of two critical things before I left:

Shower and change OR vibe up.

Tonight's fate seemed to depend on what decision I made.

Vibe up, I decided.

I slipped into the bathroom and switched on the halogen light. My face in the mirror looked doped already.

I was already halfway there.

Through deep concentration, I started to delve deeper into that attitude, further reclaiming those thoughts with that feeling—

*I am so bored. My boredom is invulnerable.*

*My boredom drains the seriousness out of life. Anything that comes my way has already lost its life. When it all stops meaning anything, then nothing can take over me, nothing can affect me, nothing can change me. I am free of it all.*

*An empty world, however, is not that easy to live with. Its emptiness can be painful, frightening, anguishing. It can be hard to carry around and can drag you down. It can force upon you so many questions. What will you do now? Who are you now? What will guide you now?*

*But if it hurts to be like this, it is because you still care, you still miss what you had and what you were before.*

*The caring has to go.*

*Once it is gone, a singular lightness will fill your life. You will realize that the sheerness of the nothing can get you high. It can take you up and out of the immediateness of your life and from these heights you are able to see everyone else down there, remote, ridiculous, in their little prisons of mammal emotions. From this distance, you cannot help but laugh at how lost they all are in their tiny soap operas, how seriously they all take them. In this way, the world becomes a top-notch comedy.*

*Comedy sweetens the arid taste of the wasteland's ash. It turns the wasteland into an amusement park.*

*Endless sarcasm loosens all the bonds you had to life. Sarcasm will set you free.*

Here I am. Let's have some fun.

## 36

I rushed out of the flat just five minutes before my date, slamming the door behind me and knocking off some of the plaster above it.

On my way to Boulevard Résurrection, I walked into Lotus Street and past Marmara Spicy Kebab. From the glass door and windows, I could see that it was overcrowded. Everyone was frantically cramming their greasy mouths with kebabs: so many overfull mouths chewing wildly away to different rhythms, taking large bites the moment they swallowed. Many hadn't even finished their kebab and were already ordering another.

The young boy was once again taking all their orders. In the open kitchen, the Arab with the bandana was preparing the plates and handing them to him over the counter. The woman with the Cleopatra bob wasn't doing anything. She was observing the clientele devouring their food from behind the till.

I was about to move on when I spotted two of Angelique's friends sitting at one of the tables. There was hyper happy Osanne and tired Nina. Both were quickly stuffing their mouths with pita and sauced lamb. Nina seemed to have gained quite a bit of weight since that night I had met them, when she had decided that Le Divin just absolutely would not do.

I arrived at Rêves de Soie at around 21.20. There were several people here in their suits and evening dresses, savagely gobbling their food as if it was about to be snatched away at any moment. No background music or chit-chatter was going on. An intense silence hung over the place. The only movement around me was the endless chewing on all the blank faces.

Angelique greeted me with a severe glance as I made my way to her table. I knew I was late. It was also at that moment that I noticed the fishy smell on my fingers, curtsey of the Arrivals encounter. So I had to run off to the toilet to wash my hands and allay any suspicions before I could sit down and give her my full attention.

"I've been sick for about two weeks," she said when I returned, and she gave me a meaningful look.

"The fever was so strong that I couldn't control my body. I was just trembling in bed from morning till night."

I asked her what the doctor said.

"I don't want to see a doctor," she said. "I hate doctors. They're all incompetent. They'll give you either useless advice or false advice. All they want is your money."

We were served an assiette royale and a spaghetti bolognese.

"Well, here's to new beginnings," I said and we clinked glasses.

We ate in silence. The assiette royale was good but nothing special.

I dipped a piece of bread in some oil and put it into my mouth. Angelique suddenly froze, her face fell, eyes popped out, mouth opened. She went all white, as if she had just bitten something hard and cracked her tooth on it. Her hand was trembling. But then she grabbed the fork again and plunged it into the pasta with a vengeance. She lifted it up wrapped all over with spaghetti, and rammed it right away into her mouth. Quickly, she dug in and lifted up another forkful, shovelling that inside as well. She stuffed her face with more and more spaghetti until her exploded mouth couldn't take in any more, until she couldn't even close it. Then, she munched and munched and munched away hysterically. The moment she managed to gulp some down, she instantly gobbled up some more.

Her plate was empty before I had even finished half of mine. She signalled to a waiter close by with her chin all splashed with sauce and bits of meat.

"Another!" she managed to say.

Eating induced Angelique to *let go*. Its rhythms and flow of tastes gradually took over her and she gave in to them. Eating brings with it the gift of release, the gift of self-abandon. For Angelique, it held the promise of a way out of the thought.

But on that night, as on so many other occasions when she ate and slipped unwarily into forgetfulness, she suddenly *caught herself* forgetting. She *surprised herself* in the process of being carried away. And at that split instant she realized very acutely what she was doing. I'm getting clandestinely away from what owns me, she'd tell herself.

To forget simply meant to remember again later on. It was only there to postpone.

Sometimes it was the thought that remembered her. It would often come at the most unsuspecting moment. When she would be at her most forgetful, when her guard would be completely down—it would strike then.

And the more she forgot, the harder it would strike. The more distracted she had become, the more shocking its revelation would be.

If eating led to abandon, this abandon turned to acid in her mouth. Eating woke her up to the alarm of herself.

Just as you forget completely, you remember. The moment it's over, it's not. It has begun again.

# 37

Straight after our dinner at Rêves de Soie, we headed to The Wohoo! The Wohoo! was the only bar in Endymion Street, a street chockablock with glass and steel office buildings. The bar was very popular with university students.

Tonight was Jager Pong night. Students were throwing little balls at glasses with shots of Jager. Teams had to take a shot whenever they missed. We joined a team and played for some time. I sank a couple of balls but Angelique missed almost all of them.

"Wohoo!" she shrieked whenever she missed and then downed a shot.

In her kitchen a few hours later, she clung onto me, stark naked with her legs wrapped around my waist, her nails digging into my back, her mouth open and her eyes rolled upward. That was the last thing I remembered on that night. At one point her burning body was all over me, the next I lost consciousness.

And then I was climbing a window that led into the attic of my family house in Cardiff. From the attic, I went down into the washing room.

Now I was dreaming. That dream again.

The bay windows in my parents' bedroom couldn't be opened. Downstairs, the entrance door of the house was locked from the outside.

I stayed still and listened. The house was silent. I could hear nothing.

Then it started again: one vicious clatter followed by a light tap. The limping was on the landing upstairs.

The entrance hall opened on my right into the sitting room, with its iris blue curtains drawn over the windows. I took a closer look at the photos in the wall unit. They were photos of my family and myself when I was younger. On one of the little shelves stood a statuette of the Virgin Mary with her palms opened outward. It was surrounded by several flowers and I could recognize white and purple lilacs. The flowers had all wilted away. The largest shelf in the wall unit held an old television that faced the sofas.

As I crossed the entrance hall back to the stairs, I caught myself in the huge baroque mirror suspended on the wall. A younger me looked back, wearing a dark blue tracksuit that said "Sahara" on its top.

A gargling noise suddenly broke out from upstairs. It went on and on. I couldn't tell if it was someone making this noise or if it was the rattle of some machine just switched on. The limping joined in. Both sounds were now at the very edge of the landing, about to descend the first stair.

I passed by the stairway and the corridor leading to pa's study and kept on walking straight on. A long corridor stretched out before me, veiled in a thin mist of tobacco smoke. All along the brown-painted walls were small wooden tables, a lit kerosene lamp on each one. In the smoky haze, the lamps looked like the pious halos of saints. A landscape painting hung over every halo.

The gargling and limping were now coming down the stairs. They were going down very carefully, one stair at a time.

The corridor finally turned around a sharp corner. There was a grandfather clock ticking away in the corner. It was showing 02.05.

Right beside the clock, facing the hallway, was a door screened with wire meshing. I looked through the mesh to a view of our garden. It was a tangle of weeds, ivy and overgrown grass and plants. A mist seemed to fill the garden with a deep eerie hush.

*David Vella*

Above the intertwining branches and thick treetops spread a grey sky. This hour could be an early morning or a late evening.

I pushed the door to the garden. It would not open.

# 38

I woke up late one morning to her whispering in my ear.

"Wake up. Wake up."

The first thing I saw as the sleep wore off was the gleam in her hazel eyes.

She got out of bed and stationed herself in the kitchen. She put her hands on her hips and gave me a strained smile.

"I made you breakfast. French style."

On the table were several jars of jam and marmalade, freshly baked croissants, three ham-and-cheese baguettes and a large jug full of hot black coffee. Two slices of toast popped out of the toaster.

"You must be famished," she said as she inserted two more slices inside. "Come and eat before it gets cold."

I told her that I didn't usually take breakfast.

She didn't reply but simply looked at all the food she had prepared.

"Maybe some coffee? You always drink coffee in the morning."

She poured some in a mug and handed it over.

It was very strong and intense. She knew exactly what type of coffee I drank.

"I bought you something," she then said. "A late Christmas present. I think you'll like it."

She fetched me a parcel with a colourful wrapping, tied with a lot of ribbons. Inside was a pair of Agnelle leather gloves lined with fur.

"Your hands are always cold," she said. "Those will keep them warm."

I put the gloves inside my jacket.

"Thanks—but oh, look at the time!" I exclaimed. "I'm late for a date with my blank canvas. Milady," and I bowed and kissed her hand, "I must make haste."

I left the flat before she could say "stay."

It was windy and bitingly cold outside as I left her block. I trudged toward my place, unaware that in my hurry I had forgotten to button up half my shirt.

I was dizzy and very tired by the time I arrived, but it was nothing that a short nap couldn't fix. On waking up an hour or so later, however, I realized that I had caught a bad cold.

The next two days I spent moping around in my room. I was too feverish and drained to do anything that required concentration—which meant no sketching or painting of any sort. Most of the mornings were spent in bed listening to classic rock and watching prank videos on YouTube, while the afternoons and evenings were spent napping and watching *Face and the City* episodes. Three days in and I finally managed to be somewhat productive by writing a new blog for my webpage. Other than that, there were absolutely no highlights on those days, save a peculiar *Face and the City* episode I watched once every day.

# 39

By Thursday I felt well enough to start painting again. Early on that day, I found a message on WhatsApp.

> Sent by: Angelique Duval
>
> Thursday, January 21, 2016
> 08.02
>
> Hey, I've taken leave today.
> I'm having a relaxing day.
> Just chatting and chillaxing.

> 10.23
>
> I just bought a shisha with 4 different flavours of tobacco.
> They all taste so good!

> 11.36
>
> Today we can have a shisha evening.
> We smoke shisha and relax and tell stories about when we were kids.

> 12.03
>
> Oh, poor Gabriel. I'll make you feel better.

I answered her every message while working on a new series of pastels which I had named *The Lounge of Curtains*.

Eight of these paintings portrayed a woman in lace lingerie, dancing in a dim hall surrounded by plush sofas and windows. There was no one watching her dance: the hall was empty. The wind from the open windows blew long sheer curtains across the empty space. In each scene, her pose was different. In each scene, the buffeting curtains enveloped and veiled different parts of her sinuous body. A curtain, however, always hid her face.

In #2, the dancer had a radiant headlamp embedded in the place where her heart should be. In #3, she had a ventilating fan springing out of her veiled head like an aureole with blades. In #4, she had iron brake cylinders for bracelets on her wrists and ankles and in #5, her arms had become pistons. Then there was #6, where her swaying body was wrapped all over with intertwining tubes and pipes, while #7 showed her with a bra and panties of aluminium. In #8, two pairs of wheels had sprouted out of her shoulders and waist like round wings stretched back.

The four other works that made up the series were entitled "The Three Passions of King Herod" and all were set in a decadently ornate lounge twinkling with candelabra.

The first one showed a plump middle-aged man chained to a sofa, wearing a crown on his head and an Armani pinstripe suit. The dancer was being escorted into the lounge by three oiled muscular men in thongs. Like a mummy, she was wrapped from head to toe with curtains, the tip of each curtain held by one of the men.

In the second painting, one of the men was violently unwinding the curtain he was holding from around the dancer, making her spin and uncovering her whole left leg from manicured foot to hip. The third showed a second man unwinding his own curtain from around her, this time revealing her right shoulder, her red-nippled breast and her ripped stomach. The crowned man was now gawping, sweating and struggling to break free of the chains.

In the fourth painting, the last curtain had been almost stripped off. The chained man was in hysterics, his crown fallen. The dancer's black hair had been unleashed and she was lifting her arms up in the air, brandishing her long red fingernails. The right half of her face had been revealed, her green eye fixed on the viewer with a razor gleam, her wet purple lips grinning. The curtain now only hid the left side of her face.

I had wanted to draw someone else, another character perhaps, but I ended up drawing her—again. I didn't mean to.

A strong wind kicked up on that evening. I could hear it howling from my room. The opened shutter of some apartment outside kept slamming against the wall every few minutes.

At around 18.00, someone buzzed at my flat. I opened the door. Angelique strode in.

She handed me a shopping bag with a firm resolve.

"This'll make you feel better," she said.

Inside were a box of chocolates, two illustrated hardcover books on famous artists and a Forever Friends teddy bear. I put the presents away on the bed.

"I like taking care of people when they're ill," she explained. "Life has no meaning if you don't take care of someone."

She trembled all over.

After that, she sat on the bed stiffly. But her right hand was vibrating.

She rummaged through her handbag and got out her cigarettes. She lit one up and took a deep and long drag.

"Life's too horrible if you don't care for someone," she confirmed, staring at nothing.

She took another very long drag.

"It's the most beautiful thing in the world to have children," she added. "You can live for them. You can give yourself to them completely. Three would be a good number. Perhaps more. I like crowds."

Her shoulders twitched and her eyes fluttered. She clenched her teeth and shook her head fiercely.

The shutter outside slammed viciously against the wall three times.

"I know what I'll call them. If it's a girl I'd call her Laila. Laila sounds wild and exotic. If I've another girl, I'd call her Rafaela. But only if she has dark eyes and hair."

She took another drag on her cigarette.

"The boy would be Castiel. The name reminds me of someone very brave . . . a hero. But I also like the name Gabriel."

She gave me a strained smile.

"Maybe I'll call him Gabriel."

The shutter banged persistently against the wall.

After a while, she said she was hungry and offered to go buy a slice of pizza for each of us.

She stood up and started walking toward the door. She watched her every step carefully, as if at any moment she could slip and fall. But she made it across the room without any interruptions. When she returned around a quarter of an hour later, her mouth was full and busy munching. She gave me my slice and soon after she stuffed her face with the rest of hers. Taking out another cigarette, she inhaled the smoke as if it was her only source of life.

Outside, the shutter struck the wall once with a sharp crack.

# 40

When Angelique left on that evening, I had a sense of déjà vu. I didn't know why, but there was something urgently familiar about her visit. Only much later, when the fly appeared on my face, did I make the connection. The name came to me on the same day I met Dina for the first time at the Noli Noli Club in Cardiff.

Charmeine.

Angelique had unconsciously reminded me of her. Come to think of it, what she said and what she did on many recent occasions were also similar to Charmeine's behaviour. But it seemed to me that their characters were at their most similar on that windy evening when Angelique came bearing gifts.

Charmeine was the closest cousin I had. She was the kindest and most compassionate person I've ever known. As well as being a volunteer for several charity organizations in Wales, she also used to spend a good deal of her free time taking care of many of her young nephews and nieces. Most of her salary she'd spend on expensive gifts for her relatives.

Her profession suited her caring personality very well. Charmeine worked as a registered nurse and nurse practitioner in Whitechurch Hospital. I was told that she inspired a deep gratitude among many of the patients she ministered to.

Charmeine barely ever took leave. That was also well known among her colleagues and friends. On top of that, she was always more than happy to take over anyone's shift if needed. She didn't mind working unpaid overtime, because at the end of the day what mattered were her patients and their well-being. She cared for every single one of them as if they were her own children . . . even though she didn't have any of her own.

At all times Charmeine did her best to be there for anyone who needed her, expecting nothing in return. She never married. She never had a boyfriend.

There was something else to her that people never talked about. Perhaps only a few had noticed it. Perhaps one wasn't supposed to mention it at all.

Charmeine's kindness was *too eager*. In its enthusiasm, it bordered on hysterical. There was a despair to it. It was as if she *had to* be kind or else . . . or else something truly horrible would happen. Some form of unspeakable punishment.

I remember what she told me right after her fortieth birthday dinner, once all the guests had left.

"I'm very scared of being alone. When I'm alone, I don't feel like I'm really alone. I feel someone observing me all the time, studying every single thing I think and do.

"'I disapprove,' this someone is saying with its watchful eyes. 'I disapprove forever of every decision *you* take. I disapprove of *you*.'

"I know that this someone is coming for me. Very soon he *will* be here. There's nothing I can do to stop him. I don't know what will happen when he comes. What I do know is that when he does come for me, everything will change.

"When I'm alone, I remember that I'm his. I remember that he's everything and I'm nothing.

"It's the worst loneliness ever . . . knowing that no one can ever take this loneliness away."

On another visit to Charmeine's place, we watched *The Unbearable Lightness of Being*. Right after the movie, she made a confession.

"Whoever's coming for me blames me for something so awful it can't be described. He tells me that everyone's hurting because

*When Her Time Comes*

of what I've done. What I'm guilty of is so big I can't even begin to make it right.

"In the end I know. I know that what I'm guilty of is *myself.* I'm guilty of being me.

"I know I shouldn't be here. I'm not supposed *to be*. This me is a stain.

"And I try . . . I try so hard to clean myself of myself. Every single chance I have, I dedicate myself to others.

"It's not enough, of course. It's never enough but I have to keep on trying."

She looked down at her skinny feet and stooped some more. Her eyes shone with trembling tears.

Perhaps Angelique's recent behaviour had a similar motivation behind it. Maybe she too had turned kind to reach for the same thing. Giving herself to others to get away from herself.

If this were true, then her actions didn't testify to any feelings she might have started to have for me. She had clarified this on that first time I had kissed her in the elevator.

No, she hadn't really fallen in love. She had instead *made herself* fall for me. And she did so because she needed to. She did so as a means to a totally different end. She *needed* to fall for something. And there was probably no fix more effective to fall for at that point in time.

So she picked me.

But it could have been anything or anyone else.

"I can't stop giving," Charmeine once told me as she pulled her freshly baked mince pies from the oven on a Christmas Eve. "I don't want to be anything or anyone. I just want to be a giving."

Charmeine killed herself two months later.

# 41

Sent by: Angelique Duval

Sunday, January 24, 2016
08.02

Today I'm cooking something special for you.
White cheese chicken lasagne.
It was going to be a surprise. But we both know you don't like surprises ;-)
I'll bring some as soon as it's finished.
Fresh and hot is best.

Tuesday, January 26, 2016
18.42

Sometimes there's this bad smell in my apartment.
It's just there.
I don't know what it is and where it's coming from.

It stays here for most of the day and it won't go away.

Can I come over?

Saturday, January 30, 2016
10.52

What a beautiful day!

> Are you feeling any better?
> I'm going to spend the day at Park Ailes de Joie with my four musketeers.
> We're going to laugh so much and make merry all day long.
> You must come by :-)

I was quite recovered on the Saturday she had sent that message, so I made up my mind to go and meet them.

At around 15.00, I was at the park. It was a hot day and by this time, as on any other weekend, the park had become a dump of beer cans, liquor bottles and plastic cups and wrappings with people of all ages sprawled out on the grass, many passed out. Those few lying down who were still conscious lifted their arms every now and then, with a lot of effort, to put their joints or bottles to their mouths. Someone in boxers tried to play an indistinguishable song on his untuned guitar and then gave up some minutes later and settled for his beer.

Amidst all this peace and serenity, I found Angelique and her merry troupe sitting cross-legged under some lime trees. They were all in their bikinis, drinking pastis from cups. Angelique was staring at nothing with a sulky pout on her perfect face. Sybille was taking selfies of herself slowly taking off her bra, her expression switching adeptly from duck face, to surprised face, to fish-gape. Arienne, the quietest one with the look of futility on her face, had passed out while sitting. A little dribble was coming down from her open mouth. Nina was focusing all her determination on drinking and pouring. Osanne, however, true to her hyped-up nature, was active. She was playing football with a few children. She only stopped running and kicking the ball around every few minutes to gulp down from the bottle she held in her hand.

"How wonderful this is!" Angelique remarked. "This haze is so beautiful!"

She swallowed some more of her pastis.

"I'm floating in this haze," Angelique blurted out. "Inside this haze, everything is light and dancing and nothing matters.

Everything here is now a love story. Life should be like this forever."

As the sky grew dark and the birds chirped more, Park Ailes de Joie became a magical place. A secret seemed to grow in the trees. There was a sign in the purple space of the sky. It talked to me from across the silence. It told me how exciting everything was soon going to be.

# 42

For her, happiness was sleep . . . a little reprieve.
 Soon it would remind her of what it was, of where she was.
 "You are dreaming!" it would tell her. "This isn't real!
 "Wake up! Wake up!
 *"Aren't you forgetting something?"*
 And the world was electrocuted by remembrance.
 *"Aren't you forgetting something?"*
 And past and future would lose all reality.
 The past would become a series of scenes that were never hers but another's. It would become the past of a sweet and innocent girl who had lived asleep, who had lived a fairy tale of a life—before the awakening. What was no longer was remembered like a segue of mute moments from an old fading film that had been watched a long time ago.
 As the past was robbed of her, the future crashed, it fell apart, its excitement and plans and hopes and mystery all crumbling down. What was to come glared at her in a flat and explicit light absent of all doubts. Nothing could ever exist beyond that moment when the thought would return to her once more; there could be no new experiences, no new life beyond the thought of this moment always repeating itself. What was ahead promised her more of the same, the promise that the time to come would be a time of again and again and again.

# 43

I woke up at Angelique's place full of nausea and a throbbing head. I had taken a bit too much of that pastis yesterday at the park.

I turned on the tap in the bathroom and gulped down some water. That was when I realized that today was Sunday and my heart instantly sank. Sunday and I had never been on good terms for quite a while. Angelique was of the same mind. There was this one entry in her diary I remember coming across:

> *Sunday, November 10, 2013*
> Sunday is a leftover. It is what remains when something has ended. Sunday is lived as a time that has not ended completely. It is also a time that has not really started yet. The end refuses to end properly and the beginning refuses to begin properly. Between the clean closure and the clean beginning—there is Sunday.

I was about to leave but Angelique immediately called out to me from bed.

"Let's smoke some shisha today. We can chillax and tell stories of the good old times."

I told her that I had to paint. *The Lounge of Curtains* was still incomplete.

"It's Sunday," she replied. "No one works on Sundays."

Some do. Those who still have to get somewhere.

I walked to the door to leave. She stepped right between me and the door.

"Sunday is for friends and family," she insisted. "You won't get through Sunday by painting. Time here will go faster."

"I have to go."

"Good. Then go."

But I stayed. I wouldn't have been able to sketch or paint with that headache.

She started setting up the hookah. She was lighting up the charcoal when she suddenly started spasming as if someone had turned on a switch. Then she stopped and continued lighting up the coals.

We smoked some Watermelon with Mint, Blue Mist and Absolute Zero flavoured tobacco.

"Let's play Truth or Dare," she suggested as the afternoon wore on.

She fetched us a bottle of red wine to drink. At first we both chose "truth." But as the game progressed, we felt bolder and we started choosing "dare" more often. The dares, in turn, got more challenging. Soon we had finished the first bottle of wine and Angelique brought over a second. She refilled our glasses while I spun the bottle. When it stopped spinning, its mouth was pointing at me.

"I dare you to wrap something up in a sheet so that it looks like a bundled baby," she said. "Then, you have to deliver it to one of the apartments in this block."

I opened her bedside cupboard, knowing that she kept a life-sized baby doll there. I took it out and bundled it up in a bed sheet. I went out and down the stairs to the floor below. Apartments 10, 11 and 12 were on this landing. I chose 10. I placed the bundled doll on the doormat. I put my ear close to the door but I didn't hear any noise. There was probably no one inside. I pressed the doorbell and hurried off. As I was going up the stairs I listened carefully for any sound of a door opening, but it was all quiet.

It was my turn to assign the dare.

"I dare you to put on a sheet, go out and pretend you're a fortune teller," I told her. "You're going to ask the first person you meet for twenty euros for the future."

From the balcony, in the fading light of the evening, I saw her running across the concrete street, holding the sheet over her head with one hand. As she ran, the sheet blew around her in the wind like the cape of some vigilante. The first person she saw had the looks of a businesswoman. Angelique stepped right before her.

"Behold!" she called out, raising her arm, pointing up to the sky. "Your time has come!"

The lady walked around her as if she didn't exist.

But Angelique persisted. She followed her, holding the sheet carefully over her head.

"Whenever you see me," she shouted, "you must run away! You must hide and look away!"

Even now, the middle-aged woman didn't spare a single glance at her. She marched on.

Angelique started walking alongside her.

"From now on," she shouted out, "I will haunt you. I will haunt you in the streets, in your office, in the kitchen, on your dates. I will haunt you in your most secret moments. I will come when you're in bed, about to sleep, about to wake, when you're making love. I will come while you're eating. I will come while you're taking a bath. There is nowhere you won't find me."

The woman finally turned to her. She glanced at her briefly and told her something. I could see her lips moving but I couldn't hear what she was saying.

Angelique instantly turned and sprinted away. She raced back to the block with the sheet still trailing behind her. In a short while, I could hear her footsteps frantically climbing up the stairs.

"I thought you were going to be a fortune teller," I told her as soon as she entered.

"No, I was something else," she panted. "And that was more exciting."

"What did she tell you?"

"She told me to fuck off."

So we opened a third bottle to celebrate.

It was my turn. The dare was the most challenging yet.

"Strip naked and put on a scarf. Go down all the stairs of this block and back up with just the scarf around your neck."

I stripped. I even took off my boxers. She came up to me and wound a reindeer scarf around my neck. She made a knot and pulled the ends to tighten it. This, however, made the scarf too tight. She had tied it like a noose and it almost made me choke. So I loosened it a bit.

I scratched the right side of my mouth a couple of times and went out of the flat.

There were five floors in this block and this was the fourth. The stairs to the next landing were on the far side. No one was around. I moved quickly across the landing.

The landing below was empty as well. The bundle I had placed in front of door 10 wasn't there anymore. I crept toward that door and tried to listen for any noises. This time I heard something. There was a muffled thudding repeating itself somewhere inside. Someone was very angry and was banging something about.

Down the stairs was floor 2, dead quiet as well. The bulb hanging at the far end kept on flickering. It was around 18.00 on a typical Sunday. Usually there would be people going out and coming in at this time of day.

The last door on this floor was covered in thick chains set to metal rings hammered into the wall.

There were two more floors to go. I went down the stairs to floor 1.

The first half of this corridor had a dim amber light like all the other corridors above. But the furthest bulb cast an alarming red light in the second half of the corridor. This bulb was swinging slightly to and fro. Beyond it was pitch darkness with no sight of the end wall. When I stepped into the red light, I noticed that the next two yellow painted doors were made of steel, each with a glass slot at head level.

Even as I stood beside the descending stairs, at the very edge of the light, I still couldn't see the end wall. Before me and above me was a yawn of void. A thin chilling breeze came out of this void and stung my naked skin like countless tiny needles. The scarf around my neck seemed to tighten and I felt as if I was going to choke again. I had to loosen it some more.

I started going down the stairs to floor 0. Halfway down, the stairs went around a sharp bend. I was only a few steps away from turning the corner when I heard footsteps coming up from behind it. They were slow, climbing one stair at a time. One step had a firm and strong clap. The other was a light tap on the ground. A limp.

I scratched the right side of my mouth a couple of times. I returned to the landing in the red light and hurried past the two metal doors, back into the warm light of the other half of the corridor. I climbed up the first few stairs to the upper level. The limping was suddenly in the corridor I had just left.

As I walked across floor 2, I noticed that the footsteps below were getting faster. I quickened my pace as well. I went past the door barred with chains and under the flickering bulb overhead.

Along with the limping, a rattling was suddenly turned on. Once it started, it kept going on and on. It was as if some machine was suddenly unwinding. Sometimes the sound seemed to alternate to a very wet gurgling.

I scratched and scratched my mouth again. I tried the lift but it was closed and rumbling up to floor 4. I had to go up the stairs to the next floor.

Once I stepped onto floor 3, I broke into a run. I ran past flat number 10 and I thought I could still hear the muffled thudding coming from behind that door. The limping was now louder than before. It was now pounding up the stairs to this landing.

It was so sharp it could only have come from someone wearing high heels.

The lift was still rumbling upward.

I reached the stairs to floor 4. I went up two steps at a time. I arrived on that landing and headed straight to door 15. The lift suddenly rang. The doors opened. The lift was empty. In its mirrors stared back at me three replicas of a naked man with a scarf and the face of a ghost.

# 44

The moment I entered Angelique's flat, I snatched my trousers and headed straight to the bathroom. Locking the door, I sat down on the toilet, fumbled in my pockets and whipped out my earphones and phone. Quickly, I went onto YouTube, and put on some funny music from *Face and the City*. Then, I searched for my website and the blog I had written a few days back when I was still sick. When I found it, I read it over and over again with total concentration.

*The Jaded Debauchee*
Wednesday, 27 January, 2016
18.56

There are not many of our kind left in this world. Our time has long since passed.
We are the artists who don't live their life. We *perform* it. We have transformed it into a work of art. A thing of beauty.
Our every day unwinds within a story. It is the tale of a tired artist who falls for any temptation that comes his way. He falls to forget how tired he is. All his adventures are temporary medications.
There is spectacle in his life. His fallenness is a spectacle because it is spectacular. He falls spectacularly.
And he takes great enjoyment out of this. He looks at it and makes fun of it. He bursts out laughing in the dark. Laughter makes the dark shine for a while.
Humour does not know vice from virtue. It levels everything down. In its eyes, degradation is as fine as kindness, but probably

so much more enjoyable.

In the world of humour, nothing is important, everything is permitted.

This story is not new. It defined the soul of many a great person. It is also mine and me.

Whatever happens, it will *always* happen in this story. What is to come I will paint in the shape and colours of its mood. Anything can come to pass but I'll make sure it'll pass through this state of mind. That way I will always be ready for what the future may bring.

I walk into scenes and events and I see myself walking. I feel and see myself feeling. I am in this moment just as I am out. I live and I see myself living as a protagonist of one story that absorbs all stories into it.

The tired artist's paintings were the only thing that justified his existence . . . his last religion. They were the only windows left to the depths of his spirit. It was almost impossible to believe that a man who lived in such a way could produce such horrifying wonders.

*(written in a time of dire need)*

# 45

After reading my blog trice, I put on my pants and got out of the bathroom.

The moment I set my eyes on a confused Angelique, I said: "Let's party."

So we went out that very instant and headed to The Wohoo!

It was karaoke night, so we went downstairs to the clubbing cave. A small group of Japanese girls were jumping and screaming on the stage to Queen's "I Want To Be Free." There were usually a lot more people on such occasions.

"Where's everyone?" I shouted above the music.

"At you-know-who's place," she replied, as she brought two double rums with coke to the table. "Tonight you-know-who's hosting a special event. Many are going. These are the ones who don't know about it."

"Who is he really?" I asked her.

She downed her drink, stood up and in her tube top dress started swaying her hips to the song.

*I want to break free!*
I want to break free!
"We should go," I suggested.
*I've got to break free!*
"Why don't we go?"
"Because I'm not that kind of person," she shouted back, eyes closed, slowly shaking her ass.

*God knows! God knows I want to be free!*

I went to get two more double rums from the bar upstairs. It took me a long time to order because a couple of Korean students were asking for a ridiculous amount of sophisticated cocktails, which kept the bartenders busy. On returning to the cave, the Japanese group had gone offstage to their trays of shooters. Replacing them on the stage was Angelique.

A piano swooped in, followed soon after by the slow bittersweet melody of a violin. A heart-strung love song was playing. "Take Me to a Time" by a group called The Mutes. The first verse was displayed on the large screen on the far wall.

> Take me back to a time
> When everything stood still in time.
> Oh my heart breaks every time I know
> That you're no longer mine.
> So I hope to open the gates to that past design.

Angelique unclamped the microphone from its stand and pasted it to her mouth. With a very serious face, she stretched out her arm, pointing her finger ominously at her audience, the cheerful Japanese group.

The pre-singing countdown appeared next to the lyrics.

3

2

1

"Take me back to a YIIIIIIIME
When everything stood still in YIIIIIIIIME
Oh oh oh breaks every YIIIIIIIIIME."

She paused . . . for effect.

And then it came out:

"That you're no longer YIIIIIIIIIINE."

The last line went by unsung. I suppose it wasn't as good as the others.

There were a few sparse claps from the Japanese and then they went back to chugging their shots. She put down the microphone.

But then quickly pasted it to her mouth again.

"Yeah baby."

The piano and violin took over for a while, soaring and plummeting with emotion. She sprinted to our table, snatched her drink, gulped it all down, slammed the glass back on the table and sprinted back onstage. The next verse now appeared on the screen.

> Every place I go to now
> Is a shadow of that place with no time.
> Let me dance in its rain and roll in its grass
> And celebrate my soul in all its sun.
> It's like I told you honey.

With a blank stare, she pasted the microphone to her mouth again and

3

2

1

"EVERY YACE I GO GO YOW

IS A SHADOW OF YIIIIIIIIIME

YET ME YANCE IN ITS RAIN . . . AND RAIN YAIN YAIN YAIN

IT'S . . . IT'S . . . IT'S . . . "

Confused, she blinked a couple of times and stared quickly around, hoping perhaps to find some answer that wasn't on the screen. Then:

"OF YIIIIIIIIIIME."

I focused on my drinking to pretend that everything wasn't happening. The Japanese were doing the very same thing. Judging from their faces, they probably had regressed to sobriety.

"YEAH YEAH YEAH!" Angelique decided to fill in the next instrumental part of the song.

"YEAH YEAH YEAH BABY!"

The refrain was now on.

> I won't walk these streets, I won't cry no more
> But fly away and again to that other life.

In its bright days, in its dark nights
There is no place, there is no time.

And

3

2

1

Angelique pointed at the Japanese girls again with a menacing stare and they looked back at her, deeply puzzled. Angelique started rapping into the mic.

"YEAH BABY! HEAR THAT!
FLYING MY ASS TO CORFU!
CORFU BITCHES!
NO PLACE, NO YIIIIME LIKE CORFU!
THIS HOE ASS BE FLYING THERE!
THAT'S RIGHT BITCHES!
YEAH YEAH YEAH BABY."

I got up, grabbed her pointing arm and pulled her down from the stage. She stumbled behind me, still clasping the mic. I started dragging her up the stairs.

"BITCHES!" she screamed into the mic.

I snatched it out of her hand and flung it at the Japanese girls. It struck one of them straight in the head, toppling her off the chair like a bowling skittle.

Thankfully I managed to calm Angelique down with a few tequila shots by the bar. We left shortly after to Bar Infinity, a hip-hop club on L'Opéra Street. En route, she got all touchy and kept on stroking and squeezing my groin. On no condition would she take her hand off.

Infinity was flickering everywhere with purple neon. Under the giant Rubik's cubes shining with all the bright colours were several people lying on the sofas, arms and legs entangled around each other, worming their tongues along necks, chests, tits.

We threw ourselves on the only empty sofa we could see. She quickly unzipped my jeans and dug her hand into my fly. Her deft hand grabbed me and started beating away. Up above me, a neon Rubik's cube of a shocking pink and orange and yellow split into two and then into three and then joined into one again.

"Stick something inside!" she shrieked, fapping. "Make me feel something too! Feel something!"

My hand went under her miniskirt. Her body tensed, her eyes widened and her rouge lips opened up in wonder. She was once again lost to the whirlpool of sensations.

In her apartment, I climbed onto her and entered her and she held onto me for dear life. Her arms and legs latched onto my waist and back and squeezed. Every one of my thrusts she took as if it were a blade slicing into her; with every thrust, her face screwed up like Munch's "Scream," and she howled and writhed as if she was being exorcized. As I slid deeper, she threw her head back, stretching out her neck laced with veins. She was plunging into a fever that was a plea to fill her up with more of me, with all of me and more. In her fever, she was begging me to take her to an extreme point of no return where she could be obliterated into sheer joy.

# 46

Perhaps there came a time when the thought didn't remind her of a wound anymore.

Perhaps it eventually reminded her only *of itself.*

It would come to her and make her remember that it would always come again later on. At that point the thought reminded her of its own endless repetition. If it reminded her of a wound before, now its *own reminder* was a wound.

"I've come," it would tell her. "I've come to tell you that I will come again."

Now, the thought had no content.

# 47

I woke up. It was dark and I was in bed alone in her apartment. I didn't remember going to sleep. I wasn't sure either if it was very early in the morning or if it was night. I wasn't sure if last evening was the evening we went to The Wohoo! or if I had slept through the next day or two. Or maybe this was a different time altogether, a different week, a different month and so many other things had happened already.

Cosmic music with a chilled beat was playing in the background. It was coming from the bathroom. There was a light in the crack under the closed door.

I got out of bed and approached. I turned the handle and the door opened.

The smells of various perfumes rushed into my senses and I was dizzy for the first few seconds. The bath was hidden behind drawn celestial blue curtains with a Chinese floral pattern. I went toward the bath. I threw the curtains apart.

Angelique was lying down in soapy water, resting her head against the edge, eyes closed, mouth slightly opened, surrendered to the silken heat. The smoke of the incense candles around her shrouded her in a thin mist. She inhaled it and exhaled it slowly, deeply.

"Shut . . . the . . . curtains," she whispered, barely able to say the words.

I shut them behind me and she turned blue, shadowed all over with the spiraled rose patterns. I was enclosed in her little world of scents, mist and flowers.

    I climbed into the bath and sat down in the hot thick water on the opposite side. A drop fell at regular intervals from the curtain railing overhead, plopping into the foam right between us. I reclined and opened my legs around hers and squeezed them together.

    "Heaven is a feeling," she whispered from her blue lips.

On another night, I found her again in the bath like this and she whispered to me:

    "I like the water in my bath to be just a bit too hot. Just that bit.

    "I go in and it all goes away. *I* go away.

    "Only the feeling exists.

    "And all I want is to be this feeling."

# 48

I gradually came to the realization that the *Lounge of Curtains* series I had finished in January was a creative abortion. There was nothing—and I mean, *absolutely nothing*—innovative about it. For all intents and purposes, it was a carbon copy of other series I had painted, namely, my *Moonlight Striptease* series. My long rollercoaster ride with Pixie Hotness seemed to have come at the price of a long dry spell.

So one afternoon I finally decided to do something about it.

There was a public library in Lancöme Square, only around five minutes away on foot. I could go there and borrow some books on art. That could get me juiced up, perhaps inspire some new ideas. I was aiming for a couple of works on symbolism and surrealism, though anything that would catch my eye was welcome.

I reached the place at around 16.00 and it was open. It was only once I went inside that I realized that this was probably not the best of ideas. The library assistant on duty was a Romanian I had met a while back in a cab. We happened to be both pretty drunk at that point in the night. A precious few words were said, gazes were exchanged and our loins did the rest—all in the backseat and unbeknownst to the mumbling driver, who was probably on something himself. It seemed like a good deal at the time, but it was only when I met her the second time that I became fully aware of what I had unleashed upon me. And it wasn't her New Age rants about my chakra being "misaligned as fuck"; I also had a missing one apparently. Not even her self-proclaimed mission to spread the Word that meat-eating promotes toxic masculinity. No.

It was her breath.

Abstaining from toothpaste probably helps prevent an "environmental holocaust," but at the expense of your breath, which *itself* becomes the holocaust. She opened her mouth and she could've killed people.

I let it slide at first and tried to drown it all with drinks. But then the sex came, and with every "Haaaaa" uttered to presumably express her excitement, a fresh hell was released upon me. Until she orgasmed—or faked one—and her scream did what Instagram was already doing to humanity.

I gave her a couple more chances; I had two more dates with her. But nothing changed. Thankfully, she hadn't yet seen me standing by the library entrance. So I made up my mind to come back another time. I returned to the revolving doors and was out in the busy square again. Before I could make a move, however, I found myself face-to-face with a tall scrawny guy sporting an oblong shaved head. And of course that large Adam's apple.

"I was just about to do some research at the library on posthumanism and the post-literary with a special focus on Jacques Derrida's relationships between 'the human' and 'the animal,'" he pointed out. "This relationship suggests that in the process of seeing one another's vulnerability, a remodification of current oppressive ethical considerations of animals can occur. A fascinating topic, is it not?"

"There are no words," I pointed out.

"Though naturally," he said, "I'd be more than inclined to postpone the research for the moment and have a chat with you over a drink to, you know, pick up where we left off in our first rendezvous at your exhibition. I recall we were discussing the poststructuralist influence on postmodern theories of literature?"

"Most definitely," I replied. "I'd be more than happy to—ecstatic even—were it not for my grandma. She needs me. And it's urgent. She has these issues . . ."

"I insist," he said firmly. "There's no time like the present, sir."

"She has cardiovascular disease, you know, topped with osteoporosis. Can't walk without taking a fall."

"Come now. That can wait. There's a bar right there we can have a drink at. It's quiet so we can talk properly."

"I forgot about her Alzheimer's. To be perfectly honest with you she also can't see. Blind as a bat. And she has got no arms."

"Like I said, there's no time like the present."

"But *her* present is shit."

The bistro, which was only three buildings away, was called "Lounge 52." The walls and ceiling of its only room had a beige design of 3D hexagons. It was there that Samuel finally turned toward a subject that touched a chord. I remember his monologue to this very day. It was about the ways people forget.

"It's the most secret art we all have, we all use," he said. "Some of us forget by burying away. You hide a terrible memory from yourself in a place you can't find because you don't want to find it. You make believe an absence until that make-belief becomes your life.

"But burying is not killing. What you've hidden is not dead.

"With the burial comes the phantom of what you've buried. It persists and you can't explain it away. You want to believe that the phantom is some sort of sickness.

"But it's not a sickness. It's a symptom."

"Sometimes the terrible memory remains but you bury away what it did to you. You remember what happened by forgetting what happened to you, that it happened *to* you. You forget that the memory is yours, as close to you as your own skin, your own consciousness. That past comes to you as a simple flat story of what happens next and what happens after that.

"Then, at some unexpected moment, the life of that memory returns. Its pulse haunts you, revisiting you in a different body that's associated with it in some way. Suddenly that door opening, the water running into this sink, that confectionery shop, those creases on your hanging shirt are alive with an ominous meaning.

"That little crack in the wall is seeing you. When you go near it, when you pass by it, you feel its stare fixed on you. You feel it wants to share something with you. It's calling you again and again in silence, throbbing with a horrible significance. And you're furious, distressed, anxious, frightened of that little crack in the wall. It's making your life torture. But you'd rather have it so than find out what it really is, that little crack in the wall – a symptom.

"Because deep inside you know—we all know—that you can only move on when you forget. You are who you are, you do what you do every day, because you *chose* not to remember. You can only say 'I am this' or 'I am that,' you can only say 'I' because you have denied what happened to you. By denying, you've created a life for yourself. You've created who you are by forgetting. You learn to see by unseeing."

But I cannot unsee, I cannot forget.

Here, in the Glaze Restaurant toilet stall on my date with Dina, a year onward, I know that I carry around with me a piece of me that shouldn't exist for me anymore. It's an excess of awareness that makes me see too much to see properly. Upon the forgetting of this knowledge depends my living an ordinary life. But that memory *insists* on staying and feeding on its insistence, fattening itself on it.

So now it's here to stay, this fly that doesn't let me be me; this fly that's always disrupting all that I think and do. Its presence is now as constant and as intimate as the presence of myself to myself.

# 49

I'm not sure if most of the things Samuel said made much sense or if they were actually true in some significant way. I got the impression that very often he thought he saw things where there was nothing to really see. Most of the things he said could have been the product of a fertile imagination. And yet, he could prove to be quite entertaining if you were in the right mood for him. On such occasions, I had to admit, the truth hardly mattered.

If Samuel excelled in anything, it would have probably been his insistence. Since our second accidental encounter by the library, he had set his mind to meet me again at all costs. I had a feeling that was probably because the first time we had met at my exhibition, I had introduced myself as a professor.

So they started—his Facebook messages—first delivered on alternate days, and then, fuelled by my excuses, on *every single day*. I ignored some of them but they kept on coming and the excuses got lamer. Until I finally caved in. Again.

I guess I guilted myself into saying yes. You also can't make excuses forever. I told him I could do that Friday night and he was fine with that. As insurance against boredom, I brought along a third party.

I was to meet Samuel in some bar in Saint Paradis Street, the famous nightlife district of Saint Laurent. We arrived there at around 21.00 and spotted him standing at one of the Coca-Cola zinc tables outside the entrance to La Chimère. In his tweed jacket and buttoned-up plaid shirt, he looked his part. With an air of gravitas, he was smoking a joint and sipping at a green absinthe. Sometimes he would check around him to see if anyone had seen him take that drag, have that sip. He seemed to be hunching more than usual.

He greeted us with a dignified nod. His Adam's apple jolted savagely in his throat. Tonight it seemed to be very active.

Angelique bought a bottle of tequila for us. She gulped down the first shot before we had time to say cheers. Right beside us, two hippies were smoking pot while having a very heated discussion on love in the twenty-first century.

"I'm throwing another party soon," Samuel declared. "I give you, 'Before The World Ends—Once Again': May 6 at the Dream House."

We started chatting about life in Saint Laurent. But after a couple of shots, out of the blue, as he did, Samuel started talking about his PhD.

"My PhD is in fact about an intriguing theory by an obscure contemporary psychoanalyst. He's one of those few psychoanalysts who dabble in the occult and I've read and heard said that his therapy sessions are too radical for many people. Some have described them as unbearably intrusive for the patient, too excessive . . . too dangerous."

Angelique downed her fourth and sucked hard on her cigarette.

"His writing is obscure, just like himself. There are so many metaphors and riddles in his works, so many symbols everywhere. But in the end, what he's saying always comes down to the same thing."

"That this world is not real."

We refilled our glasses. Angelique swallowed hers before we could lift ours to our lips. Then she poured more into her glass and when she had gulped that down as well, she lit a new cigarette and inhaled the smoke greedily.

"In fact, according to him, everyone is on a crusade of denial of what is really real. That denial creates your world, this world you see and live in. True reality is here, right now, all around you, but you pretend you don't know that, you pretend it's not there. *That* place horrifies you. You spend your life trying not to go there."

Three girls in school uniforms, glittery faces, and pigtails were skipping by, holding each other's arms and laughing. In the greasy restaurant beside La Chimère, I spotted Gregory, the chef who never delivered. He was sitting at a table with three burgers and fries before him, furiously biting into each and every one of them in turn with a beastly hunger.

"But like it or not, you *do* find yourself in this place from time to time. You're suddenly in what this psychoanalyst calls—the Real. It comes to you sometimes in moments when you're not in control of yourself, when you're not quite yourself.

"When it passes, you make yourself forget it ever happened. You shrug it off like a bad dream. It's in our nature. But the Real is everywhere; it's always been present."

Along strode a group of men and women dressed as pirates, singing Nicki Minaj's "Pills N Potions" while raising their pitchers of black beer to the neon signs flashing around them. Following them were a group of smartly dressed women gathered around a bride-to-be with a veil and glow-in-the-dark horns. They were taking swigs of different bottles and passing them around as they marched by.

"Before you see the Real, you've already been there. Before you enter it, you already have. When you're inside it you suspect this but you don't know when, how, why you've been there before. It always reminds you of somewhere because it's disturbingly familiar. There, you always *almost* remember.

"Everything in that place is alive with a presence you can't see. Things and surroundings are veined with a mystery that has a deep intimacy to you. You feel you're tied to the spirit of that place in ways you never thought possible. There's some kind of conspiracy there, unknown, that's coursing in every single thing. And all this time you're being observed by the hidden eyes of this secret. There you're always under the gaze of this presence. Sometimes it can take on the guise of someone."

A couple suddenly stepped out in the middle of the street and started dancing. The woman whirled round and round until she was too dizzy to continue. Some people in La Chimère stood up and burst into song. They were singing Taylor Swift's "Everything Has Changed."

"Deep inside you are certain of one thing and one thing only: this presence knows who you *really* are. It knows that the 'you' you want to be, that you're always trying to be, is not really you. It knows your deepest secret—your *other* 'you.'

"The Real is the world of this presence. You are its hostage, its patient, its lab rat. It can do anything to you at any second. Already, from the very first moments, you feel it messing with you, playing at these mysterious games . . . teasing you with things that it'll do to you.

"We call it, 'the God.'"

Across the street, people were hugging each other and laughing and talking excitedly. Angelique swallowed yet another shot, crushed the filter against the tabletop, and instantly took out another cigarette.

"As you wander that world, you've a feeling that the secret that runs through its veins will soon reveal itself. Every moment there is an anticipation, a calm trembling before the storm. Soon, the curtains will fall. The revelation will come forth. The presence will show itself.

"The God will come out."

He knocked back the rest of his absinthe. The lump in his throat woke up again. It jerked up and down twice.

Angelique suddenly made a grab for my balls under the table but I pushed her hand away. I was too exhausted from a party the night before and wasn't in the mood. She tried again and I pushed her hand away a second time. She contented herself by knocking back another shot of tequila.

Now more than ever these days she was flinging herself at any promise of fun and pleasure that came her way. She grasped onto this promise with a resolve that had gone beyond exhaustion—and it could have been anything: this drink, that food, this pill, that music, this bar, that club, my body, that body. The world for her had become a landscape of glittery signs of feelgood. Any sign she spotted, she would drive into with kamikaze abandon.

"I want my night out to be fast," she would have said at the time. "I want the speed. I want the night to get wilder. I want the pace to pick up like crazy. I don't want it to give me time; I want it to overtake time. I want to get lost in its frenzied escalation. I want it to take me over till it blots out the world with its ecstatic dark. I want this blind rush to swallow me whole."

"I want that man," she suddenly stated, bringing me back to the moment as she pointed to a bald guy with bulging biceps. He was waiting in a crowd that was gathering in front of a club nearby. His head was covered in tattoos and he wore a shocking pink polo shirt with the collar turned up.

"I want that man inside of me."

The crowd waiting to enter this club was growing. It was the most popular nightlife place to go to in Saint Laurent. Club Sublime.

"It's time," Samuel pointed out.

"Yes," someone close by answered him.

"So many waiting for this moment," someone else said. "We all need this."

Angelique chugged the rest of the tequila straight from the bottle. She smoked her next cigarette while staring intently at the tattooed man, following his every step.

"In there, we'll be absolved of ourselves," Samuel said. "It's all going to go away."

By some silent agreement we all joined the crowd. We had to wait for more than half an hour before we were finally let in. We descended the stairs into the thumping darkness of Club Sublime.

# 50

The tattooed man was eight persons ahead of us in the queue. Angelique walked in complete awe of him.

We went down into a bar that looked like a giant cube aglow with a phantom emerald. Silver lightning was trembling in columns of glass that towered around us. Over the walls and ceiling, golden laser lights were forming the shapes of swirling stars, diamonds and falling comets. A muffled techno beat could be heard some distance away. The tattooed man was last seen leaving this room and going into the corridor that led to the clubbing cave.

"He is the one," Angelique proclaimed with a green glowing face.

I couldn't see Samuel anywhere. We had probably lost him at some point in the crowded stairway.

We left the bar for the corridor. The tattooed man was right at the far end. He turned a corner and disappeared again. We turned that same corner but we didn't see him anywhere. LED tubes of brilliant scarlet ran forever along the walls. Further on, on either side, there were brightly coloured beaded curtains covering arched entrances. Behind the curtains I caught a glimpse of figures spasming on top of each other. Sometimes a moan or a shriek sliced open the background beat of bass.

Angelique jumped and her body was jerking everywhere at different speeds, waist, arms and legs twisting and turning here and there, chest pushing out and in, head quivering like a picture jitter.

She shook herself aggressively and managed to regain some control of herself.

Suddenly she was running away from me. I chased after her and I just managed to catch a glimpse of her walking into the flashing cave round the last corner. I followed.

The cave swallowed me like a massive mouth, hot and reeking, biting me with its schizoid lightning and clinical techno banging. Laser beams lanced out from between raised opened fingers and moving heads. I spotted Angelique jostling her way through the electrified people. In the very centre, the tattooed man was dancing all by himself.

Then he grabbed his pink shirt and stripped it off. Ultraviolet spiral patterns tattooed his ripped back and chest, glowing neon green in the dark. In the centre of his back was a tattoo of a bird with vast opened wings, just about to fly off into the sky. The man was dancing so wildly that it seemed as if he was wrestling with some spirit adversary that only he could witness.

I stayed where I was to observe Angelique struggling to reach him. She was almost there when a group of people, raising their glow sticks in the air, shoved their way right in between him and her. They broke out into a dance and pushed her back and pushed him back as well. He left his spot and pressed onward into the crowd, deeper into the cave. Angelique in turn pressed forward to catch up with him. Suddenly she slipped and crashed face down onto the floor.

I went for her. My feet crunched on several shards of glass as I reached her. I told her that we had better go. She looked up at me and the strobes lit her face up like a ghost. A little shard of glass was stuck in the middle of her forehead and a needle-thin stream of blood was running down her cadaver face.

"He's the one," she said robotically. "I want him inside of me."

She turned and walked away to go to him. I went after her.

The cave lights now flashed rapidly, incessantly. At one

moment she was beside me and at another she had disappeared. After a while I saw her heading in the direction of the deejay stage. The tattooed man had just started dancing again beside that stage.

I pushed onward into the crowd. I managed to hustle my way to her just as she was about to pass through the last wall of people that stood between her and him. Suddenly, someone behind her grabbed her ass and squeezed. It was a young boy of not more than fourteen. A much older sweating man with a beard was standing beside him, talking in his ear.

Angelique turned to face them.

"You want to have some fun with us?" the boy rehearsed to her. "Daddy can show you a good time."

She stared at him, deadpan, not moving a muscle.

She lashed her long nails at the boy's face. He stumbled back, covering his eyes, screaming and crying. The bearded man scowled at her and he opened his mouth to say something just as the techno beat got louder, taking his words away.

I grabbed her hand and dragged her away. Her hand in mine went limp but she didn't try to break free and run off. I hurried as fast as I could toward the entrance of the cave, driving right into all the people before me, shoving away anyone who was in our path. At long last I plunged into the last few groups and before I knew it I was out. I quickly passed through the many-cornered corridor with the LED scarlet tubes, past the several archways with beaded curtains. As we finally arrived in the emerald bar with the lightning columns, I looked behind us for the first time. No one was coming after us. The disgruntled boy's father was nowhere in sight.

We reached the stairs to the main entrance. Right next to the bottom stair was a woman sprawled out, face up. A large round belly protruded from beneath her windbreaker. She must have been around seven months pregnant. She was staring at the ceiling, her face stunned, her eyes blinking and blinking. We had to step over her to climb up.

Outside, the sky was the first pasty white of the early morning.

The milky gloom exposed all the cracks and stains on the buildings and the river of cans and bottles in the deserted street of Saint Paradis. A warm breeze brought with it the sour aroma of vomit and clattered for a brief spell the crushed cans scattered on the concrete. Further on in the street, a plump red-faced man with glasses and an open shirt was pounding on a door with his fist.

"Let me in!" he shouted out, shaking. In the stark silence of this hour, his voice was the sharpest voice I ever heard in my life. He pounded again on the door and this time he wouldn't stop.

"*Please please*! Not here! Not here! I need to be in! *Please!*"

We walked out of Saint Paradis and on the way to my place went through a couple of narrow empty streets, the white ferroconcrete stacked cubes and oblongs of various residential buildings looming on either side.

"He's the one," Angelique said with finality. "I want him inside me."

She kept on saying this at different intervals during our walk. It was her mantra for the night.

"He's the one. I want him inside me."

In a street named "Our Lady of Sorrows" she pushed me into an alley full of the smell of rot. Stainless steel cans were scattered everywhere, stuffed with opened garbage bags. She came toward me with the piece of glass still protruding from her forehead. As she approached, she knocked down two of the cans with her arm. Both banged against the ground, gushing out mush like two open mouths vomiting on the tarmac.

With both her hands, she pushed me back again.

And then again, she pushed me further back.

When we were in the middle of the alley, she turned around and peeled down her jeans and then her panties. She bent down from the waist up and thrust out her ass at me. Just like that time at the Hieroglyph toilet.

She slapped her ass cheeks with the same hand that had clawed at the boy's eyes. Her fingers left bright red handprints on the cheeks. Her hand slid down and the fingers started ruthlessly rubbing herself.

Grabbing her by the waist from behind, I took her. Our hips together, we rocked savagely back and forth in tandem with a steady ferocity. One of my thrusts made her lurch forward, and she slammed into some garbage cans and took them all down with her.

I seized her up by her collar. She ripped her shirt open, spitting out buttons that pattered on the ground. She tore off her shirt and she tore off her bra.

"Grab me and rape me!" she shrieked out.

"Demolish me!"

I whirled her around so her back faced me again. I slammed her against a shutter in the alley wall, cracking her face against the plastic.

An ooze started slithering out of the garbage bags inside some of the overturned cans. The ooze was salmon coloured, crawling out from several places at once, all around us.

Pressing her against the wall, I took her once more. But this time I went slower and harder than before. Each and every thrust made her jump upward and crack her forehead against the shutter. Each and every one was emphasized with the beat of her head slamming, which she in turn accompanied with a croak.

The slime was crawling out of other cans that had been knocked down. Its sluggish streams were intersecting at various points, merging into thicker streams that kept creeping onward. The entrance to the alley was already covered with this viscid substance. It was coming straight toward us.

I wrenched myself away from her. But she grabbed my hand and stuffed all five fingers inside of her. I rubbed and rubbed until my arm went numb and I couldn't stand it anymore. I fapped trice. She noticed and went straight down to her knees. I spasmed and hotly exploded over her mascara eyes, nose and mouth. Blinded, she opened up her mouth and rolled out her tongue to receive the rest. Though her face was covered, it still couldn't hide the vivid red slit in her forehead. The shard of glass had been driven inside the flesh.

The slime was only a few steps away. Its worms were coming at us from all sides. We were surrounded. Soon . . . very soon it would reach us. It would touch us.

## 51

Angelique's hypothetical confession:
    The thought is obsessed with a wound. It likes to stick its finger into this wound. Just when the wound is about to close—just about—it sticks its finger back inside.
    Its nail is clean and polished. It cuts like a whetted razorblade. It always opens the wound in an unpredictably new way.
    Oh my, I would answer.
    Oh my, she would reply. There goes the rhythm of my life. The wound opens and then it starts to heal. It opens again and then it's about to heal again. And the only thing that changes in this oscillation is the pockets of healing, which get shorter and longer as the days pass.

## 52

I don't remember anything else from that night. Other things could have happened in the alley and afterward. I've this lingering feeling that a lot more had transpired. There might have been someone else involved. And he might have been in that alley: a man with no hair and very soft skin.

It's ironic that the most real experience of that night was the dream itself. At some point, the dream began, and it felt as if I had finally woken up from the foggy mystery pounding with techno, spinning with people, soaked with drink and sex.

I found myself, like many times before, climbing into the attic of my family house from the window. Downstairs, on the first floor, the bay windows of my parents' bedroom were locked. The main door on the ground floor wouldn't open either. In the smoky wooden corridor with the kerosene lamps, I tried the wire meshed door to the garden. This was locked as well.

The limping coming down the stairs to this corridor suddenly stopped halfway. Just like that, it stopped. There was an interval of complete silence. I didn't move. I kept on listening.

The limping then continued descending, one stair at a time. The click-clacking sounds it was making meant that it was wearing thin high heels.

I turned round the corner of the corridor and the rest of it faced me, misty with tobacco smoke, lit with more kerosene lamps on little tables. At the end was the door to the kitchen and in the kitchen there was that tiny bathroom I used to go to when I was sad or very scared. That room always felt so peaceful. I'd cuddle up in the shower tray and everything would be fine as long as I was inside that porcelain square.

The click-clacking down the stairs had almost reached the last stair. The gargling suddenly broke out and once it did, it didn't stop.

I reached the end of the corridor and opened the kitchen door. I was greeted by the beige walls and cream cupboards. A large dinner had been set on the table's gold-and-cinnamon spotted cloth. Roast chicken with boiled vegetables and a mushroom lasagne were ready to be served. An iced cake was prepared for dessert. A small cloud of silent flies hovered over all the food.

The wall adjacent to the door was completely blank. Ma and pa could never decide what painting they should hang on that wall, so in the end they left it bare.

There was only one door here and that was the one to the little bathroom. Beside it was an old radio on a cabinet. Ma used to listen to the radio while she was cooking.

The limping had finally arrived in the smoky corridor and it had suddenly just turned around the corner. The gargling sounded slimy.

I hurried toward the door to the little bathroom. I turned the handle, entered and locked the door behind me like I used to do so many times long ago. Once I was inside, I left the world behind. Now nothing could touch me.

In this room of white ceramic tiles was the gentle light of early morning. A timid mist hung in the air over the blue sink, toilet and shower tray.

Then I noticed the outline of a door in the wall between the toilet and the sink. There had never been any other exit out of this bathroom. I approached the outline of the door. I pushed it. It opened inward.

At that moment, the crackling sound of static erupted from the radio in the kitchen. A distant voice struggled against the static.

It seemed to be the voice of a woman.

"Smile . . .

. . . for . . .

. . . me . . .

. . . forever . . ."

The radio went off again.

I entered.

The new room looked like the mirror image of the little bathroom except that it was empty. A floodlight in the ceiling illuminated this space.

The walls were splattered with a slimy substance. Some of these splatters were twitching as if they were alive.

I returned to the bathroom. It had gone dark now, and formless faces of slime had also appeared everywhere. In the gloom, they glowed. Some of the viscous faces were writhing. The room was now a metal cage.

I abandoned the bathroom for the kitchen. But the kitchen had also become a metal cage. A black iron hump of a diesel engine, the size of a human, stood right where the oven had been. It hummed endlessly.

A few steps forward and I saw that the cupboards had become a complex network of intersecting aluminium pipes and valves. Liquid could be heard rushing through these pipes. I went past the table, now made up of six large horizontal wheels with axles moving in opposing directions.

There was a gigantic hole where the bare wall used to be. I couldn't see the garden from the hole. It was the purest black outside. A feeble wind blew in and touched the right side of my mouth.

# 53

I woke up to something scraping my face.

It was my hand. It was scratching the right corner of my mouth. Then, it was finished.

I was in bed in my apartment and Angelique wasn't here. The half-light entering the ashen room could have been the half-light of early morning or late evening or the light of a streetlamp. The silence around me was shrill. How I came to be here I didn't know.

I stretched out my arm and groped around the bedside table. My fingers felt a packet of cigarettes. I tore the top of the packet off, but it was empty.

My hand scratched again at the right corner of my mouth.

I made myself get up to grab my laptop from the desk. I poured myself some whisky and clicked on season four, episode seven. This episode focused on the glam world of rock and rock stars.

### Rocking the Wilde Way

Vincent enters the room of a Goth girl who goes by the name of Mara Pale Night. The walls of her ornate bedroom are full of Venetian masks and occult symbols. Doom metal is playing in the background. She's lying on her bed.

Vincent starts dancing to the music by doing a slow merry-go-round while raising his arms and waving his hands.

"I'm not getting my moves right?" he asks her. "Let's try another."

He goes for a Batusi, passing V signs across his eyes with the two fingers of both his hands.

"You're making fun of art," she replies gravely. "I'm not impressed."

"Perhaps you need some lessons in the Zen art of not-giving-a-shit. Lesson number one: don't give a shit."

"Where would that get me?" she asks back.

"Many places. For starters, you'd be able try new things. Soooo many new things. Like this."

Going 1960s again, he starts squatting up and down while doing strokes with his arms and swaying his hips to the left and to the right.

"And how exactly would it get me into many places?" she retorts.

"If you don't believe in anything, you're free to do anything. So you can do this and you can do that and it doesn't matter."

"Are you on something again?"

"'Oh it's such a perfect daaaaay,' he sings, massacring Lou Reed's chorus. 'I'm glad I spent it with youuuuuu.'"

He grabs a candlestick and uses it as a guitar.

"Oh such a perfect daaaaay
Becauuuuuse . . .
Nothing is importaaaaant.
So everything is permitteeeeeed."

He falls onto the bed and on top of Mara.

"I belong to metal." She stares solemnly up at him. "And metal alone. And you've just mocked it."

He worms his hand under her skirt.

"Your cootch," he explains. "It begs to differ."

# 54

When the episode finished, I drank the rest of the whisky straight from the bottle.

I went to the bathroom and switched on the light on the mirror.

I took in a few deep breaths and closed my eyes.

*I am the one who lives for adventures. I am the one who collects them, grows rich on them. The new is my guide, my purpose in life. It attracts me because it offers a chance for intensity, a chance to let go and be overwhelmed. Once the intensity pales, once it starts to grow old, I'll leave the journey—shedding it like an ill-fitting dress.*

*Mine is a life that's a series of presents free of one another, enjoyed without shame in all their exotic sensations. Mine is a life that's an ever-insistent hunt for new futures, even as the present is being enjoyed. A life of endless anticipation and excitement. Unmoored from all that's past, the future I envisage is a breathtaking constellation of possibilities. So many new stories can happen to me—so many worlds I can see and be and feel. "What's next?" is my first thought every morning.*

*But on this journey, I can never let go completely. I know this. Always I've to keep myself on guard against the dark side to each and every new world I discover.*

*The temptation to linger.*

*Every experience has a siren's song that will seduce me to linger in it. And I must deafen myself against that song.*

*Lingering is the great sin, the only sin that exists in my game. To linger is to miss out on all the other opportunities so close at hand.*

*Picking this experience is already at the expense of so many others waiting to be enjoyed.*

*I have to be quick and sharp. I must never stop looking for signs of lingering. When the magic of novelty starts wearing off, when its romance and thrills start turning to routine, when, above all, the experience starts growing on me, then, I'll know that it's time to go.*

*Linger long enough, and you can get addicted to the familiarity of your experience, to its predictability. In doing so, you let your experience become your shelter, your insurance, your hearth and home. You let it become your crutch, depending on it, becoming it.*

*And home—I know this—is the tumour of laziness. It comes from that one fatal decision to cave in, lay down your arms and rest indefinitely. Apathy breeds the same actions and the same lifestyle: a falling-for that always prevents a moving-onward. You would say, I've done my share of experiencing. You would reason, I'm not unhappy here. I can't expect much else. I'm too tired to move on, to take on new adventures, to feel something different. It's time to settle. Now it's time to be content with the little things.*

*Because the big things are too big for me.*

*This is who I'm not.*

I open my eyes before the mirror. The wrinkles have disappeared. My face looks calm, amused. Eyes half closed, it stares at me with a dopey smile. I address it for reassurance.

Nothing is true. Everything is permitted.

I quickly left my place and wandered around town. On the terrace of La Grotte d'Eden Bar in Sephora Square, there was a redhead in a polka-dotted dress sipping prosecco. She was alone, probably enjoying the sun. She met my eyes and smiled. I pointed at myself and made an astonished face.

## 55

I next met Angelique on the Sunday of the following week.

"Last Saturday was so fun," she said. "It was so crazy."

This afternoon, she was wearing a red Valentino cropped jacket over a Burberry floral minidress. The slit in the middle of her forehead had healed a bit and now it looked like a little brown lip.

We went to the Monoprix Supermarket on Cristalle Avenue to buy food and drinks to take to my place.

"Yesterday, my babysitter agent called," she stated as we walked past the canned meat shelf. "She told me that the two families I was babysitting have found someone else and they no longer require my services. I guess that's because I've missed a couple of sessions lately."

I chose some cheeses and a couple varieties of crisps.

"I'll have to use my savings for a while," she said. "I've no more work now."

She chose some chocolates. We both agreed on two bottles of gold cinnamon vodka with 24-carat gold leaves inside.

On the way to my flat, she stopped in front of Pygmée Concept to look at the children's winter clothes on display.

"All I ever wanted was to be a mum," she said. "That's all I ever wanted."

As we were walking in Euphoria Square, I saw a British-looking man in stripes sitting outside a bistro, drinking white wine and reading a newspaper. Occasionally, his head twitched and his shoulders jerked upward. I don't know if he noticed it when it happened. He had probably been doing this for a long time.

In my room, she took out a stash of cocaine from her Michael Kors handbag. She said she got it from her girlfriends but she suspected who their dealer was.

"You-know-who must have given it to them," she said.

I put on some house music and opened a bottle. Angelique snorted two lines before I could join her. I poured two full glasses for each of us. When I gave her the drink, she instantly gulped down most of it.

"Everything's as clear as a movie now," she said with a spark of eagerness in her voice. "Now I feel as if something exciting is going to happen today. I wonder what it's going to be."

She filled up her glass again and quaffed half of it.

"I want to get away from all this, from everything," she said. "Go somewhere far away where I'm free. Yesterday I decided that I'm going back to Corfu. I want to go back and live again like those times. Some days there were truly beautiful.

"There was this one time when we found an abandoned boat with oars on a beach in Palaiokastritsa and rowed it to Othonoi, a few hours north. It was believed that Ulysses had lived his years of passion with the nymph Calypso on that same island. We found a small cave which, long ago, could have been Ulysses's and Calypso's bedroom, full of candles, urns of grapes, fur blankets, pillows, cushions. There, the lovers must have spent long warm nights in each other's arms, watching the waves outside crashing against the rocks. At night we lit a fire beside the entrance and told fantasy stories to one another.

"Then there was that day we went to the town of Kassiopi where this feast was taking place. It was a festival commemorating a miracle that happened long ago. A boy had been blinded for a crime he didn't commit, and one night, he found shelter in the church of the town. The next morning he could see again.

"I remember there were trumpet processions until late afternoon and in the evening, the feast moved to the harbour area. I remember the people there roasting lamb on spits under the palm trees, the air getting thick with the smell of herbs. A band of street musicians were playing folk music with guitars and mandolins and several locals were holding each other's hands and dancing in circles. We joined a circle and went round and round. Sometimes we all stopped, whirled, clapped, jumped, took each other's hands again, and moved around in the opposite direction. I remember all the movements as if it was yesterday."

She opened her handbag and fumbled inside for some time but couldn't find what she was searching for. She frowned, wrinkling the little brown lip above her pencil thin eyebrows. Her lower lip trembled a little bit.

"Motherless cunt!' she spat. 'Where the fuck are those cunt cigarettes when you need them?"

I offered to go and buy some since I had finished mine, too.

When I got back, she wasn't in the room. The music was still playing. I poured myself some more vodka and had a cigarette.

I went to the bathroom to take a leak. I opened the door and she was on the toilet seat. She was spasming hectically. Every part of her body had erupted into a frenzy of its own. Her head was shaking like a spinning top, her shoulders leaping, her chest and stomach lurching up and down, her arms thrashing about, and her open legs kicking around.

"I'm okay," she said solemnly as her head twisted from one side to the other. "I'll be with you in a second."

I closed the door and went to my desk to change the music. I had listened to too much house for one evening so I went for classical rock. I chose a Led Zeppelin album.

Something heavy inside the bathroom slammed onto the floor. "Stairway to Heaven" started playing.

It took some time before the bathroom door opened. She came out and approached me cautiously. The lip in the centre of her forehead had opened again and was now a glistening red slit.

"I've made up my mind," she said. "I'm going to Corfu soon. I'm going very soon."

## 56

On the evening Angelique told me that she was going to Corfu, I had a dream—a different one. In it, the door of my bathroom inched open and her eye peeped through the crack. Then she emerged, and I saw that the lip on her forehead had opened up bright and wide and was pouring a line of blood right down to her nose. Her black-lined eyes were locked onto mine. The look on her face was grim. Slowly and steadily she shuffled toward me and not once did she seem to notice what was on her face. She approached me until she was about four steps away. Then the bathroom door opened again, and the scene repeated itself in exactly the same way.

I woke up with a start, needing to pee. I got out of bed and made my way to the toilet. I groped around for the switch and turned on the mirror light. A red stain instantly appeared on the frame of the shower tray. It was a very vivid red in the bright light. I tried to look down the toilet as I peed but I couldn't get my eyes off the stain.

*It's going to happen*, it told me.
What was going to happen?
*What was always going to happen.*
There's a long way to go.
*No, it's going to happen soon. Any time now.*
I doubt it. I'm ignoring you.
*You knew this.*
*You always knew that the time would come.*

The bathroom had a carpet, swirling with a floral pattern. I grabbed it and placed it over the stain in the shower.

## 57

As I look into the mirror of the Glaze Restaurant toilet right now, I cover the fly on my face with one hand. Then I take my hand off, exposing it again. I cover it and expose it a second time. I'm doing this to see how I look when it's not on my face. I'm trying to imagine how I used to see myself.

That's not possible anymore, of course. All my attempts at covering are now futile.

And Angelique knew this as well.

She wanted to hide herself in the fever of her parties.

It was this same fever, however, that finally revealed her. The very rush and excitement she gave herself to, at some point gave her back to herself. It led her straight into the surgical light cast by the eye.

Blind and deaf from all the fever, she would suddenly see and hear the words:

Your fever is covering. Its darkness is covering a light.

Your fever will go. The wound is there—always.

Your fever is a dream. The wound is a bone-hard fact.

Angelique caught herself hiding. So hiding led to her capture. Losing herself brought her to herself once more.

Every day was a constant hide-and-seek that she'd lose. She'd always hide well. She'd always find new ways of hiding well.

But it was all a matter of time until it found her, until it slid its nail into her—once again and always for the first time.

> Wednesday, March 02, 2016
> 11.23
>
> Today it's shopping! Just shopping!
> Oh my god! I really need so many new outfits for the next spring!
> When I'm finished, I'll leave them at yours so we can go to Electrique and have a cocktail or 3.
> Life is good!

> Saturday, March 05, 2016
> 22.50
>
> I'm at L'Essence right now wearing a plunge-front caftan from L'Absara.
> Come and see what I'm wearing underneath ;-)

> Tuesday, March 08, 2016
> 13.21
>
> Tonight's going to be AMAZING!
> It's Nina's birthday party!
> We're going to her place first and then go barhopping after that – yeah!
> You must come and celebrate! I got presents for your nosey! Oh yeah!

> Thursday, March 10, 2016
> 01.13
>
> You are so so missing right now!

By the third week of March, we were meeting three or four times a week. We'd go from one bar to the next, drinking something different in each bar. Come the evening, we would head straight to The Wohoo!—where we'd play ping-pong drinking games with some group of students. Right after, we'd go to Saint Paradis Street and pick a bar there for a couple of strong shots. But eventually, at around midnight, we always left to go to the heart of Saint Paradis.

Club Sublime was the climax of all our nights. All roads led to Club Sublime.

> Sunday, March 13, 2016
> 16.42
>
> Take off your clothes.
> I want you to put your tophat on and your leather trenchcoat and boots.
> Come here at 21.00 sharp. The door will be open.
> I'll be asleep in a white nightdress ;-)

> Tuesday, March 15, 2016
> 14.31
>
> Today I'm really REALLY spoiling myself!
> At lunch in Cherry Blossom, I'm having a rabbit in Dijon mustard sauce, three slices of chocolate-cake and mint cookies with white chocolate ginger icecream!
> Soon after, I'll be having strawberry Mojitos at Happy Days.
> You got to try them! They have the best Mojito you'll ever taste in your life!

> Friday, March 18, 2016
> 08.04
>
> From time to time I can hear something trickling slowly in my flat.
> When I look for it, I don't find it.
> It's very frustrating.

> Saturday, March 19, 2016
> 02.46
>
> I'm dancing and dancing at Odeur 53!
> I've almost reached the stars!
> Come over now! This is so CRAZY!

*When Her Time Comes*

Whenever she felt like doing something, she did it. The slightest craving, the slightest desire had to be gratified as quickly as possible. She would not wait. She could not stand the waiting. She squeezed out what little joy she could the moment she could. There had to be no time in between. It all had to happen now.

> Sunday, March 20, 2016
> 14.09
>
> And now, 4 crepes with cheese, a Cassoulet, 2 appletarts and a red Bordeaux at Boulevard Résurrection for lunch!
> You must join me and celebrate!
> LIFE IS SO GOOD! LET'S CELEBRATE!

> Monday, March 21, 2016
> 14.11
>
> I'm celebrating life, baby! This is THE LIFE!
> I just bought a Dior handbag, a Dior perfume and a pair of D&G pumps at Le Splendid!
> The assistant has opened a bottle of champagne for me to celebrate!

> Tuesday, March 22, 2016
> 15.20
>
> I need you to do something for me.
> Be a dear and drop by to Nina's for some nosey candy and then bring it here.
> Don't take long!
> RUN   RUN   RUN!   LIKE   FLASH! HAHAHAHAHA!

> 16.38
>
> Where are you? You're a bit slow today ha ha. Can you run for it?

> Wednesday, March 23, 2016
> 05.10

I can hear the trickling noise again in my room. I'm going to leave this flat and find another one.
WATCH ME!

20.02

OH MY GOD, THIS FILM LOOKS SO SCARY! It's called *The Eye* and it's showing in 1 hour at Ange Gardien Cinema.
I just booked 2 backseats for us so you've no choice but to come now! Hahahahahaha!
NO EXCUSES AND DON'T BE LATE!
IT'S VERY VERY SCARY! YOU'RE GOING TO HAVE NIGHTMARES! HIHIHIHIHI!

Thursday, March 24, 2016
13.47

THE PARK IS REALLY REALLY BEAUTIFUL THIS AFTERNOON!
SO MANY KIDS PLAYING AROUND IN THE SUN!
I'M WRITING AND DRINKING PASTIS!
YOU HAVE TO COME AND DON'T SAY NO!
THE PARK'S AMAZING TODAY!

17.10

I'm in the library of the Faculty of Letters reading a lot of Victorian novels!
THEY'RE SO ROMANTIC THEY MAKE ME CRY! OH MY GOD!
YOU MUST COME AND CHEER ME UP …
… WITH YOUR DICK! HAHAHAHAHA!

20.31

I'M COMING TO YOUR PLACE RIGHT NOW WITH LOTS AND LOTS OF GIFTS!
YOU'LL BE SO EXCITED! LIFE IS GREAT!

## *When Her Time Comes*

Friday, March 25, 2016
19.22

I WANT YOU TO FUCK ME INTO OBLIVION!

20.14

I CAN'T WAIT TO BE AT YOUR PLACE!

20.30

I WALK SO FUCKING SLOWLY HAHAHAHAHAHA!

20.40

OR YOU CAN COME TO MINE RIGHT NOW!
I WALK SO SLOWLY!

Saturday, March 26, 2016
18.04

NO IS NOT AN OPTION!
IT'S YES YES YES! WAIT TILL YOU SEE HIHIHIHIHIHI!

18.25

HURRY UP OR I'LL COME NOW!

18.44

YOU HAVE TO COME NOW!
PLEASE!

19.18

PLEASE COME!

19.40

> RUN! RUN!

> 19.51
>
> I'M COMING NOW!

> 19.59
>
> COMING NOW!

My apartment door buzzed. It buzzed again. Then I heard an insistent pounding on the entrance door downstairs.

# 58

One morning, Angelique called to tell me that she had something important to show me. I have to say I was curious, so I agreed to meet up. Designated meeting point: the children's park near her place at 21.00.

In preparation, I switched on the bathroom light. The floral carpet was still lying on the shower tray. I hadn't looked under it since I had put it there, though it felt as if it was pleading with me to take a look.

I grabbed the edges of the sink and stared intently at my face in the mirror. Taking a few deep breaths, I closed my eyes, concentrating on one idea—*the mood*.

Again, I willed my whole being to be fashioned by the mood. I forced the mood to take me over, bathe me in its world and all its colours.

I believe in you, I said to it. I believe that I am you.

My grip on the sink relaxed. The feeling ran through my veins, rich and exciting, sheer relief, like a shot of the purest heroin.

In the mirror, my face was smiling at me with that dopey look.

Here I am, it said. Let's have some fun.

When I arrived at the park, the swings, slides, merry-go-round and toy horses were all empty. She was sitting on her usual bench by herself, staring at nothing, with frown wrinkles between her eyebrows. The lip on her forehead was slightly larger than before, but it seemed to be healing. A thin line of pink crust was all that remained. She had a bisque Camilla and Marc caster coat on with a purple dress underneath that went down to her knees.

"It doesn't matter anymore," she muttered at the deserted park, her lower lip trembling now and then. "There's nothing I can do. I don't care anymore.

"I'm going to see the Duke."

We started walking in the direction of Euphoria Square. She couldn't stop talking. She was certain that her friends wouldn't be at the Duke's tonight because they had a party elsewhere. She confessed that this was a relief since it would be awkward to bump into them in that place. After a while she took out thick-framed glasses and placed them on her face. Then, she took out a net-cap which she stretched over her head. And finally, on top of it, a 1960s beehive wig.

"Sometimes," she said, "I prefer to be someone else. Like in a game."

On the way, she spasmed brutally twice as if something inside of her had suddenly woken up again and gone haywire, and on the second spasm her wig slid out of place. She had to readjust it.

Once we arrived at Euphoria Square we took Lotus Street. There, Angelique stopped right in front of the Marmara Spicy Kebab Restaurant.

"We have to be hungry," she informed me. "Aren't you hungry?"

She pushed the glass door open and went inside. I followed.

The place was exactly the same as the first time I had visited it, though it was much busier than I remembered. The little boy was serving the customers as before. The Arab was in the open kitchen behind the counter, almost hidden in a cloud of smoke. The sizzling and popping of the oil joined the hip-hop blaring from an unseen speaker.

"Almost there, almost there!" the Arab shouted out.

Behind the counter, the tall woman with the Cleopatra bob and the caked-up face was observing everyone. She was sucking a blue lollipop.

We found an empty table and the little boy soon came over. We ordered two doner kebabs and beer. As we were waiting, spectacled Angelique said: "When you get the kebab, eat it quickly as if you're starving."

The moment we were served, she grabbed the kebab and stuffed a quarter of it into her mouth, ripped it out and started munching it away hysterically. Salad and lamb and sauce and oil came out of her full mouth, toppling onto the plate, but she kept gobbling on and on. I pigged out on mine as well. It was spicy with a lot of sauce, but it was good. Once we had finished eating, we swallowed down the pints. Plates and glasses empty, we sat in silence staring at nothing. Spectacled Angelique licked her lips and chin like a cat.

Soon enough the little boy returned.

"Dessert is expecting you both at midnight," he said mechanically. I was surprised by how thick his voice was. His voice must have dropped at a very early age.

"Tonight," he added, "the dessert will be rare."

With that, he left to serve some new customers.

"Almost there, almost there!" the Arab shouted out from the smoke in the kitchen.

We stayed at the restaurant for a couple of more hours, drinking more beer but hardly talking. As it grew late, people started leaving. By around 23.00, only twelve of us remained, drinking at the Formica tables, and everyone was silent. The only noises around us came from the MTV music videos on the screen and the Arab scrubbing the dishes and saucepans. The Cleopatra girl and the little boy were nowhere in sight. It felt as if nothing was going to happen.

"Almost there, almost there!" the Arab shouted.

Spectacled Angelique looked bored. At least the beer gave us something to do while we waited.

At 23.40, the little boy appeared from nowhere. He told everyone to line up in front of the aluminium door behind the counter. As we queued, he produced a key from his pocket and opened the door with a strong tug. We followed him into a corridor illuminated by two rows of globes embedded on the ceiling like embryonic eggs. There was a black-and-white zigzag pattern on both the walls and the floor. As we walked onward, I spotted another aluminium door with a toilet sign. I told Angelique I had to take a leak and that I would meet her in line afterward.

The door led into a pale green corridor with a zinc bar on either side. The gents' and the ladies' faced each other. The gents' door was jammed, so I tried the ladies'. It opened.

I was about to enter when I suddenly saw someone hunched over a sink, gazing at the mirror. It was the woman from the restaurant with the Cleopatra hair. Her apron was hanging over another sink, and she wore a gold midi dress. She was touching the brushstroke of her left eyebrow with her pink polished fingers.

She started peeling her eyebrow off, exposing the bump of the bone behind it. Then, she peeled the right eyebrow off as well and placed both of them on the edge of the sink. After that, she lowered her head and pressed her fingertips against both sides. She started lifting the silvery Cleopatra bob up and off her head, revealing her bald scalp.

She turned the faucet on and cupped the gushing water with both her hands, splashing it trice onto her face. She washed her face, showing the grey and gaunt skin that had been hidden by her makeup. Her hollowed eyes looked at herself and then suddenly rolled away. And saw me.

I hurried off, shutting the door behind me with a loud noise. I went back to the toilets entrance and returned to the main corridor with the zigzag design. I was going to have to hold it for a while.

Walking quickly down the passageway, I finally came upon a flight of winding steel stairs at the other end. The procession of twelve was going up with the little boy still at the front. I joined Angelique, who was at the end of the line. The staircase led to another plain aluminium door which the boy opened with a

## When Her Time Comes

different key.

We stepped into a small corridor covered with gossamer curtains. The translucent whiteness made me feel as if I had entered some ethereal dimension. I breathed in the church smell of incense.

The boy pulled at a string concealed behind a curtain and revealed a frosted glass door. We were taken into a lounge draped with heavy dark blue curtains. Incense sticks burned in all four corners. Three couches quilted in scarlet lay in the centre of the otherwise vacant room.

We were asked to sit down and the little boy gave us red wine in old-fashioned crystal glasses. As we drank, he went behind one of the curtains and didn't return. I stared for a long time at the swirling patterns on the floor. I soon found myself growing calmer. Some of the others were also staring at the patterns and nodding off.

At some point, a bell rang behind the curtains. It rang once. It sounded like an altar bell.

*Pling.*

After a while, it rang again. This time it was nearer.

Some time later, it rang a third time, closer still.

The bell kept ringing and getting closer until it was right behind the curtain to my left.

*Pling.*

A man emerged. It was the Arab with a brass bell. A lime green toga was now wrapped over one of his shoulders, going down to his ankles. His chest was bare, a canvas of curly black hair. Crowning his head was a circlet that glowed a neon green.

"The. Real. Is. Awakening!" he chanted to us. "It. Is. Coming. For. Us. All."

The little boy emerged and stood beside him. His toga was a lemon yellow, matching the circlet on his head that glowed with the same colour.

"Follow. Us. To. Hide," the Arab chanted on. "Follow. Us. To. Live."

*Pling.*

We formed a procession again and followed him through the opening he came from. Behind it was another straight corridor enveloped with more gossamer white curtains. As we walked on, the Arab kept ringing the altar bell once at equal intervals. The boy walked at the rear of our procession. We passed under a few chandeliers shaped like round nets and sprinkled with several nodes of LED light. There were the vague silhouette figures of people behind some of the curtains. The forms were motionless, standing or lying down in different postures like the shadows of museum exhibits.

The Arab stopped and exposed another frosted glass door. Inside was a spacious dining room draped on all sides by dark blue curtains of damask, like the entrance lounge. There was a table with grand mahogany chairs. Two crystal jugs full of a rich purple liquid were on the table, as well as a plate and an empty chalice in front of every chair. In the exact centre of each plate was a tiny yellow polygon pill etched with the horizontal 8 symbol of infinity. I counted twelve chairs.

*Pling.*

We crossed the dining room and went out of the door at the far side. After some more walking, the Arab stopped and pulled at another hidden string. The curtain drew back to show us a third frosted glass door.

The door opened into a bathroom ghosted with smoke. From inside the thick haze, the orange coronas of several incense candles flickered. I noticed that silk cloth was covering the one window and the three mirrors on the walls around us.

As I stepped into the mist, a figure materialized out of the far end of the room. It was a bald man sitting cross-legged inside a bath that was half full of water glowing with a phosphorescent light. He didn't have a single hair on his body that I could see. His skin was as pale as an albino's and it had a waxy sheen to it. He had a globe of a belly, protruding half out of the water like a bulbous appendage uselessly attached to his otherwise skinny body. His face was soft and feminine, with skin so shiny that you couldn't tell his age, and it made me wonder if he was really a man and not a woman, or bot . . . or perhaps something else entirely. Completely still, he stared right ahead, beyond us, at something I couldn't see. He was so still that I was almost fooled into thinking he was a lifelike wax statue.

All twelve of us formed a crescent in the middle of the bathroom. The voice of the Arab came to us disembodied from somewhere in the smoke. It said:

"You must open your hearts to him before you receive him.

"Listen.

"He is knocking at your door."

*Pling.*

Pling.

"Will you open the door? Will you open your hearts to him?"

"Yes," we replied all together. "Yes we will."

"Then approach, one by one. Come forward for the miracle to begin."

The Arab pointed at one of us—a middle-aged woman in an office suit. She stepped forward timidly and he started stripping her of all her clothes. Finally she was completely naked, her pasty skin covered in various parts with inflamed patches of blisters. The nipples on her small breasts looked like a pair of little red antennas, and she pressed her thighs webbed with veins tightly together.

With ceremonious movements, the Arab proceeded to wrap a blue toga around her. The little boy then took her hand and led her to the bath. The eyes of the man in the bath were now following her closely as she came toward him.

"Kneel," the boy commanded.

She went down on her knees right before the bursting belly of the Bath Man. The boy then touched her head and bent her forward. Her head made a splash as it disappeared into the phosphorescent water. He sank her head even deeper, right under Bath Man's belly. Multi-coloured bubbles sprouted out around his love handles.

Some moments later, the boy pulled her out. The Arab rang

the bell with excitement.

"You are now ready to receive him," he chanted.

The next person to be chosen was a Korean girl with a sad face. Spectacled Angelique gave me a nudge.

"Pssssssst," she hissed. "Maybe we should go."

I didn't pay her any attention.

When the boy lifted the Korean's head out of the bath, her eyes were gleaming and she was smiling as if now she knew something that pleased her a lot. She giggled like a naughty little girl.

*Pling, pling, pling, pling.*

"I wasn't expecting this," Angelique insisted. "Let's just go. Let's go."

After the Korean, the boy chose a blonde-haired Slovakian man. His large hanging cock was pierced in several places. He wagged it about with his hips. On his left side, from pelvis to upper ribs, ran the fierce scythe of a scar. When he noticed everyone's attention turning from his crotch to his curved scar, he stopped flaunting about and hunched, his arms falling limply to his sides as he glanced down at his feet.

"You don't understand!" Angelique suddenly hissed. "We *have* to leave!"

An intense relief was on the Slovakian's face as his head was thrust out of the water before the Bath Man. All glistening, with eyes closed, he gave out a long deep sigh.

*Pling, pling, pling, pling.*

"Listen to me! We've to go. Now!"

"Or else?" I replied.

The fourth was a woman in her sixties with short curly hair dyed green. She instantly covered her breasts with both her hands as her clothes were stripped off. When she took her hands off to put the toga on, only one flabby tube dangled out of her chest.

*Pling.*

"I don't want to be here anymore! We have to leave right now! Please!"

Sheer rapture was on the green-haired woman's face as she was hauled out of the water. Her ageing face was calm, completely abandoned.

*Pling, pling, pling, pling.*

"*Please!*"

The boy now pointed at spectacled Angelique. Reluctantly, she stepped forward and let the Arab undress her. All the men in the group stared at her naked figure with hungry faces. The toga that was wrapped around her had a royal red colour. With her beehive wig still on, she was led slowly to the bath. The Bath Man's eyes were fixed on her. The Arab rang his bell exactly with every step she took forward. When she knelt, the boy took the glasses off her face. Then, he placed his hand on her head to sink it into the water. She flinched.

"I . . . I've a cold," she stuttered. "I might get worse if I put my head into the water."

The boy didn't say anything. He tried to touch her head again.

"Can . . . can I receive him without touching the water? I . . . I'm afraid of this water."

The boy tried to touch her yet again.

This time she let him.

Her head was instantly plunged into the phosphorescent colours.

*Pling.*

A second later, her hair surfaced. Without her head. The ball of hair floated about like a dead furry animal in front of the Bath Man's explosive belly. His eyes followed its rotations but then fixed themselves again to the spot ahead of us.

Angelique was pulled out of the water, her uncovered short hair pasted against her head, dripping down her face and neck.

*Pling, pling, pling, pling.*

As the bell rang, she looked up at the Bath Man and he looked down at her. His eyes suddenly glared, showing a lot more white than should have been possible. His thin mouth parted slightly and started to twitch. He shifted his haunches in the water.

The bell stopped ringing and a screaming silence fell upon the room. There was an electric tension all around us. No one dared to move or do anything. Everyone was waiting. Angelique and the Bath Man just stood there gaping at one another.

"Your heart's not ready to welcome him," the Arab interrupted. "It's closed to him. You have to leave now."

Torn by shame, Angelique quickly took off the toga and put on her clothes again. Everyone's eyes were on her, studying her. The Bath Man seemed to have recovered now and his face had returned to its solemn detachment.

The bell rang the moment she left the room.

*Pling.*

I left with her.

In silence, the boy escorted us out of the curtained maze and the building.

## 59

When we were out of Marmara Spicy Kebab, Angelique insisted that she now wanted to have some *real* fun. I was in no mood and we had to have a row about it before she finally let me go home. In truth, deliverance arrived in the form of a message from her friends who asked her to join them at La Grotte d'Eden Bar. This soon resolved our quarrel and we parted ways.

I stayed wide awake in bed for a while. I couldn't stop thinking about the carpet lying over the shower tray in the bathroom.

When I finally drifted off, the dream came again.

I went into the little bathroom in the kitchen. And the room was tranquil, safe.

But now the outline of a new door had appeared in the wall between the sink and the toilet.

The wall opened into another room.

"Smile . . . for . . . me . . . forever . . . " said the staticky voice of a woman from the kitchen radio.

The new room was tiny and empty. There was a bright light in the ceiling that filled the space, illuminating the blood-coloured slime writhing on the porcelain walls.

I returned to the bathroom and then back to the kitchen. A dirty yellow light had fallen everywhere and the walls were made of wire mesh, the floor an iron grating. Slime twitched in various places. The hulk of an engine was humming.

Along the ceiling of the corridor outside the kitchen stretched out a spine of bulkheads, each one wrapped in barbed wire and giving off a saffron glow. Rows and rows of rusty steel chairs, with an aisle in the middle, crowded the entire length of the corridor. In the aisle was a railway track that led to the sharp corner at the far end and wound around it. Large cooling fans droned in the shadows.

Around the corner, the corridor led to the entrance hallway with the large mirror and the main door. Beside me, in the corner wall facing the hall, was the door to the garden. The wire netting in its frame was now a soft pink skin marked all over with spots of inflammation. Nearby, the grandfather clock made a heavy grinding noise. Its tower-casing held an elaborate clockwork with gearwheels revolving. The face showed 02.05.

I reached the end of the corridor and walked into the entrance hall. In its four corners, instead of the columns, there were street electricity poles joined by a web of wires spread out between them. As I was crossing the hallway, I passed by the wall where the large Baroque mirror once hung. There was now a large sheet of pink skin stretched out tightly against the chain-wire. It was pinned to the wall behind the wire with a nail driven into every one of its corners.

The sitting room to my right was draped with soft curtains of inflamed skin gently moving to a warm breeze behind them. Rows of chrome shelves protruded out of the wall and there was slick orange ooze pouring slowly out of the vases on the shelves. The statuette of the Virgin Mary had become a sharp pyramid of steel. All the photos lining the shelves displayed the closed mouths of many unknown people.

Since the main door was still locked, I walked back across the hall to go to the corridor with the stairs to the first floor.

I went up the first stair. From the corner of my eye, I caught something white moving behind me in the hall.

I turned around. The sheet of skin nailed to the wall was quivering. Something behind it seemed to be trying to push itself out.

## When Her Time Comes

I approached.

Pressing behind the sheet was a bulge around my height that was moving restlessly from time to time. At any point now, it could manage to rip itself out.

I was in front of it now. I lifted up my hand to touch.

My finger was a hair's breadth away when a ripping sound began. Only it wasn't the skin before me that was ripping. Something else was, from the railway track corridor adjacent. The noise was coming from its far end wall. It was coming from the *other* sheet of skin nailed to the frame of the garden door.

From outside, a fillet knife was tearing a gash out of that sheet. When the gash was large enough, a naked leg started to slide out of it. It was sinewy and long. It was wet all over. Its smooth skin gleamed in the amber gloom. The foot was in a high heel with a strap around the ankle. The thigh was shapely curved. In a short time, the pelvis and hip were showing themselves as well.

The gargling finally poured out into the corridor.

I hurried back to the stairs and started going up. The faces on the family-tree photos hanging along the stairway all looked down at me with mocking eyes, laughing from their foggy brown world.

Down below me, the first steps clanged upon the metal grating of the stairs.

When I was halfway upstairs, the limping started banging across the corridor below.

I reached the last stair. The limping had just reached the first step.

## 60

I woke up to pale light seeping into my room through the windows. Every object in this room stared at me in silent expectation. That tap, the canvas, that doorknob, the painting, that crack in the wall were waiting for me to do something . . . to do *it*.

I scratched the right side of my mouth.

I put my hand back under the blankets. All my clothes were flung across the floor. Dirty plates piled in the sink and the tables were cluttered with empty wine bottles and stained glasses. Some of the glass rims were marked with red lipstick. A Vincent Face screensaver was floating on the laptop screen. I was naked.

My hand tore out of the blankets. And scratched the right side of my mouth.

Somewhere far away, from inside an apartment, a voice was speaking from a radio.

I waited for around half an hour. Then, I got out of bed.

I chose episode three of season five for today –

A Christmastime Tourist

One fine evening in the Christmas season, Vincent Face spots his former lover, Laura, walking in a busy street. He sprints after her as she waits by the traffic lights to cross.

"Hey!" he calls out. "Hey, it's me!"

Laura stares at him, perplexed.

"What . . . what are you doing here?"

"Do you think I asked for this?" he says. "You woke me up and I *never* wanted to wake up. You came along and you were *too much*. What you made me feel was *too much*! You were the anomaly."

"I don't understand," she replies. "Why you did what you did."

He steps closer to her.

"We were awake somewhere else. A special place. Us together. Let's go there again. You've always been the anomaly."

He's just about to touch her cheek when she stops him and shakes her head.

"You can't," she says with a fatal calm. "You know you can't."

She turns and crosses the road as the pedestrian lights turn green.

# 61

Ever since the events at Marmara Spicy Kebab, Angelique started partying almost every single day. Exhaustion, hangovers, sickness, boredom . . . it didn't matter. She held onto the fever with a ferocity that broke through all obstacles. She turned it into an obligation, a regime, a structure to her days. Every day she gritted her teeth and made herself sleep again with the liquor and the bars and the people and the music and the dancing.

The ritual began at Monoprix on Cristalle Avenue in the early afternoon.

*The smart choice to live well*, two screens beside the escalator would say before and after they showed the horoscope for the day. We'd go straight for the liquor shelves and choose a bottle of vodka and a mixer. After that we'd head to the wine shelves to get two bottles. It was always two bottles. *Feel good—with Monoprix*, the screens would say in the wine section.

Once we had bought our drinks, we'd walk to Park Ailes de Joie. On the way there, we would buy pizza from a fat man who was always sweating and complaining about the weather. We always bought the same type of pizza: the meatfest—always. At the park, we'd lie down and eat and drink in the sun without saying a single word until we fell asleep, like we always did.

The chiming of a nearby church clock would wake us up from our long nap. Sometimes it'd be 18.00, sometimes 19.00. It didn't make much of a difference. The evening cool and quiet would have fallen upon the grass, the trees, the busts. Time for The Wohoo! Time for some beer pong!

After that, Saint Paradis Street would be waiting for us. La Chimère would be our next stop and La Chimère meant tequila shots. We'd take the same Coca-Cola table on the left-hand side of the bar entrance and take a shot every time we couldn't guess the title of the pop song the bar was playing in its first ten seconds.

"Soon," Angelique would say. "Soon."

The bar always played "Can't Stop the Feeling!" after "Don't Let Me Down." We drank while watching the people passing by in the street. So many different people walking in the street.

And then the time would come. 23.00.

She would have been looking forward to this hour for the whole day. Sometimes she counted the hours, the minutes. It was 23.00 that drove her onward. She'd have that tiny shiver of excitement whenever she remembered that tonight, like most other nights, she was going to the club to end all clubs.

In those days more than any other, routine was her irresistible addiction, her everything. Its rhythms gave her the deep calm she always sought. They must have sent her into a lull like the back-and-forth swaying of a rocking-chair. Routine has a hypnotic effect: it makes you lose yourself in its numbing repetitions.

Routines also made her, make us, feel we are accomplishing something. We are progressing toward a goal: money, a toned body, a place of our own, marriage, completing a work project. When the goal is achieved, we come up with another. As long as we do the same of this or that activity, then it's all fine. As long as we're active and occupied, everything will be alright. Goals are not hard to come by, especially those which justify our rituals.

We love the anticipation of the Monday dinner with friends, watching a movie with a pizza delivery at 21.00 on Tuesdays, going to ballet classes after office hours, jogging on Wednesday and Friday late afternoons, reading on lazy quiet Sunday mornings. We look forward to a certain time because we know exactly how it's going to be, what to expect out of it.

Then there's that happiness of doing something we've done so many times before. It's a cosy happiness, a relief as well: tender and warm, like caressing a purring cat on our lap.

In those days, she must have lived for this as well – this tenderness, this gentle excitement of feeling safe.

Through routine, we try to assert control over our little worlds, to make our lives our home. We get to know every single one of our life's rooms and objects, its nooks and crannies. This Angelique must have attempted relentlessly. The prospect of looking outside routine's cushioned walls would have scared her insufferably. The unknown, the absolute unpredictable was the last thing she wanted to ever encounter.

## 62

If routines were Angelique's medicine to forget, Club Sublime was at their very centre.

In Club Sublime everyone forgot.

At the club one night, she tripped and fell down its flight of stairs. Her face slapped the floor loudly at the bottom. As she stumbled to get up, I could see that she had bruised her forehead. The crusty lip in the middle had turned an angry red. The moment she was balancing on her feet, she viciously brushed nonexistent dust off her halter top, and then staggered to the bar to get a drink.

At the clubbing cave, she met her friends and eagerly followed them deeper into the cave to dance. I lost her in the crowd. Not that I wanted to find her that night.

I walked out to go to the bathroom. On the way, I spotted a tanned girl with silicon enlarged lips and a perfectly straight A-bob. She was leaning casually against the brilliant LED tubes lining the wall, having a smoke. Her arms and legs were covered in tattoos. Her black teeshirt said, "I love you but I've chosen techno." She saw me checking her shirt. Her head suddenly lurched forward and back.

"And I love *you*," I said. "But let's settle for fun."

The girl's head made the forward-and-back bobbing movement again.

"Everything that's exciting in life is new," I continued. "Are you?"

Her head bobbed.

"Seems like we're on the same page. The one that reads: 'The past's outdated and the future might not come.' So all we have is now."

I took out my hipflask, opened it, made a toast and raised my eyebrows and pursed my lips.

Her head bobbed.

"See, if nothing else is important, then everything's a game. And the only thing that matters is the game you want to play right now. Shall we play?"

I closed in and brushed my lips against hers. She let me. So I kissed her. When our kiss was over, her head bobbed as if it agreed.

"You're a fast learner," I said.

"I don't care," she said. "Let's play." She did her best impersonation of a Kim Kardashian give-it-to-me face.

I looked into the several cubicles behind the beaded curtains along the corridor. In some I spotted a tangled ball of naked bodies on the sofas, interlocked in various ways, jerking to different rhythms, muscles tensed and faces with veined temples and necks lost to the expanding sensations.

All cubicles were taken. So I grabbed her hand and led her straight to the toilets.

The ladies' room was enveloped in a ghastly white cast by two globe lights. They were emitting a low buzzing sound. There were three stalls and all of their doors were shut. I opened the first one and the wall had caved in, filling the area with rubble, debris, shit. I opened the second and caught a woman sitting on the toilet, bent down, injecting a needle into her eye.

The third stall was all that remained. I pushed the door open. Inside was Angelique, sprawled on the floor in the middle of a shapeless star of vomit. Her body was flapping wildly around like a living fish on dry ground. The lip had burst open again. Three dark streams of blood were spilling out of it, splitting her face into three. As her body leapt around, her glazed eyes were staring up while her mouth opened a little, as if she was just about to say something. Scattered around her were around a dozen white pills.

# 63

When I found her in the ladies' toilet of Club Sublime, I called emergency and then quickly left the club with Silicon Lips on my arm. At my flat, she gave me acid and we tripped for what seemed to be a lifetime. I plunged into a universe of the most brilliant colours where Silicon Lips, always on top of me, morphed into many characters I had seen on TV.

When I came to, I found the windows of my flat all open to a sky of lead and my canvas papers tossing and turning around in the wind. The laptop was open and an episode of *Face and the City* was playing on low volume. Silicon Lips had gone. I wasn't sure if she had really been here, if I had even met her. There was the sharp bitter smell of piss in the air.

Among the papers around me, I spotted a book that had toppled over and landed open, face up on the floor. It was Angelique's diary. I picked it up, flipped randomly through some pages and read.

*Sunday, 11 August, 2013*

It's been a long time since I've written in this diary. Two months to be exact.

I've moved to Devon now because my boyfriend's British and he works there. His name is Raphael. He's a very sweet guy.

*Friday, 13 September, 2013*

I've been ill for two weeks now. I'm living at Raphael's place and he's taken a long leave to take care of me day and night. His hands are so gentle. Such patience!

I've a high fever in the evenings and I tremble a lot. In the mornings and afternoons I feel as if my life's been taken away from me but yet I'm still alive somehow. I'm awake but for most of the time I can't do anything, I'm not anything—I can't move, I can't think and I can't even be. I lie in bed still for hours and hours, cold and hot at the same time.

I'm a sick, sad girl.

*Thursday, 26 September, 2013*
It's been almost three weeks and I'm still very sick. Sometimes, the sickness makes me see Raphael in a different way. I can see him without skin now. He is walking around or sitting by me with all his insides visible. Sometimes I can even see his whole skeleton beneath the flesh. I can see his bones moving, his ribcage heaving, his muscles and tendons stretching and relaxing, his coils of intestines quivering, his organs pumping. He has become a moving meat factory, a jigsaw puzzle of muscles over a frame of bones encasing tightly-fitted meat packets and tubes. When he talks to me, it's his facial muscles and his skull that do the talking and not his face. I can hardly see the face.

It feels as if for the first time I'm seeing Raphael for what he really is.

*Wednesday, 2 October, 2013*
When he brought me water with a straw this morning it wasn't him who was coming toward me. He has never really been there. It was a compulsion that was making him move. He was being driven to do things by the meat and fluids racing inside him.

All that Raphael thinks and does is the product of his body. Raphael *is* a body.

*Sunday, 6 October, 2013*
So many rhythms make up his body, generate it. I can see every single one of them all at once all the time as he's tending to my needs or doing housework. I can see his bright pink lungs expanding and contracting as he's breathing, his heart beating, his eyes blinking in the sockets. He can't help this. He never will.

These rhythms are his energy source, his batteries. They animate him. They power the factory that gives him the drives to do and be anything. Raphael is produced by the rhythms of his body's factory.

*Thursday, 10 October, 2013*
When he smiles, it's his muscles at the sides of his mouth flexing. When he caresses me, when he kisses me, it's the bones and the wrapped muscles and tendons of his arm and face stroking my skin, touching my lips. He doesn't smile, touch or kiss me. The rhythms of his anatomy generate his smile, his touch, his kiss.

*Sunday, 15 October, 2013*
I've been feeling better these past five days so I encouraged *it* to go to work again. It works in a biscuit factory in Devon. Its job is to keep guard on a dough mixer and pour extra vegetable fat into the churning flour in the machine when required.

On the kitchen table I've left it a very kind letter. It doesn't say much except for how grateful I am for all its love and care.

At the Exeter airport, I took the first plane to Marseille and from there I headed straight to Saint Laurent. I've found a cheap hotel on L'Opéra Street where I'll be staying for a night or two until I find an apartment. The time right now is 23.30.

*Monday, 16 October, 2013*
Today, an eye has opened in my head.

# 64

Once I finished reading her diary, I checked my mobile to find a couple of missed calls and unread messages on my phone.

> Sent by: Angelique Duval
>
> Friday, April 15, 2016
> 17.34
>
> HEY! LET'S GO WOHOOOOOO! TONIGHT!

> 18.10
>
> PARTAY! PARTAY BABY!

> 19.23
>
> HELLOOOO! ANYONE AT HOME?

> Saturday, April 16, 2016
> 23.41
>
> Are you at your place?
> I can come to yours with wine and CANDY!
> BEST CANDY IN TOWN MAN!

> 13.20
>
> STOP BEING A PRICK AND ANSWER ME!

> 14.22
>
> ANSWER ME!!!!!!!!!!!!!!!!!!!!!!!!!!!!!!!!!!!!!

> 19.52
>
> KJFA; U[W3;HLAF;ZCK;L H'NGV NF'A'JADJWEA'RJWA

I didn't text back. I intended to tell her in good time that I was too busy working on my paintings. If she persisted, I'd get blunt and tell her that it was over, that I didn't want to see her ever again.

When I woke up the next day it was raining and I found several other missed calls and messages on my phone.

> Sunday, April 17, 2016
> 14.11
>
> I AM SIIIINGING IN THE RAIN! SIIIINGING IN THE RAIN!

> 15.21
>
> Rain—purest thing in the world! Oh yeah!
> Let's go to park, drink under the trees, and watch the rain fall!
> LET'S CELEBRATE LIFE!

> 15.42
>
> COME ON LAZY BONES!
> COME ON! COME ON!
> WAKEY WAKEY!

> 15.57
>
> WAKEY WAKEY BABY!
> MEET AT 18.00 AT THE PARK ENTRANCE.
> LET'S GOOOOOOOO!
> WE DANCE AND DRINK IN THE RAIN HAHAHAHAHAHAHA!

I finally caved in and answered her.

And it wasn't just because she was hot—actually hotter than most. It was something else. There was something about her that drew me to her. It was a magnetism that was animal and felt forbidden: an attraction that seized me in some terribly intimate part of me. From some horrific and desperate place she seemed to call me, and there we met—and became one and the same.

> Sent to: Angelique Duval
>
> Sunday, April 17, 2016
> 16.05
>
> Okay.

On the Sunday I sent her that message, I had already tried to approach three girls with a hangover that literally made the right side of my face throb. It goes without saying that I was rejected by every single one of them. My reflections in the glass doors and windows of the boutiques and patisseries I passed by were making a lot of unnecessary movements to try to get my attention. I couldn't help noticing this from the corner of my eye. But out of sheer determination, I managed not to give in to them. I never looked.

When I returned to my studio room, I realized that it was better if I kept away from the bathroom. I didn't want to go that close to the flowery carpet. That was when I texted Angelique. But there were still around two hours to kill before our date, so I decided to work on my blog and force some order into my world.

*The Jaded Debauchee*
Sunday, April 17, 2016
16.16

In the beginning there was the decision.
  Before you were who you are now, you made a choice.
  There could have been many small choices; it could have been one. All that matters is that all the things that happened in your

life were the direct or indirect result of that moment.

Many of you do not want to believe this. You spent your lives doing what others do; doing what was expected of you; doing what you felt like doing. "I listened to my conscience"; "I went with the flow"; "I relied on my instinct" . . . There is often a positive ring to these remarks. But the truth lies in what they hide—*fear*.

Many of you never changed much. You always had this or that quality, this or that personality. You say you could not really make any big decision because you already had a personality; you already had duties and ideologies you had to abide by. So you say, "I never had a choice." "I didn't decide." "I was made this way." "I was born with these attributes." "I take after him or her." "There's no such thing as the decision."

But there is.

At some point, your decision was still made.

You decided not to decide. You decided you were not free to decide.

There is a horror in the freedom to choose. It is the horror *of* freedom.

At the instant of your decision you realize that you are not, you never really were, *this* person with *these* qualities. You are not anything that you thought you were. You are responsible for who you are, for everything that defines you. You are your own doing.

So you can make of yourself what you want. You can make *your self*.

True reality does not exist outside you but *inside* you.

This is the only thing you can ever be certain of.

You will. Therefore you are.

Nothing is real except for your will, which creates reality. So many selves, so many realities can be forged by this force. What is true, what is important, depends only on what your will chooses it to be.

Above all else, your will desires one thing. It wants to feel itself in control of all that happens to you. It wants to be itself, perform itself everywhere. It delights and nourishes itself on its own empowerment. True happiness will be found whenever your will sees itself reflected in your experiences, when your universe is created in its image. You exist to arouse yourself.

## David Vella

Herein lies the way to the highest freedom.

Let your free will take full charge and redesign you *exactly* as you *really* desire. No conditions. No regrets. From scratch, if necessary.

Give birth to yourself.

*(written in a time of dire need)*

## 65

I think it was on the Saturday of the last day of April. The plan was to follow the same routine we always followed on most other days.

But something extraordinary happened on that day. Something completely unexpected.

"I don't want to go to the park," she said. "I don't want to Wohoo! I don't want to go to La Chimère and I just don't want to go to Club Sublime.

"I don't want."

She said the same the next day and the day after that. She didn't feel like doing anything—anything at all. So we stopped going out altogether.

One evening she came to my flat and never left it.

During the first three weeks of May, she slept for long hours in my bed, and when she woke up she listened to some tunes while smoking and drinking wine and pastis. She was drinking from the moment she woke up right until she passed out again. She'd often forget to shower and eat. The only times she left the bed were when she had to use the toilet.

I stayed with her for most of the day, leaving only to get food and booze. The windows were always left closed, the curtains drawn, removing us from the outside world and its noisy life, its passage from morning to afternoon to night. There was no time in our secluded room. We woke up and passed out in the glare of the intense halogen lights above us. They froze our four-walled world to a static present. If there was any change or any sense of time in this refuge, it was the dizzying buzz of getting more and more wasted. The only past we had was the time when we were less drunk or drunker. The present was the persistent determination to keep on drinking. The future was the thrilling anticipation of getting drunker, of finally getting drunk beyond drunk. We lived in a perpetually blurred world that dissolved now and then into long gaps when we existed by not existing.

Rarely, while she was still asleep, I would peep out of a window down at the strait Street of Our Lord. I always spotted different types of people passing below: middle-aged women in stylish clothes parading crossbred dogs, tourists with their well-rehearsed innocent curiosity, businesspeople, secretaries, bankers, estate agents, waiters, students and more.

Once, as I was looking at some passersby, something struck me about the way they were moving. It occurred to me that they didn't seem to be the ones who were doing the moving. Something else, something inside them was making them move around. Something was pushing them to do this or that—a force that was blind, thoughtless, biological. I saw a woman take some steps and sit down on a doorstep and eat a sandwich while a man crouched and took some pictures. An old man came out of a building and dumped his garbage next to the wall of his block while a youngish man in a waiter's uniform hurried past. And all of their movements were automatic, mechanical, a sequence of reflexes. Whatever they were doing was being done on repeat.

I asked myself why this was happening. Why were all these people caught in this loop that never ended, that never broke out of itself? I supposed it was because they didn't know what else to do. Because they could not, or perhaps would not, do anything else outside of their assigned thoughts and actions.

Raphael.

The people walking in the Street of Our Lord were not really people.

They were bodies moving.

By the last week of May, all sorts of trash had accumulated on the floor and tables of my room: pizza boxes, bottles, food cans, cigarette butts, ash, clothes, toilet paper, half-eaten leftovers. Eventually, a painfully sweet stench of decay was slowly suffocating our little world.

On the bed, framed by the sea of garbage, Angelique, always naked, would often lie in a foetal position for long hours. The only movement she could afford was the automatic lifting of her arm to smoke a cigarette or drink from a bottle. She smoked all the time now and her fingers were stained yellow and orange with nicotine. A mist of smoke would always envelop her. I thought that this made her look like a saint in a cloud, witnessed in an epiphany. Sometimes she would burst out hacking. At other times, her body would erupt in a nonstop spasming and flapping. She stopped showering altogether. She also gave up on talking. She only spoke a few words when she wanted more cigarettes or drinks.

## 66

Angelique's decision to stop trying, to surrender was wise in a certain sense. She must have concluded at that point that she could never really forget. Sooner or later, the thought would return, with a new face, in an unexpected way.

So she went for the logical alternative. She tried to spend a lot of her waking hours forcing herself to be aware of the thought. Even in the last few weeks before she moved to my apartment, I think she was doing her best to keep it as close as possible at all times. She held onto it no matter where she was or what she was doing.

These were the days when the thought hovered in the background and then interfered every now and then as a necessary static.

"Hello, my name is Angelique and I live in Saint Laurent but I prefer Paris" *tssssshiiiiiigggg*

"When I get back to Corfu, I'm going to do that dance again at the feast" *tssssshiiiiiigggg*

"Maybe I'll meet a strong Greek man . . ." *tssssshiiiiiigggg* " . . . and we'll have a lot of . . ." *tssssshiiiiiigggg* " . . . children.

"We'll live in a cottage by the sea . . ." *tssssshiiiiiigggg*

"He'll be a fisherman and when he'll go fishing I'll write a great . . ." *tssssshiiiiiigggg* " . . . love story about us.

"I always liked writing about a faraway . . ." *tssssshiiiiiigggg* " . . . mystical island . . ." *tssssshiiiiiigggg* " . . . where all dreams . . ."

*tsssshiiiiiggggg* " . . . come . . . " *tsssshiiiiiggggg* " . . . true." *tsssshiiiiiggggg*

But sometimes, inevitably, she slipped; she let herself go and forgot.

And there were still other times, when she wanted to forget. She dove into a sea of sensations, letting them dissolve her, absolve her. Though this plunge was always laced with dread.

I see this—or I think I see this—but in this instant, as I stare at my face in the mirror of the Glaze Restaurant toilet, I start reconsidering everything. This evening's attack during my date with Dina seems to have opened up in me a new perspective. Maybe what has happened to me has in reality blinded me from really understanding Angelique, or understanding anyone. Perhaps all my attempts at interpreting her are a projection of my own sickness onto her condition. I could be totally wrong about her.

What if I'm missing something? Or what if this wasn't the whole story? What if there was more to her fear and hiding?

What if she secretly *wanted* to keep the thought alive? What if she didn't really want to forget it, leave it behind for good? What if she harboured a suppressed desire for it, a desire that was so perverse she had to hide it from herself all the time?

Perhaps the real reason she hid from the thought was because she wanted it to find her again. Perhaps she ran away from it in order to tease it out and lure it ever closer to her. Perhaps she was unconsciously seducing it.

She hid so that it would hurt her. She healed herself so that she would bleed much more the next time.

The thought might have made her feel alive. It must have made her feel *something*. It didn't matter if her world was crumbling and falling down a vast abyss – as long as the fall was dramatic.

The thought could have made her life poetic. A drug she found irresistible.

At a certain point in one's life, any kind of intensity would do, even if it comes from Hell.

To *really* heal, to *really* go back to the quiet of the ordinary after a season of storm, would not have been that easy. The ordinary would have left her underwhelmed, empty, pointless. For her, the prospect of going back to how it had been before could have felt unbearable in its quiet.

So whenever the wound reopened, she could have smiled to herself in secret.

# 67

Soon enough, the dream came to me once more. I went out of the new room in the little bathroom of our Cardiff home and the whole house had changed. I went up the stairs and when I got to the first floor, the limping bonged on the first stairs below me. The landing was suffused with an orange light from the nickel bulkheads strapped to the wall. The doors to my brother's room, my parents' bedroom and my own room looked like the doors of high security prison cells. The pendulum clock on the landing wall had become an assemblage of rotating wheels. The largest wheel was in the centre and it was showing 02.05 as it rotated.

The limping continued. Another stair and it would be facing the landing.

I hurried into my parents' bedroom. Here, the mirrors had all turned to sheets of skin nailed to the walls and all of them displayed a bright red upward curve in their centre. The curtains blowing into the room from the unseen balcony were so thin and fragile they were transparent. The bed in the centre had become a large aluminium stretcher and right above it hung a steel chandelier with three tiers. Its candles were now fillet knives, their blades pointing up at the ceiling.

A rumbling was coming from the darkness under the grating floor. It was coming at a frenzied speed and the grating was rattling, the stretcher was rattling. The rumbling was suddenly a roaring that swallowed the room. A brilliant white light burst out from below, stripping everything of its definition and colour. For a split moment, everything was a siren white. When I looked deep below the grating on which I stood, I saw the triangular headlights of a train thundering past, a row of lit windows on each side. The lit rows seemed to go on forever. The room trembled with the booming thrum of the train's engines and the clanging of its wheels on the railway tracks.

Just as suddenly, the train disappeared into the darkness ahead, its noise growing fainter and fainter. The white light was once more replaced by the dirty yellow illumination. Everything was still as it was before.

I left my parents' bedroom and headed to the door of my room. I knew that I wasn't going to look back.

The good foot hammered on the final step of the landing. The gargling was as deep and wet as ever. It was only a few steps behind me.

I was now in my room.

# 68

By the end of the second week of June, I couldn't stand being inside any longer. It was around 21.00 on Saturday and she was still passed out from the afternoon. I put some clothes on and left the flat.

I wandered around town until I found myself in Lotus Street. On impulse, I stopped before Marmara Spicy Kebab. From the glass entrance I could see that the restaurant didn't have a lot of customers. I pushed open the door into the humid smoky heat with the familiar sizzling sound of frying oil and the smells of grilling and roasting meats. With a massive spoon, the Arab with the bandana was scooping and pouring red and white sauces over an opened kebab.

"Almost there! Almost there!" he shouted out.

The small boy was making the rounds as usual, writing orders in a notebook. The woman with the Cleopatra bob was sucking a rainbow whirly lollipop while closely observing the few patrons munching and slurping.

I sat at an empty table and the little boy was with me in no time. His denim shirt was half open and there was quite a bit of hair further down his chest. I ordered a lamb kebab. When it was brought over, I devoured it like a pig. It was spicy and the pieces of lamb were crispy, yet tender.

"Almost there! Almost there!"

The kebab was followed by three pints of beer, which I drank over the course of an hour.

By 22.30 I was still sitting at the table. The kebab grills were still rotating. The screen on the high shelf was showing *X-Factor*. That was when it dawned on me that I was waiting.

It was now around 23.00 and I was still here. No one had yet come over with an invitation.

"That was *beyond* incredible!" exclaimed Simon Cowell from the screen.

Two hours later and the restaurant was almost empty. The Arab and the Cleopatra girl were nowhere to be seen. A middle-aged woman in grubby blue overalls had started cleaning the floor with a mop, her arms jingling with bracelets. Her face had so much makeup on that it looked as if it was made of cake icing.

Still no invitation delivered.

Some ten minutes later, I spotted the young boy cutting slices of oily meat from a grill behind the counter. I signalled for him to come over.

"I want to have your midnight dessert tonight," I told him.

He shook his head sombrely.

"I'd like to see him anyway."

He shook his head again.

"Why not?" I asked.

"He's indisposed," he replied in his very bass voice.

"I don't believe you."

"He can't see you tonight."

"Sure he can."

I whipped out my phone and tapped 112.

"Or else your asses are going to jail."

"You won't do that."

"Sure I would."

"You won't."

"Watch me."

I pressed Call. The phone started ringing.

The small boy seemed to grow sad. He frowned and wrinkles appeared at the corners of his eyes and around his mouth. I spotted the stubble on his cheeks. The boy wasn't a boy at all. He was a man—probably in his forties.

"Come," he finally said.

I cancelled the call and stood up. I was easily twice his height. He led me to the aluminium door behind the counter like last time and took out the key from his trousers. We went into the corridor with the black-and-white zigzag designs and the glowing globes overhead that looked like embryonic eggs. We climbed up the spiraling stairs at the far end. Once we had arrived at the other door, the dwarf opened it for me to enter.

He took me into the first corridor again amid all the stirring gossamer curtains and the smell of incense. Tonight the floor was covered with a layer of snow-white smoke that almost reached up to my knees. It reached up to the dwarf's waist and it looked as if he was walking inside a cloud.

We entered the lounge with the dark blue curtains of damask and the hypnotic patterns on the floor. Three people with furry bear masks that were too large for their bodies were also there. Papa Bear was in a suit relaxing on a sofa with one leg on the other, reading a newspaper. Mama Bear in a long frilled purple dress was rolling some dough on the table. Baby Bear in dungarees hopped and skipped around, throwing a rubber ball in the air and catching it. He seemed happy though he was quite large for a baby bear. Three plastic bowls full of porridge were ready on the table and three beds had been prepared in a corner, one next to the other, two big and one small.

We passed the second long corridor of gossamer curtains and smoke. In the middle towered four high poles, and on the tops of these poles, almost touching the ceiling, rested a mattress with velvet sheets. Lying on the mattress was a woman in a medieval pink satin dress with bows and sequins and a glittery overlay. Her intricately curled hair was blonde and she wore a crown on her head. She also wore a mask of Disney's Sleeping Beauty. She even had the same sleeping posture as that character in the cartoon: hands crossed over her breasts, a rose lying under the fingers. A man in black spandex was struggling hard to climb up one of the poles that held the bed. The mask he was wearing covered his eyes as well. He managed to climb halfway up but then suddenly slipped all the way down to the floor. He tried again and again and every time he slipped all the way down. But Spandex Man was not about to give up anytime soon. As we were going to turn a corner in the corridor, another Spandex Man came out, groping around with his hands as he made his way on tiptoe toward the elevated bed.

Around the corner, the corridor kept on going. Beauty and the Beast were coming toward us from the other end. The Beast was chasing Beauty and both of them were moving in slow motion, as if they were in a different space-time. The girl with Belle's mask, blue dress and pinafore was waving her arms wildly in the air as if she was very scared, while the Beast, hot on her trail, was reaching out for her with both his arms, so desperate to catch her. They ran past us slowly in silence. They disappeared behind a curtain adjacent to the corridor junction.

In the dining room, ten persons sat around the central table, every one of them covered in a grey sheet. The Arab, in a monk's cassock, was walking in a circle around the shifting forms with an altar bell in his hand.

"You. Are. Nothing," he chanted. And then he rang the bell.
*Pling.*
"You. Are. Nothing," he repeated.
*Pling.*
Blocking the next corridor was a high pedestal with a wooden throne on top. Sitting on the throne, with her back toward us, was Snow White's Evil Queen. She had a cape that fell over the chair and down the length of the pedestal until its rim touched the floor.

"Mirror mirror on the wall, who's the fairest of them all?" the queen announced in her majestic voice.

We walked on the side, around the pedestal and below the throne, and confronted a forest of rubber masks hanging down head-level from strings attached to the ceiling. There were rows after rows of hole-eyed faces, all the way down to the very end of the corridor. From her seat high up on the pedestal, the Evil Queen gazed down at all of them.

I had to part masks to move every two or three steps forward. The dwarf, of course, didn't have this problem. Most of the rubber heads around me belonged to other Walt Disney characters. But after a while I started spotting the faces of characters from all sorts of popular Hollywood movies. Each and every one of them was making a different expression.

At one point I drew back a curtain of masks and a very familiar face suddenly appeared on my right, swinging to and fro. With its two holes, it stared at me with a stoned grin. Then it was gone behind the next curtain of masks I pushed away as I trudged onward.

"Mirror mirror on the wall, who's the fairest of them all?" the Evil Queen asked behind me to all the rubber faces.

Behind one of the curtains, the form of a slim girl was dancing sensually, waving her arms above her head.

Finally, the dwarf stopped, drew back a curtain, and the frosted glass door to the bathroom was before us. He knocked four times: two slow knocks, two rapid ones. Then, he opened the door a little bit.

"There's someone here for you," he said. "He insisted on seeing you."

A long silence passed by.

"Come in," a voice from inside replied.

The dwarf entered. After a few minutes, he walked out again and nodded for me to go in.

# 69

The candles were gone and the ceiling fluorescent light was on. The Bath Man was beside the sink, unhooking a heavily padded bra off his chest. He had no clothes on except for scarlet briefs that were too tight for the bulge of his crotch, half covered by his dangling belly. The silk cloths had been removed from all three mirrors and a different angle of his albino body was reflected in every one of them. There was no smoke here.

"So here you are," he said with torpid eyes. His male voice had an effeminate gentle tone.

"I wasn't invited tonight," I said. "Even though I ate the way I was supposed to eat."

"You were faking it, of course," he replied. "And last time you were faking it as well."

"So I was. And?"

"When you eat you let go," he said. "When you let go, you reveal who you are and what you're going through. If you're observant, you can tell a lot from the way a person is eating. How you eat mirrors your most intimate self."

"And I only choose those people who eat in a certain way," he added.

"So people who eat like pigs," I replied.

His face twisted into a wide, tight-lipped grin.

Then it relaxed and went back to normal.

"Their way of eating is just one of many symptoms. They're

the ones who need my help the most."

"Who *are* you exactly?" I asked.

"Does it matter . . . " and he paused for a moment.

" . . . as long as I'm not God?"

"What matters is that these people are shattered. Their reality is unhinged. They need to create a new one. I can give them that."

"A Walt Disney character you mean," I retorted.

"Not just them but they're easy to be," he answered. "In fantasy stories, everything is so black or white. Everything is so clear and well-defined.

"I give each person the character that seems to suit their personality the most. They don't need to stick to that when they're outside. What's important is what this character makes them realize—that all identities are fantasies and who they were need not be true anymore. What they *can* be is just as true. It can even be truer. The Game offers them the opportunity to end one fiction and recreate and explore a new one. It shows them that they can be whoever they want to be. What matters is that they *have* to be someone."

"And why's that?" I asked.

"Because our identity creates our reality and our reality is an armour."

"To protect ourselves from . . . ?"

A large tight smile stretched out on his face again, squeezing his eyes shut.

"We create our reality," he said, "this reality to protect us. It's a reality that's premised on denial; a reality that's designed to deny.

"See, we as a species live through denial. We live because of denial. We thrive on it. We're at our most creative when we deny. We build our lives on how strongly convinced we are of our lies. And yet, even so, we're still often affected by what's outside this illusion we've made for ourselves. Sometimes what's out there can make us angry, anguished or sad. All these strong emotions can signal to us their true origin if we're honest enough, willing enough to trace them back to where they really come from. But the truth of the matter is that very few of us really want to open our eyes. And so we're hardly ever really aware of *why* we're sometimes so sad, angry, scared . . . And it's easier that way.

"This is the Sun World," and he opened his flabby arms out wide. "This is the world we've made: the world that's in the light of the sun. Together we have woven this reality to feel safe, to see clearly, to understand. Because we all need to *pretend* that we understand. This here, the world around you, is the world where everything's the usual, where everything remains the same and can be recognized, where every day is a routine, where everyone wants to be like all the others."

"And yet," he said, "and yet, deep inside we know . . . we *all* know that this Sun World is a cover-up, an illusion, another Walt Disney fairytale."

"What are we hiding from exactly?" I asked.

From the mirror shelf he picked up a jade cigarette holder with a joint, lit it up and took a few elegant puffs. After a moment of silence, he faced me again.

"The Real, of course."

His face wrinkled up into that same tight smile once more.

"I heard that name before," I said. "A person I know told me that this is a theory created by an obscure psychoanalyst who conducts bizarre therapy sessions."

The Bath Man said nothing but simply took a few more elegant puffs from his cigarette holder and looked at himself in the mirror.

"The term's an adaptation from the famous psychoanalyst, Jacques Lacan," he said to his reflection. "It refers to an experience that's so intense emotionally it can destroy us. It can shatter all that we think we are, everything that we know. Just like that."

He turned to me. He snapped his fingers.

"And then it's all gone—the whole world. And our remains scattered in the *other* night."

He took out a half-filled bottle of champagne from behind the sink, along with two crystal flutes from the few glasses on the bathtub ledge.

"The first time we encounter the Real is in our earliest years," he said as he poured into both glasses. "We're at our most helpless at that time and so we're likelier to be at the mercy of such events. I'd wager in fact that the Real is the first reality we go through. Before we're weaned into what we call 'reality,' we've already been through another one. We've already been suffering."

He offered me a glass. I shook my head. He shrugged, placed it on the sink, and sipped from his.

After savouring the taste for a while, he continued: "The Real can come again later on in our lives. A trauma, a tragedy, a thought, a person, a place, a meal ... anything can invite it back into our world. It can come from something that we're not even aware of. It would come unannounced. But when it does come, everything goes upside down.

"It's therefore very important that we try our best to forget we ever saw it. Everything, you see, depends on how well we hide it from ourselves. We are who we are by how well we bury it. In that sense, it defines our lives."

The Bath Man then puffed out a perfect circle of smoke.

"There's a better way," he said afterward. "The way of exposure. The way of welcoming it when it arrives. But very few can bear that. So to deny its existence is often the safest route. But its memory is a cut and it goes deep, too deep for some people. Whenever they forget, they find themselves reliving it once again. Just when they thought they had healed and it was all over, the cut opens up for them as fresh as ever. There's no end to it."

His face winced, his mouth stretched out into that smile.

"The cut reopens at your most vulnerable moments," he said. "When it does, your world starts changing. Fragments of that past when the Real came into your life will morph your present in many ways and forms. As it starts giving way to bits and pieces of the past, your world will start running out of everything that's familiar, or, the same thing, fill up with a familiarity that is too disturbing. The sleepy day gradually becomes a wakeful night. Your world will turn into a mass haunting of events that happened long ago.

See, the Real is haunting you because you've been hell-bent on suppressing its memory all along. It's getting back at you. A vendetta of sorts."

He took another hit from the joint. After that, he scratched the bulge of his crotch.

"Of course," he said, "the Real can leave you for a while. But make no mistake, it'll always come back. Once it comes, it'll keep on coming. That is its way."

"So the people you gather here are all suffering from this condition and you help them forget with masks?" I asked.

He simply gazed at me with his torpid eyes.

"But you don't accept all of them," I pushed. "You turn some away."

He kept on gazing at me. As if my question was too ridiculous to answer.

"Sometimes you have to," he then murmured.

"But that's not exactly what you want to know, is it?" he added. "You want to know why I turned *that* girl away. And that's probably the real reason why you think you're here. You think you want to understand why she wasn't chosen on that momentous night because you want to understand *her*. She fascinates you."

"So what if she does?" I replied. "Are you going to hold that against me?"

"She's been here before," he said. "One time too many."

He opened the mirror and took out a perfume in the shape of a heart. He sprayed three times on his neck.

"But the Game didn't work for her," he said. "She didn't respond well to its fantasies. Not well at all. The Game made her do things . . . things that horrified all of us. She was a threat to all of my therapies. She made them fail—one after another after another. Domino effect."

"Who is she? Really?" I asked. "Because I don't know. I feel as if I can never know."

"She's someone who's too far gone. Her reality's too infected to recover. She's among the Incurables. Perhaps it's because she loves herself as sick. She might have turned her condition into a romance. There's a deep pleasure to be gained from seeing yourself as the victim of a tragedy. It's easy to fall in love with the idea and the pain of being doomed, to turn this into the purpose of your life, your identity."

The Bath Man put out the joint on a rose-shaped ashtray. Then he slipped into an ankle-grazing leopard printed robe.

"The Real disfigures many forever," he said, his mouth pulling into that thin-lipped smile one more time.

"I've said enough. I've to attend to some patients."

He went to the door and was about to open it.

"This Real, you said it comes for everyone?" I asked.

He went still and slowly turned his head, looking at me with his lashless, droopy eyes.

"No one is spared.

"You know that.

"You just don't remember."

"Don't remember what?" I retorted.

He stared at me as if the both of us were in on a secret.

"This place."

# 70

"Make me remember then," I told him. "I know you can."
I didn't believe him.
"I don't think you'd want to," he answered.
"I want to."
"Why dig up what is better left buried?"
"There's a reason it's buried."
"I want to know *that* reason," I said.
"It's of no use to you anymore."
But I insisted. I threatened again that I'd call the cops. Finally he agreed, though I very much doubt it was my threats that changed his mind. The police probably went to him as well.
He gave me a drink that looked like fizzy milky water in a glass chalice. He said it would help me relax. I drank it. It tasted of nothing, though I felt the faint burn of alcohol. Then he took me to a cinema room that smelled of plastic. It was curtained on all sides with royal blue damask. A large screen was on the far side.
I was asked to sit in the middle of the second row of seats. He didn't sit next to me. After a while, I realized that he was standing right behind me. He smelled of expensive perfumes.
"Lie back," he said very slowly. "Contract and then relax your muscles. Clear your mind of *her*. Clear your mind of all your needs and longings. All your confusions, questions, anxieties. It all must fall away. Welcome what's outside."
The screen suddenly switched on. A large eye stared right at

me. It had a grey iris with a few purple flecks, long eyelashes, a thick eyebrow. The eye was the only thing on the screen. Sometimes it blinked.

"Now I want you to watch the eye. As you watch the eye, relax all your muscles. It is very important you relax your muscles. Tense a little. Now relax. Watch the eye. All weights are dropping away. You are about to fly away, light as a feather—as you watch the eye.

"Can you see that there's an eye's reflection in the eye?"

There was in fact another eye reflected in the pupil of the eye.

"And there's an eye within that eye?"

And yes, there was another eye inside that reflected eye.

"And the eye in that eye?

"And the eye in that eye . . . "

I recognized the gigantic eye staring at me on the screen as mine. And it reflected itself forever in its pupil. In this labyrinth of self-replicas I got lost. At some point, his voice, the texture of the curtains around me, the rows of empty seats, the room's gloom, all withdrew, and then dropped out of my consciousness. There was only my eye before me—isolated, as if I was observing it from a telescope. The eye was floating in a kind of void that it emanated and yet also came from. I was watching my eye and my eye was watching me. There was nothing else in the world. Just us: two entities equally suspended in nothing. The nothing was pure and glistening. Both the eye and its halo of void had neither meaning nor feeling. There was only the sensation of that moment.

Slowly, the void gave rise to a new sensation. I sensed that it was attending to something—listening. A tension, an expectation: a waiting that was a waiting for something unknown. I didn't know if what I was waiting for was something I could hear or something I could see. But it was trying to come and I was trying to understand what was coming. There was no longer an eye anymore. The void was all: darkness and expectation.

And then the void flickered as if it was static. And it opened. It opened to what was arriving.

And it finally arrived.

I am standing in a room surrounded by scarlet curtains that match the scarlet of the pillows and blankets of the bed on the side. A tall black-haired girl in a laced corset and leather pants is sitting on the bed, staring at me with a curious amusement. Over my head and face is the rubber mask of Vincent Face with his stoned smile. I am jumping and whirling around and waving my hands in the air as I dance about to a music only I can hear. She doesn't take her eyes off me for one single moment. She looks very interested in what I'm doing.

"I'm not getting my moves right?" I say. "Let's try another."

I make a V sign with two fingers and start moving them across my eyes and then I do the same with my other hand.

"Perhaps you need some lessons in the Zen art of not-giving-a-shit. Lesson number one: don't give a shit.

"That'd get you into many places."

The girl doesn't say anything but smiles in a teasing way.

"You'd be able to try new things.

"If you don't believe in anything, you're free to do anything."

I spin around and squat up and down while doing strokes with my arms.

"Oh it's such a perfect daaaay,

I'm glad I spent it with youuuuu!"

She nods and smiles some more.

"Oh such a perfect daaaaay . . ."

I skip toward her, take her hands and lift her up to dance.

"For nothing is important," I tell her.

"So everything is permitted."

A flicker—quick, barely discernible.

The scene had changed.

I'm wearing Vincent Face's rubber mask as I enter a toilet. A petite slim girl wrapped only in a towel is about to step into the bath.

## When Her Time Comes

The shower above her is on. Her wavy brown hair is so long that it touches her thighs.

She spots me and jumps, confused, surprised.

I point at myself and put on an astonished face.

"*You know you remind me of Arwen the half-elf in* Lord of the Rings *when she saves Frodo and she's all glowing and shit,*" I tell her.

I extend my arm and offer her my hand.

"'I've come to help you,'" I announce. "'Hear my voice. Come back to the light.'"

I close the door behind me.

"I'm sure the big guy up there would approve."

She looks about and doesn't know what to do. She covers her breasts with her hands.

"He'd probably be high-fiving me if he were around. 'Good one!' he'd say. 'That's a damn good one!'"

Her face is growing more alarmed. The water behind her patters away in a frenzy.

"See, I only pray to what's beautiful."

She takes a step back. With one hand she gropes around the little shelf behind her. There's just a sponge there.

"Don't get your hopes up, though, about your beauty."

She knocks the sponge off the shelf. She backs up against the wall. Her wide eyes are riveted on me.

"It all depends on which angle I see you from."

I turn the key in the lock behind me. It clicks.

I take out my hipflask, open it, make a toast, and raise my eyebrows and purse my lips.

# 71

I was asked to leave the building shortly after I recovered my second memory. It was quite late; the streets were empty, the bars were closed. The town was a graveyard. Back at my place, I couldn't sleep, so I spent some time writing a new blog for my *Jaded Debauchee* site and then a couple of more hours browsing the net. On Facebook I came upon the event page of Make Music Day in France. Make Music Day, better known as "Fête de la Musique," is an annual music festival where musicians and deejays, amateur and professional alike, play in the streets and public areas of every city and town all over the country from afternoon until late at night. The motto of the festival is "to bring the music everywhere and the concert nowhere." In two days' time, the town of Saint Laurent was going to be transformed into one massive party.

I had a good feeling about this. I just knew that something exciting was bound to happen on the day of that festival.

Enter Gabriella on the morning of the day in question, the 21 June. She was from Malta and was living in Saint Laurent with her boyfriend, who worked in some financial planning company. I saw her as she was protesting against the Maltese Prime Minister, whose minister and chief of staff recently had been discovered to have opened secret companies and trusts for their own wealth management purposes and future earnings.

"Shame on you!" she yelled over and over again from her

loudspeaker. "Shame on you!"

Every now and then, she raised her placard that said, "A Maltese Government of Greed and Hypocrisy. I demand Justice!"

She was by herself.

Two hours before the festival began, in Park Ailes de Joie, she was on top of me with her shirt all open. But then I heard a deep rumbling high above her and when I looked up I saw the piercing blue sky being drained of all its colour and light right before my eyes. In a few moments, a ghoulish white waste was spread out all over us from one horizon to the other.

The drizzle started spitting down a few seconds after we started banging. The rain was thin and rusty and it shivered the bushes and leaves, soiled the ponds and streamed down and smeared the busts' faces with its brown filth. I could feel it hitting my back like so many unseen fingers poking me. It rang relentlessly on the empty whisky bottle beside us. I focused on Gabriella's tense face.

When we had finished, a woman's voice boomed out of a microphone, echoing across the town.

*In town there is life. Monoprix.*

They had set up a stage nearby and were playing adverts over the amplifiers. In around an hour, the whole town would become a stage.

Gabriella popped a speed to sustain her energy for her stand-alone protest part two. We parted ways as soon as we were out of the park. She had more hours of protesting to do. I was probably not going to see her again.

I headed to my apartment in the brown-red drizzle. When I opened the door slightly, a stench struck me, rushing into my nose and down my throat. It was a new, deeper stench of rot.

*Dulcolax in the evening, relaxed in the morning.*

I opened the door wider and went inside. My feet squished in a yellow mush that had somehow caked various parts of the floor.

Naked and motionless over sheets covered with ash, Angelique was sprawled face up on the bed, her belly heaving quickly, her eyes staring upward wide open, barely blinking. Her short hair was wet and plastered to her head. In between some tufts of hair right above her eyes, a scab protruded out like a little horn. Every now and then she lifted a bottle of vodka to her lips. And swallowed.

*With Carrefour, I'm positive.*

"I get out. Get out of here," she mumbled in her new raspy voice. "Too much. This room too much."

I went over to my computer without saying anything. I didn't talk to her anymore these days.

But she persisted.

"I go away. Must go away tonight. Somewhere. Away.

"Dream House."

*Lysopaïne transforms the aarrgghh to the aaahhh.*

# 72

As it happened, from Facebook, I discovered that I was invited to another one of Samuel's end-of-days parties on this very same evening.

> Before the World Ends—Once Again
> Soon. Always Very Soon.
> Today at 19.00

The invite was tempting. I confessed that the one time I attended Samuel's party, it had been quite interesting. I could go to the Make Music Festival afterward.

In preparation, I reabsorbed my new blog. I read it carefully with a complete surrender of mind and spirit as if it was a prayer.

*The Jaded Debauchee*
Tuesday, 19 April 2016
18.12

Your life is how you see your life.
The dice is cast. We are all playing at a game of perceptions.
No perception is truer than any other. What is true is only what *you* decide to be true.
Whatever I see is my image of what I see. Our experiences and our very being depend on necessary fictions. There is no way of knowing what is outside my fiction, what is outside of yours.
Some perceptions have more value than others. These are the fittest ones, the elite. The fittest will trample over the weak. They will triumph because the weak are less conscious, lazy, resigned.

## David Vella

The elite perceptions are those which have recreated the self from a clean slate; the ones that leave nothing to chance, to nature. They are the absolute architects of their world and as such they live to enjoy themselves as absolute. Theirs is the endless joy of pure authority and power. They are the closest to godhood.

*(written in a time of dire need)*

# 73

Angelique put on the sweater and leggings she had been wearing when she came to my flat over a month ago and we left straight after. The rusty drizzle was still spitting out of a sky that now looked like a smoke-infested war zone. On the way, she stopped in front of the Lovely Mum boutique to contemplate the children's clothes on display. As she was studying them, she exploded into violent, wet coughing. She gripped her knees and bent down as her body spasmed forward with every cough that ground out of her. When it was over, we kept on going.

By the time we had arrived to the Dream House, the desolate sky had grown even darker. Its leaden vagueness gave out a vast rumble, like cosmic drums signalling an impending doom

The door to the Dream House was ajar like last time. We walked into the stark ceramic corridor with the grey doors on either side. Over us, the fluorescent tubes made the whiteness of the walls and floor glow. There was music beating from the main room up ahead. Someone or something was pounding urgently from behind the door right next to the entrance. The banging stopped for a while but then it started again, insistent, desperate. Sprayed hastily across this door were some red words that I couldn't read.

The corridor leading to the common room was hidden in a wall of smoke that sometimes flickered with a cold lightning. We walked into the smoke and saw a few people in patchy reggae clothes sitting against the walls, passing joints and drinking from bottles. Angelique bought two X from one of them.

"That's all the money I had left," she rasped. "Now I'm free. Free as a bird."

She swallowed both pills at the same time.

A few weeks before, after buying groceries, I had lingered for a while at Lunaris 383, a minimalist lounge with walls of glass. Samuel happened to be there as well and after a brief chat, he started explaining it all to me—what this was, who they were.

"We of the Dream House," he had said, "know that it's all over. And yet we keep on having our last drink, our last smoke, our last pill, our last shag. In the Dream House, we prolong the instant. We stretch out a moment of joy for as long as it's possible. We know that this might be the last moment we'll have before the end; all we have before it all goes away."

In the common room, we were swept up by the jackhammering of industrial techno, a strobe-light blitzkrieg raining a spectral white upon everything. The deejay, dressed up in a Wizard of Oz Tin Man suit, was doing a robot dance to the rhythm. Eager girls in floral pyjamas were jumping on the sofas, arms stretched up, trying to reach out and touch the glittery paper stars hanging from the ceiling. Stainless steel trays lined with cocaine were being passed around a circle of people. Dancing on a brass chair at the far end of the room was a young girl, not older than ten years old, in tiny shorts and a tight red crop top. Black streams of eye paint stained her cheeks and she was rolling and twisting her stomach, making waves with her raised arms and swaying her hips while tossing her hair from one side to the other.

In a few rapid blinks of light, Angelique disappeared from beside me. A few blinks later, she appeared near a far table filling a thermocol cup with gin. A quick pause of darkness and in the next prolonged flash of light, the cup was raised to her lips. Darkness again and in the next flash, she was dancing in the centre of the room. Her dancing was as hysterical as the schizoid lights.

"Our time is the time of postponement," Samuel had said in Lunaris 383. "We suspend and keep on suspending. We throw a party in this snug haven in between two worlds.

"One more, one more, we say . . . before the God comes."

Angelique was dancing as if she was having a seizure, as if all the parts of her body were moving of their own accord. All this jolting seemed to be taking place in order to get rid of something inside of her body, to get it out, dance it away, keep it away. As long as the dance went on, it couldn't come back and take over her again. So her body wasn't going to stop moving. It *could not* stop moving.

I went to the drinks table and poured myself a double black absinthe. A flash of light and Samuel was suddenly before me with gleaming eyes. He came closer and his mouth opened, forming words that I couldn't hear. The ball in his throat lurched up and down all the time.

In another flash of light, I spotted Gregory sprawled on a sofa, staring into space with his baby smile. He was much fatter than usual. His whale belly and hips sprouted out in tyres from under his teeshirt and they wobbled as he grabbed one of the three half-eaten hot dogs on his lap and stuffed it furiously into his mouth. Mayonnaise squirted out and poured down his dangling chins.

I downed three more shots of black absinthe.

A woman in her late forties, wearing nothing from the waist up, was suddenly skipping around the guests. Her silicon tits jumped around tirelessly like jelly melons. She had Indian feathers in her hair and a hippie shawl around her legs.

"I'm so full of love!" she shouted out, laughing, lifting up her hands full of bracelets, barely able to contain her joy. "I've so much love to give! I'm all love!"

Angelique suddenly slipped and went down like a dislocated doll. She clapped her face flat against the floor.

Many rapid blinks later, she was up again, dancing, the scab sticking out of her forehead stamped with a red mark.

"We of the Dream House have the Midas touch," Samuel had said. "We turn the last hour into the greatest passion. We turn it into our be-all end-all. We'd give up everything in the world to let the last moments take over us and take us where they will. See, we of the Dream House are romantics."

Gregory was suddenly in the open kitchen, his belly nodding eagerly out of his top. He jerked open the fridge door and its light shone like a pure sun on his baby smile. He reached inside with both his arms and brought out fistfuls of food. Quickly, he crushed the food into his mouth, and then reached out for more as he munched and munched.

A scruffy bony man right in front of me suddenly unzipped his jeans and started wanking fiercely at the hippie woman with the silicon tits.

The wall of smoke in the corridor was thinning out. Beyond it, I could just see a door at the far end opening. A naked, meaty man slowly came out on all fours, covered in a grizzly forest of body hair that made him look like some species of chimpanzee. Horn implants rose out of his pink scalp and his crescent erection was scraping the floor as he came forward. He was crawling toward us for a while but soon disappeared into another opened room along the corridor.

Angelique slid and slammed facedown onto the floor. The crack her head made against the floor was timed exactly with a techno beat. A few more lightning blinks after and she was suddenly standing up and dancing again, more frenzied than ever before. The inflamed scab on her forehead was now glistening with red beads.

I downed another double absinthe. I found myself staggering into the passageway, making my way toward the bathroom. Something or someone started banging again from behind that door with the sprayed red writing that I couldn't read.

"The Dream House," Samuel had said, "is a church built for those who refuse and deny. It's a sacred palace built to hide us from the inevitable. There we pretend and our pretence is *the* sacred. St. Pretence.

"We all know this. The God *will* come for us all."

I opened the bathroom door. Inside were three beds and tied to their bedposts were a man and two women in white tunics lifted to the waist. They were rolling up their eyes and opening their mouths in rapture. All their bare legs were spread wide open. A person, whose sex I couldn't identify—with spiky hair and glittering with piercings—had just released a snake from a casket. The snake was slowly crawling between the legs of one of the tied women. It was covered in a tar-like substance and it left a trail of black behind it on the sheets. Underneath the black dye, its skin was a spotted purple. I shut the door.

I started making my way back to the common room, stumbling against one wall and then the other. Behind me, a soul-shredding scream ripped out.

Back at the party, Angelique was still lost in her epileptic dance. I downed another double absinthe.

"Where's the bathroom?" I asked a forgettable person who was close by and then another forgettable person close by.

"Where's the bathroom?" I asked the hippie girl skipping about with the tits skipping about.

"We're all the same," she replied, her face wrinkled with joy. "We all need love to run away. Love will set us free."

A hunk of a man picked up the ten-year old girl with the red crop top from the chair. He heaved her up onto his shoulder and she clung onto his trunk neck as he carried her away across the room.

"Where's the bathroom?" I asked the hunk. But he didn't say anything.

"It's there," the little girl said, pointing to someplace far away at the end of the corridor. "It's over there. Right over there!"

Angelique fell onto the floor again, smashing her face against the tiles. Once again, she hit the floor at the exact time as a techno beat. A few more blinks of light later, she was struggling desperately to get up again. But she kept falling down. The scab on her head had now burst open and a streak was slipping out gently from the opened wound, crawling down between her pencil eyebrows and lined eyes. Some blinks of light later, a few more streaks had decided to start sliding down her face. It was as if a blind eye had opened on her forehead and it was steadily crying.

I poured some absinthe in a mug. I gulped it all down.

When I looked at her next, she was dancing again, her face a jigsaw puzzle of vivacious red.

I staggered back into the corridor. A skinny naked old man with a patch on one eye slowly crawled out of a door on both hands and knees. The discoloured skin of his body hung loose like drapes, swinging to and fro. As he dragged himself forward, I could see needle holes riddling his arms. He turned his saggy ass to me and headed toward the door at the far end. That door was slightly ajar and through the crack I could see a tangle of naked bodies spasming in so many different ways.

I finally stumbled into the bathroom. There was no one inside. I grabbed hold of both sides of the toilet rim and bent down.

A tiny kitten crept out timidly from behind the toilet. It tilted its head to one side and stared up at me with large inquiring eyes.

I lurched forward and the brightest, yellowest vomit exploded out of my mouth.

# 74

Hard cold bars were pressing against my cheek. I was prostrated on a floor of steel grating in the middle of the tiled corridor of the Dream House. I was lying on my stomach but my head was turned toward the side that led to the main room. But I couldn't see that room. The further the corridor went in that direction, the darker it grew until it seemed to disappear into a void.

On my right loomed the entrance to the Dream House and next to it loomed the door with the red writing sprayed across it. No one was banging from behind that door any longer. I could now read what was written on it.

*In the centre there is a hole.*

Someone was coming. Footsteps were clanging on the grating from the darkness ahead. One step was heavy. The other was a light ring.

The footsteps were getting closer and closer. They had a rhythm.

*Ping clash. Ping clash. Ping clash.*

Only someone wearing high heels could make that sound.

I tried to move. My body didn't respond. It was a lump.

The limping footsteps kept on getting closer. There was a relentless determination to their banging.

*Ping clash. Ping clash. Ping clash.*

I tried to move again but it was hopeless.

I caught a glimpse of who was coming.

A tall, tall figure that glowed all white in the darkness.

# 75

I shuddered awake. The cool glossy surface of porcelain was against one side of my face. I was back in the bathroom of the Dream House. I was sitting down on the floor, leaning against the toilet. Beside me, a splash of vomit.

Mystical music was sighing out of a room outside. From time to time, a slow heavy thudding intruded into the music. The thudding followed its own dull rhythm. It seemed to be coming from the same place as the music.

My hand crept up to my face. The fingers touched the right side of my mouth. And scratched.

With some effort, I got up and went out into the corridor. As I trudged forward, I held against the walls for balance. I passed by the door sprayed with the red writing and once again I couldn't read it. One of the fluorescent tubes lining the ceiling ahead was flickering on and off. Glass cracked and crunched under my feet. When I looked down, syringes were scattered about the floor. The mystical music was coming from the common room, along with the slow thudding.

Around me, a few naked bodies were sprawled out on the floor in different positions and angles. A dark young woman with braids was leaning against the wall, unconscious, and her pelvis was twitching, thick foam gushing out of her mouth.

The main room was lit up, like the passageway, with a cold white fluorescent light. All the tiled walls here were slashed with a radiant slime, orange and yellow, streaming down to the floor and slithering to the sofas in the centre. The place was warm as a heated oven and the stench of rot was suffocating. Naked heaving bodies were entangled with each other on the sofas, limbs and heads jutting out from every part. Other bodies were stretched out on the floor. The music was being played from the deejay's laptop at the far end, though the deejay was nowhere in sight. The dull thudding wasn't coming from this part of the room. It was coming from behind me. The open-plan kitchen in the corner.

I turned around. In the kitchen there was a naked slim girl, of average height and with short hair, standing up with her back toward me.

She thudded her forehead against the wall. She thudded it again. On the white ceramic she left a splatter of dazzling red. It was growing every time she thudded.

I went to her and pulled her away. She turned to me. Her face was a running anonymity. One living white eye blinked up at me in all that viscosity. Above it was another that was round, black, large. Its nothing glared at me as it poured profusely.

I pushed her away. As far away from me as I could. She fell backward, slipping, banging her skull against the wall behind her. She let out a faint groan. Gracefully, she slid down the wall and crumbled face down onto the floor. She didn't move from then on.

Her handbag was beside a table nearby. I opened it, rummaged through and took the three pink round pills I found there. Soon after, I called the ambulance and left the Dream House.

# 76

Sent by: Angelique Duval

Wednesday, April 20, 2016
20.02

I want to go to sleep.

77

# 78

I didn't hear from her anymore. I didn't bother texting her or calling her either. I suppose I saw it all as a closed chapter and it was now time for a new story, a new adventure.

It took me around a day to clean up my place, though I stayed away from the carpet with the swirling flowers. The bathroom was still a place that made me rather anxious. In fact, I was spending less and less time in there. I had stopped using its mirror for my meditation exercises and now I just used it for daily tasks: to do my hair (and these days I'd fix it rather quickly) and on those few occasions that I had to use my beard trimmer.

I noticed that I was also avoiding looking too closely at my face in mirrors or glass surfaces of any sort. As soon as I caught myself in a reflection, I would focus on any *other* detail in that reflection besides my own face. Usually it'd be my hairline or people behind me if I happened to be outside. Twice I remember staring fixedly at my Adam's apple. That was quite risky since the Adam's apple is very close to the face.

I also stopped meditating on my attitude altogether. Instead, I resorted to writing more blogs for my *Jaded Debauchee* site. They almost had the same effect as my former exercises. I can safely say that sometimes the effect was even stronger.

*The Jaded Debauchee*
Sunday, 26 June, 2016
18.23

*When Her Time Comes*

*How to create your own elite perception*

*Step 1:*

Nothing is true, important, or real. Everything is permitted.

You start from there: a conviction that must persist like an obsession.

This is the foundation. And on it you will build your church.

*Step 2:*

An elite perception has no conditions, no restraints. It is created exclusively out of what you and only you desire.

Invoke the qualities. All those traits you never had but always wanted: invoke them now.

These will be the elements of your new self; the atoms for its formula.

*Step 3:*

Explain your new qualities. Why do you have them? Relate them to one another. String them into a story. I am this and this because . . .

The story can be basic, vague, a bare plot. It doesn't matter.

It need not have happened to you. Its only purpose is to *make real.*

You can invent it. Or you can model it on someone else.

*Step 4:*

Feel it. Feel your new story.

Its interlaced ideas emit a special glow. All throughout it resonates with a certain mood.

There is an *aesthetic* to this story that you have woven yourself with.

Let this aesthetic take over you from now on. Let it be your inner core. You'll carry it around like your personal halo.

*Step 5:*

Now you are ready.

You are prepared to face what is to come.

Nothing should hurt you as long as you keep the new halo around your head.

Your aesthetic can permeate anything that crosses your path. It is a chemical A that can infuse with any other chemical B and turn it into a species of A. Without exception.

So whatever can happen *can* happen. Because it will always

blend in with this mood.

Whatever can go wrong *can* go wrong. Because it will go wrong through your new state of mind.

Anything can be tuned to your aesthetic. Your pose welcomes all contingencies.

Let the future make its random moves. Its accidents will *always already* take place on your board, in your game. Always already.

Your aesthetic will save you. It will make everything yours.

# 79

My disquiet went on for days and it didn't look as if it was going to go away anytime soon. In this state, I started working on a new series of paintings, which I thought of calling *Skin Deeps*. I worked on them day and night without sleeping, so that by the third day I had finished four paintings in total. I didn't even try going to sleep because I knew I wouldn't be able to. I was too wide awake all the time.

Maybe there was another reason why I avoided sleeping. Maybe it wasn't that I didn't want to sleep . . . maybe I was just afraid to.

At all times, I worked with the *Face and the City* soundtrack playing on repeat and a bottle of whisky close at hand. By the time I started on the third painting, I was quite drunk.

All of the paintings focused on a man and a woman having sex in different positions among the pale pink sheets of an ornate double bed surrounded by blown gossamer curtains. The two coiled bodies were spotlighted by circular headlamps attached, close together, right above them. The walls were covered with a vast mosaic of machinery: an intricate maze of interconnecting cooling water pipes, flues, tubes and shafts embedded with exhaust valves, ventilating fans, cylinders, generators, fuel tanks and a massive diesel engine looming over the headboard.

The woman displayed was the same woman as in all my other paintings: the diamond face, the black hair, the piercing green eye, the sculpted cheekbone, the dirty purple-lipsticked grin. Only this time she was completely naked, her body in plain view of the onlooker from diverse angles. Smiling, she showed you her body curving over the man's, the muscles stretched as she arched her back, her long hair whipping the air or falling on her face, breasts pressed against his chest, her legs and arms wrapped around him like winding cobras, hands buried in his hair or clutching his temples, pelvis and waist joined with his. In the first two paintings, the only part of her that was hidden from view was the right side of her face. The man's hand was covering it.

In the third painting, however, his hand had withdrawn. Her whole face exposed.

And the right side was exactly the same as the left side of her face. It showed the rest of her high forehead, her other sharp eye, the second half of her straight-edged nose, her other high cheekbone, her full grin.

Then you went to the fourth painting and in this scene, the man was slowly peeling off the skin right under her right eye. He was pulling it away as if it were a useless layer, a stuck tape that had to be removed. She was letting him do this while staring at the viewer. A patch of an intestinal pink muscle was revealing itself behind the skin that was tearing off.

# 80

It took me two more days to finish the series. I was working on the last one when I made up my mind to take a quick shower to revitalize myself. When I had turned off the shower and was drying myself with a towel, my thoughts were still absorbed in my works and I absentmindedly wiped my feet on the carpet. At that very instant, I realized *which carpet* it was. I looked down without thinking.

I had moved the carpet with the swirling flowers away from the shower tray frame!

I quickly pulled the carpet back onto it. Gabriella, I thought.

I gave her a call and she said, yes, she was up for some drinks at La Chimère. She sounded exhausted. She must have run out of speed.

I saw her waiting for me at one of the tables. She had bought a bottle of vodka and a mixer for us, which we swigged.

"I've put two green pills into the vodka," she said while we were drinking. "They'll free us from our politics and their corruption."

The whole world now seemed to plunge into some warped dream. In this dream, there were different laws of spacetime and a mutating physics. Sounds came from far away and they sounded like foreign melodies and the hyper-colourful places and beings around us split and merged and danced and pulsed with so many possibilities of meaning. We swam and swam in this new world for hours, or it could have been days.

Until I woke up in the little bathroom on the ground floor of my Cardiff family home. In the bathroom, there was once more the new door to the new room, which looked exactly like the bathroom, but was bare and lit up in a flat surgical light.

When I climbed upstairs and I was facing the door to my bedroom, I noticed that the limping had just climbed up onto the landing behind me.

It rang on the first step on the landing of the first floor.

It was only about two metres away. The gargling was turned on like a malfunctioning emergency alarm. It had never been this close to me.

I walked into my room and quickly closed and locked the door.

My room was swamped in a dark red gloom and it was very hot and stuffy. Everything was rippling with the long striped shadows of a cooling fan's rotating blades. All walls were of barbed wire and stretched taut and pinned against the wire were more canvases of skin. Instead of my two beds occupying the east wall was a pair of stretchers with rows of empty steel shelves above them. My Playmobil castles and pirate ship on the uppermost shelf had become iron sculptures of abstract sharp-edged solids with jagged spikes. Slime was creeping all over the space, squelching and burping in the background drone of the fan.

The rumbling of the underground train was coming. The metal floor and furniture started rattling. When the rumbling was close, the headlights flooded the room and the wheels were grinding against the railway tracks and the engines were roaring. Deep below me, the endless train was now rushing by at a terrific speed. In a few more seconds, it was gone, the lights and noise fading into the underground distance. The fan's drone took over, the slime squelched.

Someone banged against the door of my room. Silence. Then it banged again.

I made for the door on the other side, which should have opened to the peach bathroom that led to the washing room and the stairs to the attic.

I opened the door. I went in.

The other door burst open.

Instead of the bathroom, I found myself on an iron grating bridge which disappeared a few metres away into a blood-red space that was above me and all around me. The bridge was suspended in this space and there was nothing else existent anywhere.

I walked forward.

The limping came clashing on the metal floor of my room.

I picked up the pace. The gloom prevented me from seeing for more than two metres ahead of me.

The limping pounded on the bridge. The bridge trembled. The limping advanced right behind me, one light ring quickly followed by a heavy one.

It went faster and faster.

I broke into a slow run. Soon the sound was growing distant.

The bridge went on and on. It didn't seem to ever end.

I started running faster now, until I was running as fast as I could. Soon I was leaving the limping far behind. It was getting ever fainter. From far off, it sounded like a timid ringing.

I looked back. It was the first time I looked back. All I could see behind me was the blood gloom.

My foot hit something hard on the floor. I lost my balance, all control. I was falling in the air. The sky and bridge wheeled about me. I hit my back against the grating with a bong.

Supine on the ground, I stared at the blank space above. It was deep and had no depth.

The timid ringing was getting closer. It was slowly turning into a clanging again.

Beside me, sitting down on the edge of the bridge, was the hunched body of a young man. I must have tripped on his legs when I was looking back. He was hunched over so much that his forehead almost touched his open knees. He was completely still but his eyes were wide open, staring vacantly at the grating. There was something familiar about his face.

I noticed that the young man was wearing a dark blue tracksuit. On the front part of the tracksuit was the word "Sahara."

I could hear it too clearly now. It couldn't be more than ten metres away.

I tried to get up. My lying body didn't respond. Only my head and neck could move.

I tried again. My body was paralysed. It was the same as at the Dream House.

The bridge under me started trembling again with the savage clanging of the one good foot.

The underground rumbling of the train was coming now. The roar of the engines and the grating of metal were here right beneath me, piercing, deafening. Dazzling light burst out of the bridge like a brilliant shapeless hologram switched on from the darkness below. The train was rushing past. And in the blinding white, I saw the figure limping toward me. Tall and lean. I couldn't see more in the glare.

Then the train passed, its headlamps carried away.

The figure was still there, coming forward, but it now seemed further away, blurred by the distance. It was tall and lean and seemed to be completely naked, its skin of a ghost white, except for the high heels on its feet. One hand grasped the fillet knife.

The figure was walking onward in disjointed jerks: one savage jerk after another. This made its long black hair whip to and fro.

Its approach was inevitable.

## 81

I woke up in my room. My hand lunged out from under the sheets and clawed away at the right side of my mouth. Then it slowly lowered itself onto the blankets.

It was dark. Was it early morning or late evening? How did I get here last night? What happened last night? Was there a last night?

I snatched my phone and it read 09.00. I had no new messages on my WhatsApp or Facebook. The only cigarette left in my packet was sodden.

This had happened to me before.

My hand went to my mouth and scratched again.

I found Angelique's three pink round pills in the pocket of my jeans. I swallowed all of them.

I had to see her. There was no other choice. We *shared* something unspeakably important. And because of that, she knew me better than most people. She knew me without knowing it. And this always gave me a reassurance that I barely ever felt in anyone else's company. Somehow, it resolved who I was. She held the answers. I had to see her.

She was offline. So I called her but her phone was off. I threw on some clothes and took a bus to her place. In Sommeil de Diamant Street, I pressed the flat 15 buzzer several times. But no one answered.

"Looking for someone?"

It was a woman's deep voice a few steps away from me. I turned.

Standing next to me was a woman with a blonde ponytail, wearing a suit and carrying a briefcase.

She had a diamond-shaped face with prominent cheekbones, but only a mouth was on her face. Instead of her eyes and nose there was only blank white skin. The mouth had full luscious lips in purple lipstick. Its right end was ripped open right up to the earlobe. But even around this upward gash there was purple lipstick. The mouth seemed to be grinning.

I could sense the rattling about to come out. Any moment now.

A few blinks later, however, her eyes and nose had appeared, and her mouth had contracted to normality. She now had pale pink lipstick on and she seemed to be in her middle age. The professional stiffness of her demeanour reminded me of a businessperson or a lawyer. That's when I recalled her as the woman Angelique had accosted in the street with a sheet on when we were playing that truth-or-dare game.

I described Angelique to her to see if she had seen her around lately, but she said she didn't live here.

"I just drop by sometimes after work to visit a friend," she said.

I asked her if her friend knew a girl with a pixie cut.

"I don't think so,' she answered. "Plenty of her friends have long black hair.

"And bright red nail polish."

I noticed that her lips weren't synchronizing properly with what she was saying. In fact, it was as if the lips were moving badly in an effort to imitate a prerecorded voice. It was doubtful if this was even hers. Another's voice, an unknown's, seemed to be speaking through her mouth and what it was saying had already been determined.

"It's in again. Bright red nail polish," she said or someone else had said.

I thanked her and left the area.

Close by was the playground and I decided to take a look there just in case. It was desolated—as it often was. So I called the only other place I could think of. The only public hospital of Saint Laurent: Coralina Hospital.

They told me that currently there was a Ms Angelique Duval staying there. I could see her during visiting hours. She could be found in the Psychiatric Ward.

Coralina was a labyrinth of bare blue-grey corridors and empty halls. There were no windows anywhere except for the rare little window when a corridor came to a dead end. It would look upon the hospital tarmac grounds with a few parked cars and an overcast sky. Occasionally a nurse or relative could be seen moving a patient around in a wheelchair.

I finally found the Psychiatric Ward. I was directed to her room by a receptionist who was constantly bending her neck sideways.

"Room 303," she said, and she bent her neck sideways.

The room was another blue-grey space. Angelique was stretched out on the wheeled bed in a grey hospital smock, a drip attached to her hand. A spotlight in the ceiling threw its harsh light upon her but she didn't seem to mind. She was staring up blankly.

I went closer.

Where the wound on her forehead had once been was now a new scab that protruded out from one side to the other like a large, thick chunk of salami. She was utterly still; she didn't react to my presence in any way as I approached her.

"You know, you remind me of Arwen the half-elf in *Lord of the Rings* when she saves Frodo and she's all glowing and shit," I joked. "You kind of look like you're glowing from here."

She could have been dead had her chest not been rising and falling ever so slightly. She remained staring at the ceiling.

"Don't get your hopes up though, about your beauty."

"That depends on which angle I see you from."

She now turned her head to look at me. Her left eye moved but her right eye stayed staring up at the ceiling.

She turned her face away again.

"I'm sure the big guy up there would approve.

"He'd probably be high-fiving me if he were around. 'Good one,' he'd be telling me. 'That's a damn good one.'"

I had bought cigarettes on the way here and I felt like having a smoke, but the nearest exit to the grounds was too far off. And it was probably not a good idea to smoke next to her. I went to the toilet and locked the door behind me.

I sat on the seat and lit a cigarette. It felt very peaceful in here, so I smoked two instead of one and took my time with it. The peace I found in toilets was a saving grace. It came from the comforting awareness that what was past was gone and what was future hadn't yet arrived. Toilets gave you time because they postponed it. Once I was done, I stood up, dumped the cigarette butt in the water and opened the door. Angelique awaited.

A bloody gloom had fallen. Barbed wire had replaced all the walls and there were long shadows of bars across the ward. She was still face-up. But she was now spread-eagled on a complicated framework of iron beams. Right above her, a human-sized cooling fan was revolving slowly, weaving swirling shadows on her body.

I went to her. Again, she didn't react to me at all. As I got close, I took her left hand and lifted it up.

"Let's have some fun," I told her. "Nothing is important. So everything is permitted."

Her one eye moved toward me again. The bad one kept looking up.

"Smile for me forever," she said in a thick voice with a strong accent.

She lunged at my face. Her nails ripped out the right corner of my mouth like knives and kept ripping up to my ear. I felt my cheek opening up like a flower.

I pushed her away from me with all the strength I could muster. She tumbled off the bed, banging her head against the iron grating floor.

I retreated to the entrance. I could feel the gash burning, its throbbing, the caress of what was hot and sliding on my face. She was struggling to get up with the hysteria of a possessed person. I opened the door, got out and slammed it shut behind me.

Before me was a long corridor of metal grating and barbed wire, with streetlamps on the sides lit up a dark red. The numbered doors that lined the walls looked like the steel doors of a prison.

I started walking away from her room, but it was hot and humid and it was making me very nauseous. The corridor was empty. I passed by several side corridors that came to a dead end on which was nailed a square slab of flesh.

Her door suddenly flung open.

And it began. The high heeled limping banging on the metal floor. The beginning of a rhythm that had no conceivable end. The relentless approach.

I walked quicker.

But so did the limping.

A turning in the corridor. I went around it. A new corridor of blood glows greeted me. I took the 312 prison door. I pulled at its large brass barrel bolt and slid it back. The door opened inward. Inside were corroding machinery, wheels and engines. Broken pipes stuck out of the ceiling, trickling.

There was no other way out of this room.

I had to return to the corridor. The limping was just behind the corner I had turned.

I started running. This time I was moving only straight ahead, taking no side routes. The underground rumbling of the train began. It grew louder by the second. Soon the bright light of the headlamps burst out everywhere from below, followed by the roaring. The train rushed by in a split moment. It was gone in the next.

I was still running.

The limping picked up its pace. By the sound of it, it was almost running. If it was not possible, it made it possible.

I went for room 320. Its barrel bolt was heavy. I had to use both my hands. I finally managed to slide it back. I pushed the door. I went inside. It was an operating theatre. Steel skeletons of stretchers were scattered everywhere, their pads made of tender pink flesh. Above me and around me was barbed wire with more chunks of flesh nailed here and there. Embedded in the far wall was the bust of a diesel engine, thrumming.

No other door here in sight. Once again, I had to get back to the corridor.

From the corner of my eye, I could spot the figure around three metres away. Parts of its naked body were twitching quickly to different rhythms. Its head was shaking rapidly, tossing the long hair all around.

I ran away across the corridor until I saw the end. A junction lay ahead. I reached it. I turned left.

The underground rumbling of the train returned. The headlights flooded the junction. The world seemed to shake with the vibrations of its deafening noise.

Then the limping was back. And it was coming at me even faster than before. In fact it must have been running. The impossible it had again made possible. It had suddenly entered the corridor I was in. It would catch up very soon.

I stopped by room 326. Slid back the barrel bolt. Kicked the door open.

Inside, heaps of broken machinery caked in black oil. No exit either.

I got out. I kept on running.

The gargling now poured out like a siren. It couldn't be more than five metres away from me. The limping was suddenly even faster than before. It now sounded like one continuous savage ringing. A deafening alarm clock of metal pounding. It was as if a machine had been turned up to maximum effect.

I sprinted. At full speed. The harsh burning in my cheek. The torn flesh flapping against my face.

Past all the doors, I saw a lift at the end of the corridor.

I got to the lift. Two buttons. Arrow showing up. Arrow showing down.

It wouldn't stop running. Always ever running.

I pressed the down button.

I pressed it again. Twice, trice, four times.

The iron grating underneath my feet was now shaking as it closed in.

The lift rang. The doors slid open.

A quiet descended everywhere. The frenzied banging had ceased. I dared to look across the corridor behind me—and it was empty. The corridor seemed longer than before. Everything lay perfectly still.

I stepped inside the lift. I pressed a G.

The doors clunked shut.

The dark cell trembled. Then it started going down.

## 82

The elevator doors opened to the hospital parking. This large tarmac space enclosed by low walls of steel was also completely empty; there wasn't a single car parked anywhere. A drizzle slashed the black air. It was about to start raining. The thin water drops stung my skin.

To get out of the hospital grounds, I had to walk up the road on the rising slope ahead. That would take me straight to the Saint Laurent town centre.

I knew where I had to go. There was nowhere else to go.

In town, all the narrow streets, boulevards and squares were also illuminated by red glowing streetlamps. All the cluttered buildings looked like train carriages stacked on top of one another, each carriage as high as a storey. The paint was peeling off their aluminium walls.

"*Hey you, Sahara guy.*"

It was the booming voice of a man with a hard accent. The voice was coming from somewhere high above me.

I looked up and then around the street where I was walking. Nothing.

"*Yeah, I'm talking to you.*"

I looked up again. A loudspeaker was fastened to the ceiling of a train building close by.

I ignored it and moved on. I tried to find shelter from the drizzle where I could by walking under the wheels jutting out of some of the carriages that made up the building floors. I should be in Anges Ascendants Street.

"*Where're you off to so late?*"

I reached Boulevard Résurrection. A few people that were completely naked crossed my path in complete silence. Their bodies were so pale they were almost blue. All their faces looked stunned, their wide open eyes vacant. Something inside them was making them walk in short erratic movements and sometimes a part of their body erupted in violent quivering and then stopped.

"*It's past your bedtime already.*"

Another loudspeaker was planted on the roof of a nearby building.

I hurried across Euphoria Square, bathed in the red twilight and empty. Attached to the square was a parking lot and the cars and bikes there were broken shells, wrecked, covered with rust, their windows and windscreens smashed, their seats ripped, some of their doors fallen off the hinges. In the square, I spotted the opening that used to lead to Lotus Street.

"*Your mama wouldn't like this.*"

I entered Lotus Street. Finally. There, a few blocks away, was where I had to be.

I made a run for it.

And there it was.

Or, at least, where it was supposed to be.

The façade of the ground floor had become the front part of a platinum painted train, while the first, second and third floors seemed to be its coaches. Up some stairs, the entrance was a prison metal door with a barred window located just below the snout of the locomotive. The sign was still there, now etched into the wall.

Marmara Spicy Kebab.

"*No, she wouldn't like it at all.*"

I climbed up the stairs and lifted up the crude door latch. The door creaked open. I could hardly see in the gloom inside.

"*Not. One. Bit.*"

I entered. In the dim red illumination, I could just make out the walls blackened with soot. The tables and counter had changed to chrome grid panels supported by rusted spikes. In the shadows of the open kitchen, the Arab was frying some eggs on a stove that looked like a large intricate engine. I couldn't see the dwarf or the Cleopatra girl anywhere. There were no clients around either. It must have been too late or too early.

I went straight toward the counter.

"Where is he?" I shouted out at the Arab.

He jumped, turning around to me in surprise.

"Where is he?" I insisted.

His expression relaxed as he saw me. Without a word, he turned back to his eggs, sprinkling some salt on them, as if nothing was the matter, as if *I* did not matter.

I reached the counter. I climbed onto it and leapt into the steel kitchen. I grabbed one of the saucepans by the sink and bashed it against his head. He stumbled against the cooker, hit the saucepan on the hob and poured all the frying oil and eggs over his hand, waist and thigh in one shrieking hiss. He cried out in agony.

I grabbed one of the butcher knives hanging on the wall and pointed it at him.

"*Take me to him!*"

He gave me a death stare as he blurted out a litany of swear words in Arabic.

I moved a step closer to him with my knife.

Suddenly something round and heavy grabbed hold of my left leg. I looked down and I saw the dwarf wrapped around my leg, hugging it with both his arms and his legs, trying to prevent me from moving any further. He had obviously been behind the bar all along and I hadn't noticed him.

"This is as far as you go!" he warned me.

I smashed my other knee into his face, cracking open his nose. The blow flung his face upward. He let go of me and toppled backward onto the floor. But just as he touched ground, he was instantly struggling to get up again. I smashed the heel of my boot into a side of his face. He went down again, hitting the floor with his chin, blood spurting out of his frowning mouth.

I knelt beside him. I stuffed my hand into his trousers pockets—and found them. The keys.

I spotted the grimacing Arab about to make a move on me. I instantly flashed the knife at him again.

"Get out!" I ordered him.

He raised his hands as a sign of surrender—one white, the other red as a ruby and steaming.

I made way for him. Eyes fixed on the blade, he walked past me and tried to help the dwarf up.

"Both of you! Get out!"

The dwarf, however, was in no position to stand on his feet. From the nose down, his face was caked with gore, and he was barely conscious, mumbling incomprehensible things. The Arab had no choice but to lift him up and slump him on his shoulder.

"Now!"

The Arab walked to the entrance and gave me another death stare before he opened the door and left. The moment they were out, I locked the door with one of the keys.

Then, I quickly headed to the door behind the counter. Like the entrance, it was now another prison door.

I tried the keys one after another until I found the right one. The door creaked open easily.

Before me, there was no longer a corridor with zigzag patterns under embryonic egg lights. Instead, another metal bridge stretched out in a dark red space. Further on, on the right edge, I could see a door leading into pitch-black darkness. It was probably the one that used to lead to the toilets. The bridge went on for a few metres and then simply disappeared in space.

## 83

I took a few steps forward on the bridge. The Bath Man or the Duke slowly emerged out of the darkness ahead, tall and scrawny in a trailing velvet gown. Underneath he was only wearing tight leather trousers. His smooth white skin seemed to glow in the dark. Just as he saw me, he gave me a benign smile and stopped, waiting, his belly protruding out like an imperial balloon.

"What's happening to me?" I cried out from across the distance of bridge and void.

My voice sounded powerless, hoarse. So I tried again.

"What is this?"

"I knew you'd come back," the Duke replied. "But I just don't care anymore."

"You invited *me* before. I was one of the twelve."

"I invited you only once. I suppose it was because I was curious and wanted to see if you remembered."

"Remembered *what*?"

"The time you were my patient."

And a tight smile wrinkled his face and squeezed his eyes shut.

"Above all," he continued, "I wanted to see if you had changed in some way. Perhaps you had been cured. Perhaps you had cured yourself somehow. But then you invited yourself over a second time and now a third. And it's clear—your visits confirm what I had already guessed."

He raised his hand out of the gown's long sleeve and wagged

his finger at me.

"There is no curing you!"

"But I don't remember!" I shouted out with all the strength I could muster though my voice was fast fading.

"I tried quite a few treatments. Oh believe me, I tried. None of them worked, though.

"You're one of them.

"The Incurables.

"So I had to let you go."

"But I don't remember!" I shouted. "What if you're lying? What if you're making all this up?"

"Either way, does it matter?"

"What happened there?" I asked. "What happened when I was your patient?"

I pointed the knife at him. I started walking toward him. I stopped until we were only at arm's length.

"It doesn't matter," he said. "I can do nothing for you now."

"What happened?"

I aimed the knife straight at his throat. I took another step. He retreated back, eyes riveted on the blade.

"You don't have to know," he murmured. "Don't you know that? You don't have to ever know."

"What happened?" I repeated.

I slashed the knife suddenly right before his face, and then pointed it at him again. He looked disturbed. I came even closer. The length of a forefinger now separated the tip of my blade from the waxy skin of his throat

He fell silent. His eyes glared at the reflection of his own eyes on the blade.

"You showed up around three years ago," he said. "A close friend of yours in Cardiff had told you about me. You came to France . . . to Saint Laurent . . . because of me. You wanted to be cured.

"So I commenced the treatment. You entered the Game. I showed you a self that'd suit you, a self you'd want to put on. I gave you a someone you always wanted to be. The Recreation was initiated.

"See, you were going to be *him* in the Game. You were going to be *him* perhaps even after."

A memory stirred at the back of my consciousness. It was a vague sensation at first, an urgent nagging, but as I focused on it, it seemed to grow, intensify and form its own images and movements and sounds and emotions. I kept focusing on it with a stubborn insistence—until it was suddenly opening up and pulling me inside of it.

*A place. A dim place with rows of chairs before a large screen. All around, curtains of royal blue damask. The strong smell of plastic. The Duke's cinema. I'm sitting in one of the seats. I'm alone except for someone standing up beside me.*

*On the screen, some* Face and the City *episode is playing. I don't know how long I've been here. A scene on the screen is playing itself over and over again. A girl is sitting on a sink with her legs wrapped around Vincent Face's waist, her feet and ankles pressing against his butt. He's sticking it into her, heaving her up against the mirror when he pushes forward, and sliding her down when he pulls back. Her nape and back are making a squeaking rhythm as they rub up and down against the mirror.*

*A figure in a white toga suddenly looms in front of me, blocking the image of the rocking bodies. He presents me with a little scarlet pill. I open my mouth obediently and receive it on my tongue.*

I flipped back to the present moment. The bridge in space, the right-hand door further on and the Duke right before me.

"But you," he was saying, "you went too far."

"You took him to an excess.

"There was another guest of mine at the time. A very pretty girl. You got obsessed with her. You see, she looked like Laura, Vincent Face's long-time lover.

"So you *had* to have her.

*When Her Time Comes*

"But you couldn't. You couldn't because she didn't want you. It was against the rules anyway. She wasn't in *your* Game. She was in another Game, a different one, with its own characters and stories and themes.

"But . . . " He sighed loudly. "But you wouldn't have it. You wanted her because she was Laura and you were Vincent.

"You followed her everywhere. She was what you wanted the most in the world. And by that time you were too far gone to be convinced otherwise. By then, you had become *too* him to be him. You had turned into his extreme, his caricature. You had become something else."

Another memory struggled to get my attention. This time I didn't need to concentrate on it. I just let it arrive.

*A bathroom. Porcelain furniture. An AC making a loud whirring noise. A lot of water on the hexagonal tiles. Someone is humming. They won't stop humming.*

*I have my Vincent Face rubber mask on and I'm straddling a girl in a white dress lying on the floor. Her very long, brown hair is spread out all around her head like a large tentacled halo. Her panties are down around her knees. We are beside the bath.*

*"It's me," I tell her and I lift her skirt. I unzip, take it all down. I'm so hard, it's painful.*

*"You woke me up and I never wanted to wake up."*

*She hums as I enter her.*

*I strike deeper, then retreat, and she jerks up and then down as if a brief electrical voltage has suddenly gone through her. She hums in reply. And wriggles a bit.*

*"And you came along," I say, "and you were too much. What you made me feel was* too *much."*

*Another thrust and retreat. Another jolt up and then down.*

*"You . . . "*

*Both her arms are stretched up above her head. Her wrists are tied together with duct tape and so are her ankles. Her mouth too is taped.*

*". . . are the anomaly."*

*Now the girl is sitting on the sink. Her mouth and ankles taped.*

"We were awake somewhere else," I tell her. "A special place. Us together."

*Her arms are crucified against the wall with duct tape around the palms.*

"Let's go there again. Let's go back.

"You..."

*With eyes wide open, she shakes her head again and again and hums. And hums.*

"... are the anomaly."

I found myself waking up to the present.

"It all went wrong," the Duke was saying. "The whole thing blew up. So I gave you a drink to make you forget. Everything that happened here—you forgot."

"But you don't understand!" I told him. "I'm still trying to be Vincent Face! I'm still watching him. I've been watching the episodes zillions of times! I've turned to him so many times!"

"That must be an unconscious effect that the Game leaves behind," he replied. "Deep inside, you're probably still attached to him. You still believe you're him. Your consciousness might not remember but your unconscious always does. You can't lie to your unconscious.

"Besides," he added after a while, "you're naturally attracted to him. He is what you never were. His series is a hit worldwide, so it was only a matter of time until you rediscovered him. With or without the Game, you two were bound to meet each other at some point along the way."

"But why?" I asked. "What do I need him for? What is this?"

I waved the knife wildly around me at the bridge and the space and then pointed it back at his face. He moved back by three steps.

"Why?" I insisted. "Why come to you? What did I want to ... cure?"

"When you came here you were in the state you're in now," he explained. "But you didn't know *what* had caused it. You didn't know what your state was a symptom of. I don't think you ever did."

"You're lying!" My hand was shaking. "Your drink made me forget that as well!"

"It wasn't the drink," he replied. "It was *you*. *You* made yourself forget it."

"Bullshit!" I cried out. "You know!"

"I can make a guess. But you'd have to see for yourself."

He walked to the prison door that used to lead to the toilets. He opened it.

"Go inside," he said. "Take a look."

His face winced and made the funny smile.

## 84

I entered the once pale green but now corroding metal corridor leading to the toilets. The gents' door was jammed like the first time. I tried the ladies' and it opened. I had caught the Duke here rubbing off his makeup and taking off his wig and he had caught me watching him. He had known all along.

The toilet was bathed in an intense red light and its walls, once a spotted peach, were now all stained with black soot, the iron floor caked with rust.

I went to one of the sinks. I looked in the mirror. My face looked back at me.

And then I saw it.

And it came back to me. It all came back to me.

On a Saturday night in Cathays, Cardiff, I'm climbing up the stairs of a bridge near the train station. My mind is racing with so many images of the late-night premiere I've just watched.

The film is called *The Laughing God*. It is the story of a man called Elohay, known by many as "the Surgeon." Elohay has a peculiar passion. He captures people and with a knife opens up their mouths from the corners right up to the earlobes. All his victims are found with a joker's wide smile carved out on their faces.

I take out my phone from the pocket of my dark blue tracksuit. It's the same tracksuit I often wear at home because it's so comfortable; the one with the word "Sahara" printed on the front. The time on the screen says 02.05. The movie is almost three hours long.

On the bridge the streetlamps loom over, hunched. Their round bulkheads cast little islands of orange light upon the metal grating floor. From the wire mesh walls on either side, I can see a large field scattered with discarded train parts. Mounds of steel pipes, cooling fans, engines, fuel tanks, side plates, water tanks, generators and other unknown wreckage rise up from the grass: a graveyard for trains. A railway track crosses the junkyard, passing right under the bridge.

Stilettos are climbing up the metal stairs behind me. I can hear the rhythm of their sharp ringing.

"Hey you, Sahara guy!"

A man's voice. The accent is strong, foreign . . . Slavic?

I don't look back at first. But then I do.

Two hunks with shaved heads and tattooed biceps have just climbed onto the bridge. The person making all that noise with the heels is right behind them. They're still coming up the stairs so I can't see them yet. The older man of the two gives me a sly grin.

"Yeah, I'm talking to you!" he calls out.

I look away. I quicken my pace.

The high heels are now pounding on the bridge. They're so loud that I can't hear the two other men walking ahead. They've taken over every other noise around me.

The rumbling of a train is approaching from the railway beneath us. It gets louder in a second. I can spot the dazzle of the headlamps below, coming from my left. In the next instant, the train is thundering under me, vibrating the bridge. Then it's rushing away to the other side of the junkyard, away into the distance.

"Where're you off to so late?"

The older man is walking right next to me. The other one is on my other side.

The stiletto clanging is almost right behind them.

I seem to remember these men from somewhere. I still don't answer them. I push on. We've just passed the middle of the bridge. Very soon I'll have arrived at the other end.

The man to my right shoves me away from him. I almost trip. I stagger toward the right-hand wall.

But the other man is suddenly right before me.

"It's past your bedtime already," he says.

He pushes me away. I stumble backward in front of them. Somehow I regain my balance and manage not to fall. I keep on walking quickly away. The end of the bridge is only a couple of more steps further.

"Your mama wouldn't like this."

I feel my hood being grabbed. I'm wrenched back. They're suddenly around me again.

"No," one of them says, "she wouldn't like it at all."

The other one suddenly smashes his fist into my stomach.

All my breath is snuffed out of me. I bend over, clutching myself, vision watering, as I gasp and gasp for air. The stiletto clanging feels as if it is chiming this unbearable time, setting the beat of its endlessness. Even though I'm choking, I still manage to stay on my feet.

"Not. One. Bit."

Knuckles bang and crack my head. My knees give way. And I'm crumbling down, my life pouring out of me, my whole body going limp. The next thing I know is the frigid grid of the floor pressing against half my face. I can't move any part of myself. I can't feel myself. My body has stopped being mine. Vomit is creeping up in my throat as I gasp and gasp but I still can't take in any air.

Both my arms are grabbed and I'm raised from the waist up and dragged to the edge of the bridge. They make me sit against the wall.

The high heel clanging now slows down. It stops. And looming before me are the two legs that wear the elegant shoes. They're

## When Her Time Comes

toned and smooth, with crisscrossing straps around the ankles. A black miniskirt squeezes the upper thighs together, rising up to a figure-hugging high-necked dress. The rich sweetness of expensive perfume rains upon me.

She crouches down and half of her diamond sculpted face fills my world, the other half hidden in the shadow of the man standing beside her. I can't look away; I'm riveted to her feline eye piercing me with its metallic green. She's smiling with lips that are so purple they are almost bleeding the colour into the air. As she's squatting down, her miniskirt is pulled up so her tight round ass slips out.

She is beautiful and horrifying.

In that instant, I recognize her. I recognize them all.

I was watching *The Laughing God* at the cinema when I turned to look at the people in my row. And I was met by her face staring at me, some six seats away, with her striking eyes, high cheekbones and mischievous smile. She likes me, I had thought. But then I noticed the two men sitting beside her, staring at me as well, and I had looked away. When the credits were rolling and the lights were on, I checked her seat again just to see her for one last time before she left. But she had gone already. She likes me, I kept telling myself.

My head is grabbed by powerful hands, slammed back against the wire netting, and held steady. A shining mirror of a fillet knife is handed over to the woman from one of the men. She curls her spidery fingers with the brilliant red varnished nails around the handle. Her eye keeps on watching me hungrily. She grins so much that she almost looks deranged.

"My love," she tells me in her Slavic accent.

"Smile for me forever."

She slips the blade into my mouth. I don't resist. I open up and receive the blade as a hard and sharp communion wafer. Everything is numb but I can still feel its edged iciness on my tongue, taste the bitter metal. She turns and wiggles the steel around in my mouth and it scrapes and rings against my molars. Then, from the inside, she slides and presses the blade against the right corner of my mouth. She presses hard. She presses even harder. And then suddenly something gives way—and she's ripping through. And through. I just see her doing this and I don't feel as if she's doing it to me.

The rumbling arrives again. A brilliant white light bursts out from below, and everything is swallowed in the white. The ground is rattling. The walls are rattling. The roar of the train passes by beneath us.

The gloom and silence return. I see one of the men touching the girl's shoulder. For the first time since forever, her obsessive attention on me is broken. She looks up at him.

"Someone's coming," he says.

She turns to me again and pouts.

"Such a pity," she tells me in her sensual voice. She caresses my face with three fingers. "Such a great pity, my love."

She gets up and tugs on her skirt as she shakes her ass. There's some more talking above me and it has an urgent pitch to it but I can't understand what they're saying. All I can see are their slim long legs around me.

And then they leave. They are gone.

I hear the clanging of the stilettos hurrying away into the distance.

There is no one beside me anymore. I am alone.

With no grip on my head, my head falls down. The new silence is thick and ringing.

But then I realize that there is some other noise that keeps sounding in this silence. It's coming from far away. Sometimes it comes slightly nearer but then it retreats again. It doesn't stop for a single moment.

It's the sound of someone breathing through a thick fluid inside the throat. A gargling.

It takes me some time before I realize that it's me who's making this sound. It's coming out of my mouth.

But somehow, it's also no longer a sound *I'm* making, no longer *my* mouth that's struggling to breathe, no longer *myself* over there.

I've risen above it all. I've elevated away from the people, the knife, the bridge, the trains, the junkyard, the movie . . . I can see them all from up high, from this shining lightness that's so free and away. I can see *me* now. Look. That's me, hunched, head bent down to the knees, sitting against the wall in my Sahara tracksuit on the bridge.

That young man over there—that's me.

He's scared and feels this guilt all the time. He doesn't know what he wants, where he's going. He often doesn't like others but what would he give for them to like him. He's quiet and nervous around many women because they can show him how ugly he really is, how inadequate and lost. On so many evenings he feels lonely and sad and on some days he likes his sadness, it makes him feel safe, even special. But more often than that—so much more often—it breaks him. It breaks him one step further. And when it does he knows that everything is over before anything has even started.

Look. That's me on that bridge.

But now I'm also no longer there. I've left him there by himself, stranded, useless. I'm gone.

In the mirror over the toilet sink, I finally saw the *other* mouth. Out of the right corner of my old mouth, a slit, like a stretched pink gum, curved up across my cheek till it touched my earlobe. The slit had thinner lips than mine and they were dry and chewed up. It looked like an attached, second, half-smiling mouth. My alien mouth. My parody. The fly stuck to my face.

## 85

The ghoulish light of day slowly dawned in the toilet room. The walls and floor returned to spotted peach tiles, the sinks to clean white porcelain, the partition doors to a slate grey. From outside came the buzz of people and traffic.

The door swung open. Two security guards marched in. I dropped the knife. It made a sharp ringing sound as it struck the floor. I raised my hands. They seized my arms and locked them behind my back. They took me out and shoved me across the zigzag corridor from behind so that I was sliding most of the way. We arrived at the restaurant door at the far end, which was wide open. They pushed me inside. Gazing at me solemnly were the Cleopatra girl, the Arab with a bandaged hand and the dwarf with a bandaged nose.

"Take me back!" I cried out, twisting my neck to address the Cleopatra girl. The security's grip on me tightened. "Try again! *Please*, try again!"

"There's nothing else to try," he replied quietly with his caked-up face, silver wig and vintage dress.

"As I said before . . ."

A security opened the glass entrance. The other one dragged me toward it.

" . . . you're incurable."

I was flung outside onto the pouring street. So much rain was whipping down on the world in a mindless fury. All I could see were the lashing curtains of water and all I could hear was their static. I stumbled around, blind and deaf, with no idea where I was going. Someone suddenly knocked me in my face. A tooth juddered. I felt my legs leaving me. And I was falling down, splashing suddenly into pools of freezing water. I struck the hard pavement stones.

# 86

I left Saint Laurent and France a couple of days later and returned to the UK.

I will go back to Cardiff, I decided. I will dedicate myself completely to my paintings. I will get some job at an art museum or as an art teacher. Perhaps I will continue my studies at university, do a PhD, get lecturer tenure. I will make new friends, form my own circle of art connoisseurs, organize debates on contemporary art. I will find a girl I really like. We will travel together to Asia and South America. I will make a fresh start. I will have a new life.

But new was not so easy after Saint Laurent. When I was seeing her, something had been slowly waking up inside of me. She had changed me—her disease had changed me—in such an insidious way that I couldn't see it happening. Her sickness had reminded me, brought out of me what I had buried so well before. Knowing her had turned me into someone else . . . someone close to what I might have been years ago.

Sickness begets sickness: a law of attraction. And this attraction had revealed to me, once more, my second mouth.

Now the second mouth exists as the centre of my life. The presence of what has gone but not quite. The twisted souvenir of a past that refuses to die. The remains of what is gone but would not let go of me. The second mouth exists for one reason only—to remind.

"You have me," it says. "You will always have me. New things can come but I will always be there, present, at the heart of them. And you will know this. In the midst of forgetfulness, in the midst of letting go, I will sprout out for you, and you will see. You will remember."

Angelique the necromancer.

But perhaps it would have been all the same had I not met her. Sooner or later perhaps this was bound to happen.

# 87

I'm still in the Glaze Restaurant toilet, recovering from that attack of memory. It has taken me a while to recover this time. My mobile reads 21.25. I've started smoking a cigarette to calm myself down some more. In a minute or two, I'll be back again to normal.

Dina, my violet-haired date, would have definitely left at this point. I've been here for over twenty minutes. I don't think I've ever had a lapse this bad. It might be the beginning of something. I'd probably have to hit a bar or two after this. Then wrestle with the blank canvas. Or perhaps crash some party, pick up another girl.

In that very instant, I receive a message on my phone.

> Sent by: 029 23 440 500
> Noli Noli chick
>
> Sunday, June 11, 2017
> 21.29
>
> Are you okay? Dinner's boring without you.

I don't reply. I simply put the phone back in my pocket. I look up at the mirror. The cigarette is sticking out of a corner of my mouth like a burnt-out fuse. I put on a weary, dopey face. And then smile.

# ABOUT THE AUTHOR

DAVID VELLA is a lecturer on modern and contemporary literature at the University of Malta and on philosophy at St Edward's College. His research interests range from mysticism and ethics to contemporary dystopian fiction, existential phenomenology, the sociology of late modernity, and identity studies. He has written essays on Michel Houellebecq, mainstream consumerist identities, and conscience. He is the author of *Refiguring Identity in Corporate Times: Or Rediscovering Oneself in a Consumer Culture*. He lives in Malta.